Close, but No Cigar

A Street Urchin's Tale

Terence O'Brien

PublishAmerica
Baltimore

First printing

ISBN: 1-4137-3609-2
PUBLISHED BY PUBLISHAMERICA, LLLP
www.publishamerica.com
Baltimore

Printed in the United States of America

The contribution of Sharon Ross to this book is gratefully acknowledged.

Cover designed by Liam O'Brien B.F.A., M.F.A.

Contents

Terry (himself)

Chapter I
Childhood Wartime Adventures
in South Boston

South Boston is an interesting place to grow up in during the Second World War. My little sister Sharon and I live in a housing project on Eighth Street at the bottom of Dorchester Heights. There is a pub at every corner of every block – enough to drink in a different one every day of the year. Pubs are interesting places for a child – seeing all the men lined up, smoking, drinking and talking about baseball, politics and the war. Once in a while I walk into Ryan's pub across the street and try to join in the fun, but they don't seem to like me and "shoo" me out the door. Children are not allowed in without a grownup – *how rude!* Dad takes me in with him sometimes, and I stand there watching the men drink and smoke. I don't know what they are drinking nor why they are blowing smoke from their mouths; but that is what grownups do and Dad tells me that I will be a grownup some day. Some of the men puff on a cigar. Dad tells me that a man puffs on a cigar to celebrate his success – like winning money on a horse race. Dad never puffs on a cigar, just cigarettes. *Some day, I would like to do that too,* I'm thinking.

Across the street from my house is a grocery store run by an old man. I call him the "old man" because he has gray hairs growing out of his ears and nose. Like the other shopkeepers in the neighborhood, he wears an apron and a straw hat – a straw hat has something to do with being a shopkeeper. When Mom buys groceries, the shopkeeper puts the food on a scale and reads the numbers. He then writes the numbers on a paper bag, and my mother gives him money. She also gives him stamps from a ration book.

Mom tells me that we are at war and food is rationed. I don't know what that means, only that whenever she gives him money, she also gives him a stamp. When I ask Mom or Dad why, I always get the same answer that I do for all my questions – "Because, we are at war." I don't understand what a war is. I know that the year is 1942, and that I am five years old and we live in South Boston.

I love horses – I watch them every day pulling wagons, all sorts of wagons. Some wagons deliver milk – others coal or ice. When a horse comes into the neighborhood, it's a treat for us kids to see a real live horse. The ragman comes by with his horse crying, "any old rags," and people give him their old clothes.

Mom says that my clothes are not old enough to give away, and there is still good use to get out of them. I wear knickers all the time with high socks that come to the knees – I hate wearing them because the socks keep falling down to my ankles, and I'm constantly pulling them up – *I wish I could give my knickers to the ragman.*

The iceman chops blocks of ice, which he then delivers into a house. The kids gather around to pet the horse, and when he is gone, grab a few chunks of ice chips to suck on. The grownups come out and shovel up the horse dung to use as fertilizer in their Victory Gardens in the park near by. Mom has a Victory Garden too – she grows all sorts of things, and tells me that we are helping out in the war effort by growing our own vegetables. This sounds like a good idea, because I then have lots of vegetables to feed the horses when they come around – I don't like carrots but horses do. There are the usual cats and dogs around, but a horse is something special – something we see cowboys riding in the movies. We dash into the house to retrieve carrots and such, to have the pleasure of feeding a horse. We aren't allowed a dog or cat where we live, but I feed them too when one comes around. Mom says that someday we will have a dog and cat when we move away from Boston.

Sometimes the umbrella and scissor repairman comes around pushing a cart. He wears a black mustache and talks funny like the strange people who live in the North side of Boston, called Italians. Another strange Italian fellow comes around playing an organ with a monkey on a string, holding a cup.

Having never seen a monkey before, except in Tarzan movies on Saturday afternoon, I stand there in amazement as the monkey with a cup walks around the people collecting pennies. I watch in fascination as the children run into their homes to fetch pennies, just so they can give them to a monkey. Musicians occasionally visit our neighborhood playing accordions or violins and collect pennies thrown down to them out of windows. The Salvation Army Band serenades us from the street on occasion. As the pennies fall from heaven to be picked up in a tambourine, I get a bright idea – I retrieve my father's bugle from the house, and join in with the band, hoping to cash in on the rain of coins. My musical contributions are unwelcome by the band and they shoo me away – *how rude!*

From the movies we watch at the Broadway Theater on Saturday afternoon, we learn about the world: the bad Japs and the bad Germans. The Japs have buckteeth, yellow skin, sneaky, slanted eyes, are stupid, and cruel to Chinese people. The Germans wear nice uniforms, are clever but mean, and are cruel to all different kinds of people in Europe – especially Jews. Our guys, the good guys, live and train at camp McKay near my home. The soldiers march through the neighborhood in long columns with all of us kids in the neighborhood marching behind. Practice air raid drills are held once in a while. Wanting to do my part, I run to the rooftop in my Superman suit hoping to spot a Messerschmidt or a Heinkel. I'm wishing that the Germans would attack so I can fight, but the air raid warden is the only one who comes, and he chases us off of the roof – *how rude!*

My best pal Kenney Walsh and I are roaming around Southy one day when we decide to visit "our guys" at Camp McKay. We come upon the camp and suddenly see something new. The camp is now surrounded by barbed wire and watchtowers. Most extraordinary of all, inside the camp are German prisoners of war being guarded by our soldiers. Suddenly, all the war movies that we have seen on Saturday afternoon come into focus, right in front of our eyes, real live German soldiers here in Boston – *something seems out of place.* What had been fantasy has somehow become reality. Kenney and I need to get to the bottom of all this, and immediately devise a plan of inscape.[1] First, we have to survey the objective and make a map. Nonchalantly, we walk around the compound – noting the barbed wire, watch towers, buildings, gates, guards and such, then we spot an opening under the barbed wire just big enough for two 7-year-old boys to crawl under. We devise a plan. "Wait – a guard is coming!" We cower in a ditch not moving – "He doesn't see us – good!" The guard passes and we proceed to invade the enemy, crawling towards the barbed wire. We reach the depression under the wire and pass through to the other side. The guards in the towers haven't seen us. We are safe at last, inside the compound, surrounded by the enemy – Nazis, and real ones at that. Quickly, we move to blend in with the Germans so we won't stand out. The Germans eye us with curiosity, but are otherwise not impressed by our presence. I want to communicate with them, but can say the only German I know from the Saturday afternoon movies – "Heil Hitler!" They are amused and return the salute. They laugh and talk about us but I don't understand a word – *I wish I could speak German*. One of the prisoners speaks some English, and tells me that I look like a teddy bear. From then on, they all call me Teddy Bear. We make our way around the camp giving the Nazi salute and getting smiles and salutes in return. They all have something in their pocket to trade, and want to know what Kenney and I have for barter. Strange, but I don't hate them like I do in the movies. There, they are just the bad guys, but here they don't seem so bad. I trade a chocolate bar for a bead-link rifle cleaner, which he says he doesn't need any more now that he is a prisoner. We trade what we have, and decide to come back another day with more barter. After a while, fantasy returns to reality as we begin to get hungry and realize that it is time to go home for supper. We will have to suspend our operations of rounding up and interrogating the enemy since Major Mom is waiting and doesn't like me coming home late for dinner. We retrace our path under the barbed wire and escape unscathed and undetected, but tired and hungry. We always seem to have food on the table, but it never seems to be enough and I am always hungry. Mom tells me that because we are at war with the Japs and Germans, times are tough, and there isn't any meat.

In order to help the war effort, she has enrolled me in the Clean Your Plate Club, and to do my duty and eat every thing I don't like. "Think of the poor children of China," says she. I do, and so my little sister and I obey our orders and eat the usual macaroni and cheese during the week and fish on Fridays – *holy mackerel!* We eat fish because we are Catholic, and vegetables from the Victory garden because we are at war.

One day, I get a surprise and a treat – Mom takes me to a White Castle restaurant on Broadway where she buys me my first hamburger sandwich for 25 cents. It comes with mustard, relish, raw onions, and it is love at first bite. If that weren't enough, later that night, my pal Kenney steals a cigarette, and we puff on it in a back alley. For a little boy in South Boston, smoking one's first cigarette is a like being a grown up – like the guys who hang out in Ryan's Pub across the street.

During the following weeks, I frequent the P.O.W. camp regularly, and establish a trading post. Sneaking in and out becomes routine and even some of the G.I. guards trade with me. Mom begins to wonder why things in the kitchen are disappearing and where I am getting all those war souvenirs. I tell her that I trade with the other kids whose dads came back from the war. One day, Dad takes us to the Franklin Park Zoo on the trolley. Trips to the zoo are always a treat for Sharon and me. Except for dogs, cats and horses, one doesn't see animals around South Boston. Also at the zoo are German prisoners of war from the camp in South Boston who spend the day digging, cutting and trimming the grass. Dad is conducting us on a tour around the zoo, explaining about the wonderful world of birds and bees, flowers, trees, animals and such. Suddenly, we come upon the German POWs who see me, and begin to wave and call out. My mother thinks that they are waving to her and waves back. My father mumbles something anti-Germanic as we continue on our way to see the elephants. "What do they mean by teddy bear?" asks my mother. "That means they like you," says my father with a smile – I am smiling too.

*

Almost every one in our neighborhood comes from Ireland, or so it seems. In my small world as a child in Boston, there are only the Irish, the others, and the enemy. I know there must be lots of other kinds of people in the world, because I see them in the movies on Saturday afternoon at the B-way Theater. I know that Italian people live in the North end and that Polish people live down the way in City Point, because my father told me so. I have never seen a Black person except in the movies. I even heard that there are Jewish people who live in Mattapan, an area South of us where my father sometimes takes me to buy a foot long hot dog for 15 cents, but I don't know what Jewish people are.

Dad teaches me how to ride the busses, trolleys, and subways of Boston. My pals teach me the fine art of doing it without paying. With a bit of practice, I turn sneaking onto the M.T.A.[2] into an art form. From then on, my quest of exploring the city of Boston takes on new dimensions. Although I never know where places are exactly, I do know how to get there. I am driven by a little boy compulsion to find out what is around the corner or over the hill. In the summer of my imagination, I hack a trail through the jungle of 8th street, in winter mush ahead with my team of dogs over the frozen tundra of Broadway, or freezing and exhausted, scale the summit of Dorchester Heights. We are a wild bunch, prowling the streets and back allies: observing, fantasizing, exploring, testing, probing for an opportunity, some fun or a free meal. Our recognizance around town usually ends with sneaking into a movie house.

Some of the ticket takers have gotten to know us and let us in – knowing that we don't have any money anyway. A double feature only costs 12 cents for kids, but that is beyond my means, unless I can beg a few pennies or find some on the sidewalk. Action movies and cartoons are our favorite. Love movies are boring and kissing is yucky. Some movies I like so much that I stay in the theater and watch the double feature twice, sometimes getting out late after the air raid curfew – thus having to negotiate a perilous trek home through the empty streets of Boston while evading the air raid wardens. Going home from the theater during a city black out evokes fantasies of a mass escape from a concentration camp with the guards and dogs in pursuit. Carney Hospital is along the way home, and a great place infiltrate and explore. No one seems to notice a couple of kids walking around the corridors. Since we seem to know where we are going, no one pays attention to us. Is it because, like The Shadow on radio, we are wearing our invisible cloaks? In a flash we are outside again, going down the street with that good feeling of mission accomplished.

We sniff the air like animals in the forest as our imaginary army patrols the back streets of Boston. Boston has an aroma all of its own – a bouquet of fragrance from various sources: essence of exhaust from factories, sensuous soot from chimneys, captivating carbon monoxide from cars and buses, a rapturous whiff of garbage and urine in back allies, vapors of steam and coal from railway locomotives, a multitude of blends and concoctions, both exciting the pallet and inciting nausea. Certain areas have certain smells, both pleasant and foul. It is all part of my world and I know no other.

For an occasional treat, Dad takes us to Chinatown: a strange, but inviting, place right in the middle of Boston. Like in a Charlie Chan movie, exotic oriental intrigue lurks around every corner. I discover that I have a craving for Chinese food, and find myself there with the gang quite often. We like exploring the back allies of Chinese restaurants where we spend hours standing in front of the exhaust fan of the kitchen, absorbing the odors of the Orient and dreaming thoughts of far away places. Frequently our mood changes, and we seek out the back alley of an Italian restaurant where we enjoy the fragrance of the Mediterranean (emitted by a ventilator) by inhaling a banquet with each breath thus invoking romantic, Italian images of Nero burning Rome, the eruption of Mt. Vesuvius, or lions eating Christians – all sorts of raunchy, little boy things.

From Carson Beach near our house, we get the smell of the ocean, the salt air, and of course, fish. At the end of the beach is City Point and Kelley's Landing where boats tie up and people fish. I often go there to visit the aquarium and watch the action going on at the pier. Most of all, I like to stand by the kitchen fan of the fish and chip shop and dream that someday I will eat one of everything in the shop. It won't be until 30 years later when I return to

Kelly's Landing that my wish comes true. Such joy for a kid to grow up in Bean Town – so much to do, so much to see, so much to smell.

*

Kenney and his two brothers, Jimmy and "Wee-wee," and I are roaming about town one day. Although his real name is Richard, "Wee-Wee" gets his name from the fact that he still wets his pants. We disappear into a back alley to piss, then upon emerging, Kenney spots a house with a funeral wreath on the front door. A wreath on a door in South Boston means that an Irish Catholic wake for the dead is going on inside, and all friends of the departed are invited to enter, pay their respects and partake of refreshments. It is the refreshment part that interests us the most as we approach the house and knock on the door. Like alter boys, we file into the house to kneel at the coffin and say a prayer or two. After giving our condolences, we make a beeline to the kitchen and stuff ourselves with sustenance. Soon after, we make our adieu and depart from the departed – feeling good inside all the while for having made the noble gesture of holy consummation – *the cookies were great.*

Families who had a soldier killed in the war hang a banner with a gold star in a window. To a little boy in Boston it translates – like the funeral wreath – "lunch time!" We spot a golden star in a window then go into our alter boy routine, consoling the mourners then stuffing ourselves with the usual amenities. Of course, Christmas is the best of all when people in the neighborhood invite children into their homes to see their Christmas tree and enjoy refreshments. We are also the uninvited quests at wedding receptions, family picnics, office parties and other social gatherings where food is served. The Salvation Army is always good for a bowl of soup. Although we raise some eyebrows as we stand in line with the winos and bums, they never shoo us away. We are not exactly starving, but the sport of hunting and surviving in the jungles of Boston is the name of the game. We know of all the bakeries in town that give free samples and the open markets where a piece of fruit can be stealthily acquired.

We learn the value of money and decide to acquire some. I find a crutch in a dump one day and our new, sensational, crippled kid's quartet is born. After singing on a street corner about an hour for a few pennies, we disband the act, and decide to incorporate ourselves into a business. I become a paperboy, selling the Boston Globe on street corners. Dad was a paperboy once himself. Although I cannot think of Dad as once having been a boy, he insists that it is so. "All fathers were once boys and all boys will become fathers," says he. This thought is something for me to contemplate as I shout – "get your daily paper here." The newspaper business is flat – I'm making nickels and dimes. It is more than I had before, but I need to increase my profit. I gather up all the old papers I find and stuff them into boxes to be recycled. The paper stock pays by the pound, so I strive to hedge my margin by loading up the bottom of the box with rocks. Sometimes it works, sometimes it doesn't – *it's a good thing I am a kid – I'm protected by law.*

South Station is a wonder of excitement and adventure for little boys – a place to hang out on cold, bleak, rainy days during winter. We watch multitudes of grownups and kids, soldiers, sailors and marines, all going about their daily lives, coming and going to who knows where. I find it fascinating, especially the movie theater where for 10 cents people can wait for their train and watch nonstop cartoons. In the train yard outside, steam locomotives, huffing and puffing, put on a great show as train cars are coupled and shunted about. Walking along railroad tracks while looking for flares and dynamite caps gone astray is something that we love to do. The caps and flares are used to warn the engineer of danger. One of our war games is to place a cap on a rail to stop the train. Like the partisans of France fighting the Nazis, we wait for an on coming train, fix the cap on the rail then run like hell. When there is no train, we just drop a rock on it to make it explode or, like in a war movie, toss a flare at a trestle as if it were a potato masher grenade. I have never been anywhere far before, and as I walk the rails, I dream of riding a train into the wonderful world beyond Boston – a world I know all about from the movies I see on Saturday afternoon.

It's a wet, wintry day as I stride along the railroad tracks. From behind, I hear the chugging of an approaching a steam locomotive. In my reverie I ponder whether to blow it up or let it pass by. Suddenly, the locomotive stops near me, and the engineer offers me a ride. I am in ecstasy as I climb up the ladder into the cab. He leans with his elbow sticking out the window like engineers do, pulls some levers, and the monster chugs forward belching smoke and steam. We chug along the tracks, and he invites me to pull the whistle cord. The wail of the whistle and the hiss of steam excite me as we rumble along – I'm in little boy heaven. All too soon, he brings the monster to a stop, and I climb down. I stand there all smiles and waive as he chugs away in the choo-choo. My head is in the clouds as I hop on a trolley car, and make my way home – *Such a nice fellow – maybe I won't be stopping trains with dynamite caps any more.*

One day at home alone, I get a visit from Kenney and Jane. Kenney has a new trick he wants to show me, and asks Jane to take off her pants and lay on the bed. Kenney who has two brothers and a sister is the expert on girls and having babies and things like that.

I don't know anything about girls or babies. I only have a little sister whom I tolerate. She is just my sister, a companion, a playmate and she is a girl who likes dolls and baby carriages and other girl stuff – *yuck!* Jane has a silly grin on her face and giggles. Kenney lays on top Jane and humps up and down. I watch fascinated, but I'm wondering what is suppose to happen. Kenney invites me to try and so I do. I hump away, but whatever is supposed to happen doesn't. Jane doesn't say anything, but just smiles. I think she likes me, but I'm a boy, and don't like mushy kissing and stuff like that. Cowboys in the movies don't kiss girls. Jane wants to play doctor. I don't know how, but Kenney does – *interesting!* However, soon we grow tired of the game, Jane puts her pants back on, and the kids depart. Then, it's on to more important business – like making myself a peanut butter and jelly sandwich.

I am in the 4th grade in a St. Augustine Catholic school. My teacher-nun, Sister Margaret, is short and looks like a penguin in her habit. The nuns carry a homemade wooden clicker in their pockets, which they use to make a click sound thus signaling the class to stand up in unison or to sit down. She clicks her clicker, and we kneel on our seats to pray. She clicks it again, and we stand up. Again, and we file up in the corridor and march outside to a record playing a Sousa march. The nuns say that I am a soldier in God's army, trained to go out into the world and fight the Devil. I don't know if I can handle all of this.

Not only am I fighting Japs and Germans, but now the Devil himself. Besides the usual school stuff, we have to learn catechism and how to pray. The boys are segregated from the girls in class so that we soldiers can keep our minds on our work. I notice on occasion that one of the lads across from me has his mind on playing with his noodle under the desk when Sister Margaret is otherwise preoccupied – the Devil indeed if she catches him. For general punishment, the nuns whip the palms of the hand with a stick of rattan. The word sounds like Battan thus conjuring up terrible images of Japs whipping American prisoners; not only that, but the all-black habits remind me of the black uniform of the *Gestapo.*[3]

Special punishment is to stay after school on Friday. For not doing my homework, I am told to not only stay after school, but to return on Saturday to complete my sentence in the corner of the brick wall surrounding the convent. There I spend hours, my face against the wall, looking for bullet holes while awaiting the firing squad of the Wardens of Waifs – not even baby Jesus can save me now – *Was it something I said?* My feet are getting tired and I'm getting so hungry. Maybe I'll get a nice hamburger as a last meal. The noon whistle blows, the gate surrounding the courtyard is opened and I am released on parole – *holy moly!*

I hate school, except of course the occasional instruction given by Jane who wants to become a school teacher when she grows up. Her class is always well attended. Attending Mass on Sunday is a torture that must be endured. I think I must be wearing holes in my knees from praying. Praying, I think, is a waste of time since I never get what I pray for. The nun tells us that someday we will go to heaven, but I'm not sure that I want to leave South Boston. In preparation for First Communion., we dress up in a white suit with red tie, and march in a parade like soldiers going to war against the Devil. I once saw a devil on Halloween so I don't understand what the fuss is all about. He seemed like I nice fellow to me. My Nana even calls me a wee devil.

When school is out, the little bad boys of Boston continue to prowl the city with our toy guns, raking havoc and mayhem like Genghis Kahn and his hordes wherever we go: tipping over ash cans at the public housing incinerator to make a roadblock against invading troops, unscrewing light bulbs from public walkways to toss like hand grenades against unsuspecting spies, setting booby traps like leaving a bottle sitting on a radiator in the hallway with a string tied from it to a doorknob. After a knock on the door, we run away and listen for the crash of glass. Best of all, I like the occasional tripping of the fire alarm on the corner then retreating to our bunkers to watch the fire engines and police converge with their lights blinking and sirens wailing. We are like Robin Hood and his merry men – a legend in our own time.

My parents had moved to Boston from Fall River, fifty miles south where I was born. My dad is a musician and plays piano in a nightclub called Blinstrubs. Mom works as a waitress in a Pub called Dorgan's. When Mom is working, I have to stay home and babysit my sister. Although she isn't bad as little sisters go, she plagues me with thoughtless questions to no end. This must be a ploy, for I'm sure she is a mole for Mom, a sleeper agent, an informer who spies into my private little boy world and reports back all she has seen and heard. It must be so, because Mom always seems to find out what I'm up to, then I suffer the wrath of Mom. Good thing she doesn't find out everything or I would be in big trouble. I go to great lengths to keep my little sister in the dark about things only a little boy should know, and avoid her when I can. Little sisters cannot keep a secret. Once in a while, I am forced to take her with me to the movies at the B-Way Theater on Saturday afternoon. Rather than stand in a long line of kids waiting to buy a ticket, I deposit my sister in the line with the money for the tickets where she patiently waits while I invent an excuse to walk across the street and explore the Five and Dime store. I return in time to meet her with the tickets, and we walk into the theater together. Sly fox that I am, she never catches on.

*

I hardly ever see my dad since he works nights and sleeps days. Such is the lifestyle of a musician, which isn't easy. Everybody at the nightclub wants to buy the boys in the band a drink. After work, in the wee hours of the morning, Dad staggers home drunk, makes a lot of noise cooking in the kitchen, then plays records on his Victrola while writing music for vaudeville acts. Mom gets up out of bed angry, and then there is the Devil to pay. They argue, they fight, then Mom calls the Boston police, and they come to take him away. At first my little sister and I are frightened by all of this, and hide under the covers. After a while it only becomes annoying. One night, while Mom and Dad are fighting, there is a pounding on the door – it's the sailor from across the hall. He is angry that my dad is flirting with his wife. They argue, they fight, then Mom gets involved. The police arrive and take my father away for the night. On occasion, I spend so much time roaming the streets of Boston that my mother reports me missing to the police who find me and take me home. Boston's finest are frequent visitors to my house – either to take me home or to take my father away. I am stressed out, and find refuge and escape at the movies on Saturday afternoon.

One day, Mom announces that she is getting a divorce. She brings home an Army Major and tells us that he is going to be our new father. He turns off my favorite radio program, *Clyde Beatty in Darkest Africa*, and tells me that I need discipline and have to shape up. I dislike him right away. As I listen in silence, he talks about good times we are going to have. The Major soon discovers that Mom is an incessant talker when she's in a good mood, and a nag when she's not. He leaves, and we never see him again. Mom does not divorce, but Dad has mysteriously disappeared.

Meanwhile at school, I continue to fail in spite of the efforts of the nuns. I flunk the fourth grade and have to repeat it again. I know I must not be too bright when one of the kids on the street swaps me my pet turtle for 5 turtle eggs, which turn out to be rocks. Mom decides that I am running around with the wrong crowd and enrolls me in the local Boys Club and the Cub Scouts to keep me off the streets. She also enrolls me in public school. I am delighted – not for repeating the fourth grade, but for my release back into civilization from the penguin penal colony for little lost boys.

One day my dad reappears in a sailor suit like the one I use to wear when I was a little, little boy. He had not run off at all but had enlisted in the U.S. Navy and is home on leave. He is stationed in the Brooklyn Navy yard as a piano player with the all-black Navy orchestra and cymbal player in the marching band. We are all glad he is back and all is well.

Although sounding strange being the only white man in a black band in Brooklyn, it does present opportunities. Because of his musical abilities, the boys in the band take a liking to my father, and when they go on leave to Harlem, they take along a fellow musician of the "Caucasian persuasion." He gets to meet none other than Count Basie, Duke Ellington, Nat King Cole, and forms a friendship with Fats Waller. Dad also returns with a beaver fur coat, which he bought at a bargain from a fellow musician down on his luck – Mom is overwhelmed. A beaver fur coat is something worn by movie stars – something to be worn on a special occasion, but Dad never takes her anywhere, except the club where he works – what to do? With a flair of the theatrical, she proceeds to hang out the laundry to dry in the public housing cloths drying area in her new coat, and on a Sunday at that – all the while scanning the windows of the housing project, hoping to be noticed. Mom is acting out her fantasy – she's in housewife heaven – a movie star.

*

Dad takes me on a train ride to New York City where he shows me the Navy base and all the other sights around town. I see Times Square and notice that there are men in uniform all over – just like in the newsreels at the movies. He shows me the Waldorf Astoria where he and the band play for the service men and women. He tells me about the time he rode up in the elevator with Bing Crosby – *wow, I'm impressed!* My eyes are aglow with visions of grandeur. My dad knows movie stars, and I never knew.

We visit the Empire State building where my mind flashes back to King Kong – climbing up from below, and I look for the airplanes coming to shoot him down. All the while during my tour, I'm craving hamburgers. He takes me to an automat restaurant where you drop in a coin, open a door and take out a meal, but I would rather eat a hamburger. He looks at me in disbelief. He doesn't understand little boys; grownups seldom do. We take the train back to Boston where I settle back into my familiar lifestyle.

Dad takes us to see the circus at the Boston Garden. I see Gargantua the Great – a monstrous gorilla in a cage, captured in the wilds of Africa by Frank Buck himself. We enjoy a performance given in 5 rings, filled with people in glittering costumes, doing impossible things – and animals, all those animals doing tricks. I can't believe my eyes; it is the most wonderful thing I have ever seen. When I grow up, I want to be in the circus. Dad returns to New York to fight the war, while Mom works at home, retouching negatives for my Mimmay's (Grandmother) photo studio in Fall River. Sharon plays with her dolls and dreams of becoming a ballerina; I dream of being in the circus – time passes.

I continue to live in my little boy fantasy world, and dash along the rooftops of the housing project in my Batman costume, fighting evil villains and such. I still don't like going to school, but I tolerate it while Mom helps me learn at home by forcing me to do my homework – even though I would much prefer to join the Army and fight Germans. Suddenly one day, the war is over. The German prisoners are sent back to Germany and life is suddenly different. I don't quite understand why there is no more war.

There has always been war – I have never known anything else. Is this the end of civilization, as I know it? I notice that we no longer need ration stamps to buy food, and that there is now meat on the table. Mom explains to me how I am growing up and changing. And so, as people change, life changes. Dad comes home from the war and returns to play in the band at Blinstrubs. He goes back to his old routine of coming home drunk, cooking, writing music all night and sleeping all day. Some things never change.

Terry with playmates Jane and Kenny (1941)

Dad with little sister Sharon (1943)

Chapter II
Adolescent Passions and Family Life

Mom and Dad sometimes take us on train rides to Fall River to visit Mimmay[4] who came from Canada and speaks French, which I don't understand. Mom tells me about her dad who came to America with a pony and would walk around the towns, taking children's photos while straddled in the saddle. He died before I was born, and my Mimmay has carried on the business ever since. I think she doesn't like me sometimes as there are so many things that I am not allowed to touch. She always wears a big hat and drives a big car to the studio where I watch her taking photos of people. I watch my uncle Ernie stand behind the camera under a big black sheet of cloth, with one hand clutching a rubber ball, and in the other, a rubber duck that squeaks when he squeezes it to make a baby laugh. It is a busy place, a strange place. All day long, Ernie takes people's photos: babies, men in uniform, weddings, graduations and portraits. When we are in town, they love to take photos of me and my sister, and we love the attention. My Mimmay always buys me new clothes when we visit, which makes Dad happy.

Mom and her five sisters all grew up without a father. Dad says that is the reason they fight all the time. They all work in some way or other at the studio. Some of my uncles work there too. Mimmay says that if it were not for the studio, we would all starve. She doesn't like my dad because he is a musician and drinks. She calls him an "Irish sonamamitch." Likewise, my uncles are all sonamamitches. "They're all after my money," says she – "sonamamitch!"

At first, I look forward to a family dinner gathering. After a while, formalities fade, and the dinner dissolves into a mad hatter's tea party. Like elephants that never forget, my aunts still hold old childhood grudges that must be avenged. Subtle barbs are tossed between sips of tea, catty comments between helpings of mashed potatoes, cutting remarks while carving the turkey, a dash of salt in the pea soup and then another sprinkle in an open wound. Each compliment spiced with a pinch of criticism.

The temperature is rising – the potion is brewing – the air is tense. Mom stirs the pot with glee while adding a little pepper of her own. Emotions rise as I help myself to more white meat. Barbs fly as the cranberry sauce is passed. My aunts, brandishing fake smiles, are having a great time while my uncles steam under the collar. They blush and squirm as each in turn is picked apart at the banquet table until only the skeleton is left. By the time I get to my dessert, a full-scale "war of the sisters" boils over. Insults pour like gravy. Slights are slung to the sound of crunching celery. Slurs slither like snakes with the slurping of soup. Casualties mount as each sister is cut to the quick with verbal vile from mouths filled with sausage stuffing. A din pervades throughout the room from the sisters all talking at once. Laughter erupts as an epithet hits its mark and a point is scored. One-upmanship is the name of the game. I am not really paying attention to all this as I have my thoughts elsewhere, but my poor little boy brain can't take any more. Although we are used to this family thing by now, Sharon is still uncomfortable, and I find it annoying. Why do moms and dads and uncles and aunts have to argue all the time? Perhaps it's a family thing. By now, Dad is getting a headache and so am I. With the battle raging on all sides, I eat my pudding and sink lower into my foxhole to avoid being hit by a stray, patronizing projectile. "Sonamamitch!" Mimmay bellows, as she proceeds to restore law and order among her daughters of disarray. A truce is called as Sharon and I disappear to play with our cousins. While the scrapping siblings clean up the battlefield, the brother-in-laws retreat to the parlor to lick their wounds and smoke cigarettes. Later, Dad suggests we leave, and so we do.

Mom says that she had a great time – a la fois prochaine![5] I am always happy to visit my mom's family, but then I'm always glad to leave – *sonamamitch*!

*

Round two: a visit with Dad's side of the family in a section of Fall River called Corky Row where my cousins, the O'Briens, the O'Sullivans, the O'Laffertys, the Doyles, and the Cavanaughs, live. The neighborhood reminds me of South Boston. Dad says that a Bostonian is an Irishman who can swim.

Apparently in Fall River they can't, though I don't know what swimming has to do with anything. My Nana is an endearing lady who drowns me in love and tea. I never knew my Irish grandfather as he also, like Mom's dad, died before I was born. He had 3 wives and so I have lots of cousins. Like Mom, Dad, his brother Donald and their four sisters were raised without a father. Like Mom and her sisters, they fight among themselves like alley cats – about things in the past, things that I don't understand and don't want to know. Mom loves to get involved, giving unwanted advice, telling secrets and otherwise meddling in her in-laws' lives – someone to be both loved and feared. No skeleton remains secure in anybody's closet for long if Mom has any say about it. Although my Dad's sisters are usually the target for gossip, poor uncle Donald suffers the most from scrutiny by his sisters and my mother.

Uncle Donald, the youngest of the O'Brien clan and Nana's darling, had come home from the war as a technical sergeant, having won his stripes as an altar boy for the Padré of an air base in New Mexico. He brings home a wife much older than himself with a daughter from a previous marriage. Nana thinks the wife is crazy, and so is Donald. Nana McCabe throws them out of the house. Such shame on the clans of O'Brien and McCabe, decedents of Irish kings, the Hibernian royalty of Corky Row. *Will the family honor be restored; and what about Dad's sister Madeleine?*

Through it all, I suffer in silence while eating my corned beef and cabbage and sipping my tea. Like a serine sow ignoring her squealing piglets, Nana just looks on from above it all, clutching her rosary, and uttering "Jesus, Mary and Joseph!" while listening to the soap operas on radio as she pours more tea. All of this family stuff is more than I can handle, and I can hardly wait to return to the peace and tranquility of South Boston – *Jesus, Mary and Joseph!*

*

Things are looking up. Dad now has a car, and drives to New York, where he plays piano with his jazz musician friend, Fats Waller. Mom tells us that Dad plays a white piano while Fats plays a black piano. This sounds wonderful, and I wish I could see them play together. Unfortunately, it doesn't last long. Fats travels to Hollywood by train to make a picture, and dies en route. Dad loses a friend and his big chance to be in a movie.

Dad continues to play piano in the band at Blinstrubs with headliners like Patty Page, Louis Armstrong, Jimmy Durante and Eddie Fischer, but show business is beginning to change – the soldiers and sailors are all going home.

Without customers, nightclubs, which catered to servicemen, no longer have floor shows and big bands. Things are changing, and I am changing too. By now I am almost eleven years old, almost a teenager.

*

Mom and Dad buy a house in Swansea on the other side of the Taunton River from Fall River. Mimmay says that Dad has been banned in Boston, and that she lent Dad the money so he could get out of town. This is a family joke, I think. Nevertheless, I am overwhelmed to move to the country, live in a big house and have a dog and a cat. We also have a piano, and when Dad comes home from work at night, he cooks, drinks and pounds the piano all night long. Mom gets up angry and they go at it again. Sharon sleeps away. I suffer in silence.

Dad tries to teach me to play the piano, but he is not a good teacher. He says "watch me" then sits down and plays and I watch. Then he tells me "now you try it" – I do, but I can't. "Watch me again," says he. I watch and I watch. Once again I try but only plunking comes out. Dad is frustrated and so am I.

We both give up. Perhaps I don't want to learn or is it something about being a musician that I don't like? Not only does Dad drink, but he also smokes Camel cigarettes as he plays, and leaves cigarette burn marks on the keys of the piano. Mom is not pleased. She erupts like a volcano and accuses Dad of playing patty cake with Peaches and Cream, one of the strippers at the club. The nag and the drunk go at it again – dishes fly. Sharon and I hide.

One night while cooking a pizza, Dad takes a slice of finger off with a knife. We all rush him to the hospital but Dad is feeling no pain. The finger is saved and the piano playing resumes, but Dad is in the dog house again. Things are quiet for a while until one morning while Dad is still asleep, we see in the paper a photo of a wrecked car found by the police, sticking out of a wall of a farmer's field. The photo of the wreck in the paper looks strangely familiar. We look in the back yard and our car is not there, yet Dad is upstairs sleeping as usual. Anticipation grows as we wait for Dad's arrival on the scene. Mom sits silently in deep thought waiting for Dad to wake up and explain. It is the calm before the storm. I feel electricity in the air as Dad awakes and descends the stairs to face the music. No doubt about it while driving home drunk, Dad wrecked the car. Emerging unscathed, he then stumbles home and goes to bed as if nothing had happened. Mom is furious. She unleashes her terrible tongue, lashing like a whip while Dad tries to

27

defend himself. Mom goes through the list of his past sins and indiscretions once again.

After an exhausting review of all Dad's misdeeds, she goes through the list of his sisters, criticizing each one in turn as if there were some sort of family conspiracy afoot. As usual when she reaches Dad's sister Madeleine, it signals that she has run out of ammunition – I've heard it all before – *Jesus, Mary and Joseph! I wish I could run away and join the circus.*

*

We live in a section of Swansea called Ocean Grove by Narragansett Bay. It is a working class neighborhood, mostly of former Canadians, who are Catholic, speak French and dig clams for a living.

They are considered to be low-class people and the butt of jokes. Kids who live on the hill above the Grove are Protestant. They go to the public school on the hill and like to trace their families back to the Pilgrims. They snub the Frenchys (Dad calls them "Canucks") who attend Catholic school in the Grove at the bottom of the hill.

The O'Briens, descendents of the Celtic warrior king Brian Boru, live at the bottom of the hill with the Frenchys. We are in a social class of our own. I attend public school on top of the hill while Sharon goes to Catholic school at the bottom. The Catholic school suits little sister Sharon. She says that when she grows up she would like to become a nun – *Jesus, Mary and Joseph!* As I struggle in school, Mom tries to help me by giving advice, but it is the advice that only a mom can give – broad and vague: "try harder," "find out," "ask somebody," "do your best." I never learn how, or who, or why. Mom tries, but she just doesn't know. She is better at nagging than teaching.

In the eighth grade above me is a girl named Ursula who is pretty and speaks Portuguese. I'm always fascinated by people who can speak a foreign language, especially a pretty girl. I want to approach her, but I am shy. I have mixed feelings about her – I think I'm in love, but her dad sells clams for a living, and she has a boyfriend – a Frenchy in my class called Jiggy. Although I've never had a girlfriend, I know all about them from the movies: things like holding hands while walking together and kissing when no one is looking. Kisses are something I get when I visit my grandmothers and aunts – something yucky that grownups do to children. Something that a child must endure, like going to school. Only a sissy kisses a girl and holds her hand. Hopalong Cassidy, my favorite cowboy, never kisses girls, just his horse. I'm not sure I want a girlfriend. Girlfriends are for sissies not cowboys.

And yet, as I see Ursula every day going to school, there is something about her that attracts me: something strange, something wonderful, something compelling. I begin to formulate a plan to meet her and become her friend. I devise the classic plan of infiltration: get to know the boyfriend, then through him, meet the girl, move in with her and move him out. Cleverly, I conspire to befriend Jiggy.

First, I express interest in his father's septic tank cleaning service by talking about my own septic tank and sewers and sludge in general. His eyes sparkle as I weigh the advantages of deep pit pumping over chemical additives. Then, I just happen to show up in places where I know he hangs out – it works. We become pals and he takes me along while he visits his girl. Soon the three of us are walking home after school or all going to the malt shop for a black cow. Ursula begins to warm up to me as I display my primary school charm. I'm getting ready to make my move and invite her to the record hop, when one day, Ursula's family unexpectedly moves to the big city of Fall River. Alas, evil parents snatch her away from me – *sonamamitch!* I am heart broken, but after a Saturday afternoon at a movie theater watching The Three Stooges followed by a hamburger, her memory begins to fade, and I survive another of life's little boy tragedies.

Dad writes music for acts: singers, dancers, acrobats, dirty comics, strip tease artists and all forms of other entertainers who need band arrangements for their act. I am fascinated by my father's friends who sometimes come to the house. One of Dad's clients is a puppeteer who in exchange for a musical arrangement for his act, gives Dad two marionettes: a white face clown and a Black tap dancer. Sharon and I decide that we are going into show business. After constructing a puppet theater in Dad's garage and borrowing Dad's microphone and record player, we put together a show of sorts and advertise to the neighborhood kids. Things seem to be going well until Mom decides to get involved. She changes the whole routine and rewrites the script. Helpless to object, I am forced to comply and hope for the best.

Mom is not only directing the show, but invites her mother and sisters to attend. This project of mine started as a fun thing, but is now getting out of hand. Saturday afternoon arrives, and reminiscent of Our Gang comedy movies, Sharon and I attempt to present a backyard puppet show in the garage. The show has a script with music and dialogue, which we recite on a hot mike while we work the puppets. Mom is right there prompting; but unknown to her, the audience hears every thing she says.

The audience is rolling in the aisles, listening to Mom prompt, correct and direct as we try to work the puppets and say our lines. By the end of the show, I'm ready to sneak out of town. Everything goes wrong, and the audience loves it. The family gives us nothing but praise for a good show, and an opportunity to laugh at Mom. Undeterred, Mom books the puppet act at a Christmas party for kids in a housing project in Fall River where I have to repeat my marionette misadventure. We are a hit again, but Mom steals the show. By this time, I am not only fuming through the nostrils, but frothing at the mouth. My entire production taken over by my mother – *how rude!*

Dad writes music for Hal and his wife Jean. They do a vaudeville act and live in the neighborhood. Hal still tries to make a living riding a unicycle and juggling, but times are tough in show business. Television makes its appearance in America and the movie houses begin to close. Hal takes a job as a butcher in a market while Jean opens a dance studio in her home. Times are tough so Mom and I dig clams to make ends meet. The big bands are becoming a thing of the past as rock and roll moves in to take its place. Dad is reduced to playing piano in bars around the city – not a healthy environment for a musician who drinks.

Jean comes from a family of carnival entertainers. Her father once did an act of plunging from a tower into a tub of water with fire burning on the surface. He made his last performance at a county fair when he misjudged the leap, and made a big splash, hitting the edge of the tub – killing himself. Jean rivals my mom as a nag and Hal is an alcoholic – another volatile combination. With so much in common, we become family friends. Our friendship intensifies as one day Hal offers to teach me how to juggle. I jump at the chance, and juggling becomes my passion. With visions of performing in the circus, I practice constantly in the backyard, gradually becoming the focus of attention of the neighbors. Friends begin to think I am odd, strangers think I'm amusing and my family thinks – *Jesus, Mary and Joseph!*

Show people, of course, are out of the loop of local society, and are viewed with suspicion and indifference. Dad and Hal, of course, don't encourage a favorable image, neither does their friend Happy the Clown who fancies himself another Lou Costello, entertaining at all the bars in town. Poor Happy abandons his family, drives to Hollywood to be discovered, only to face failure there and ridicule at home. While deep in despair, he resorts to the big sleep – a rubber hose connected to the tail pipe of his car with the other end protruding in through the window. As the engine runs, the deadly fumes seep in, and it's curtains for the clown. Undaunted by all of this, I practice juggling every day and dream of performing in the circus.

*

High school in Swansea is typical of the lifestyle of the '50s. Kids form teen social groups according to what their parents do for a living. Some of the girls in high school go steady and some don't. Those who do wear each other's clothes and jewelry, hang out with members of the clique and snub other such groups. There are unwritten rules for going steady: one cannot be seen talking in school hallways with the wrong person, socially acceptable clothing must be worn, certain high school sports become a religion.

The captains of the sporting teams and the cheerleaders are the elite of the teenage world. The boys fight, the girls cry. Emotions and passions are aroused with a bad joke, a misinterpreted gesture, a secret being revealed; thus teenage dramas take on soap opera proportions between classes. The boys flaunt their girlfriends and the girls strut around gloating, showing off their guys like a moose trophy hanging on the wall. A sheep mentality of conformity persists with gossip, of course, the usual entertainment.

I don't seem to fit in, but am resigned to my status and content to play the tuba in the band. I do attract attention with my juggling skills, but the reaction I get is that of curiosity rather than amazement. Tossing a football, hitting a baseball or sinking a basket is what turns on the girls, not juggling 3 balls.

Juggling is my passion however – after all, the O'Brien clan, like all the Irish from South Boston, are in a class of our own. I take on the image of a loner – actually, I'm just shy while yearning to be noticed.

One summer day, the carnival comes to town where I meet Darryl the Sky Master from Texas who performs atop a sway pole as a free attraction. I have never seen a carnival before, and I find it exciting. It reminds me in some way of my love, the circus. Now that I have my driver's license, I yearn to travel. My dad had taught me to drive at the town dump since I wasn't yet legal to drive on the highway. I would practice between mounds of garbage and pits of swill while being scolded by thousands of screeching sea gulls, which obviously were annoyed by our presence – or was it my driving? Finally, the day comes for me to take the driving test at the registry of motor vehicles where Dad's sister Peggy works. Thanks to Auntie Peg's aura of power, the test is a a piece of cake.

And so, I think back on that day as I stand with my new driver's license in my pocket, gawking at the carnival and wishing I could travel. Spying me standing there, Darryl walks up and asks where he can find water. I fetch him his water and we begin to talk about show business. Darryl has a problem: he is all alone, and after this engagement has a long jump to Prince Edward Island in Canada. He can't drive it alone, and asks me if I know anyone who wants to drive on a long trip. "No problem," say I without hesitation, "but I'll have to get permission from Mom and Dad." He agrees to pay my expenses, but there is no talk of salary – at this point in life one doesn't always do things for money, and I am eager to leave home. Mom and Dad approve and I am off on my first teenage adventure – driving a carnival truck a thousand miles to Canada. Facing us is a grueling, four-day non-stop drive in a one-ton truck containing Darryl's sway pole (disassembled into sections), cables, wenches, costumes and a bunk bed. Darryl doesn't seem to mind that I have never driven a truck before – no problem, he will teach me along the way.

The trip is mostly boring, uncomfortable and tedious. We drive day and night, changing drivers every few hundred miles. In Canada, road signs are not always obvious, and I manage to go miles out of our way while Darryl is sleeping. We pass through one town that is having a celebration and a parade, causing us stop for hours waiting for the parade to pass – *sonamamitch!* Already a few days and nights have passed, and we still have 2 days to go – *am I sleeping and dreaming that I am driving or am* I driving *while asleep?* The road seems to go on and on, until we reach the ferry that takes us over to Prince Edward Island and the Great Charlotte Fair. The fair has a grandstand for horse racing, and inside the track is a stage for a vaudeville show, of which the sway pole act is the top attraction. We spend the day setting up the pole, and Darryl allows me to climb the pole to set the fireworks near the top. Behind the stage are dressing rooms providing a place for the performers to sleep. This is my first exposure to big-time show business and I am impressed, also I've never been to Canada before – a double treat.

Darryl, at twenty one years old, is quite a lover; I notice a carnival girl visiting in his truck every night. I like his style with the women, but alas, they are not interested in a young squirt like me. There is something about a death-defying performer that attracts women. *Someday when I am a performer, they will come knocking on my door too*, I'm thinking. The week passes fast with two shows a day, followed by horse racing. Between shows, I enjoy the midway and other exhibits offered by the fair, then I retire to the dressing room behind the stage where I sleep. The engagement flies by, and soon it is time to reload the pole then drive to the next fair, which is unbelievably a couple of thousand miles away in Tennessee – show business is losing its appeal.

The trip is a back breaker as we retrace our route through the eastern states and into the South. In Virginia, I notice something I had never seen before –

Black people and segregation. Signs on the walls of restaurants and truck stops say "White only" and "Colored," something I had learned about in school in Massachusetts. Darryl tells me all about Blacks from a Texan's point of view and briefs me on the social customs of the South. I'm getting an education as well as a sore back.

We arrive at the fair in Tennessee where I get out of the truck like a zombie. I don't know where I am and I don't care, but there is still work to be done setting up the pole and getting ready for a show. A few days of rest puts me in a better mood, but now Darryl[6] doesn't need me any more, and puts me on a bus back to Providence. I'm having mixed emotions at this point: I love show business, I hate show business – another long trip, *sonamamitch!* This time however, its in the relative comfort of a bus where I can sleep, read and ponder where I have been and where I am going. Mom and Dad greet me at the bus station in Providence then take me home. Again, I have mixed emotions: I'm glad to be home, I hate being home.

*

My juggling improves to the point where I evolve into an accomplished performer – sort of. Actually, I'm just good enough to entertain at birthday parties and such, but the realization of having my own act inspires me and feeds my ego. After my family realizes that I'm serious about performing, they decide not only to encourage me, but to actively participate in producing and directing my act. Hal and Gene put together a routine for me, Dad gets involved and writes music for a band accompaniment, Mimmay designs and sews me a costume and uncle Joe takes my photographs. Mom does her bit by volunteering me for the Catholic Church annual variety and minstrel show – my show business career is on a roll.

Each Sunday, I watch a television program called *Candy Carnival* where amateur performers, like myself, strut their stuff, each hoping to be chosen the winner and get a booking at George Hamid's Steel Pier in Atlantic City. After writing and sending photos, they contact me to appear on the show. Not only am I overwhelmed, but I'm a nervous wreck – supposing I drop a ball (the jugglers' nightmare) while appearing on national television – *oh the shame!* Practicing every day helps relieve the stress Then the big day arrives when Hal and I take the train to Philadelphia to appear on live television. I continue to be tense, but not nervous as the cab drives to the studio where we rehearse with the band. The complexities of producing a T.V. show are greater than I had imagined;

also, I discover that the illusions seen on the screen at home are far nicer than the reality. As the ringmaster announces me, I step out into the ring relaxed and serene – the act goes well and I don't drop anything. Backstage again, I have a great sense of relief and disappointment. Mr. Hamid has watched the show and phones in his two favorites: myself and the trampoline act; but the audience chooses the trampoline act the winner – *sonamamitch!* I will have to wait another 25 years until I get to perform at the Steel Pier in Atlantic City. Back at high school again, I suddenly have a reputation, and those who would never talk to me become warm and friendly as I bask in the sunshine of my sudden notoriety.

Dad takes me to Boston to meet some agent friends, and I begin to get a few $35 Saturday night jobs. The engagements, however, leave much to be desired: smoke filled bar rooms with a four-piece band, a strip, dirty comic, singer or dancer and a novelty act. Disillusioned as I am, a gig is a gig – I'm in show business. Dad tries to help me along with my new career. For a high school graduation present, he buys me an old Kaiser Traveler – my first car, which looks good, but isn't. I have a fair date in Maine on the Canadian border. My passenger, a girl tap dancer, accompanies me on the job. As we chug along north of Boston, I notice smoke coming out of the tail pipe.

I am not too concerned since I don't know anything about cars. When I stop for gas, however, I discover the we are out of oil – an ominous sign, but the show must go on, and so we continue our trip, stopping frequently to check the gas and fill up the oil. With the car now belching smoke, our apprehension is relieved somewhat as we pull onto the fairgrounds where the car, now out of oil, promptly dies – *Jesus, Mary and Joseph!* Well at least we made the date, but how are we going to get home? A sympathetic fair manager who has a trip scheduled to Boston, offers to take us home after the date – which he does. My first car turns out to be a lemon. Dad arranges for the car to be towed back to Boston where it is repaired, and soon I'm back in business again.

*

Northeastern University lies on Huntington Avenue in downtown Boston near Symphony Hall. It's there that I begin my college life, not for any special reason about the college, but the location is convenient for me to get work. Many nightclubs that still feature a floor show permeate the area. I play trombone in the college band, excel in the German language and enter a freshman talent contest at school – winning first prize. My spirits soar as I experience being on my own and able to survive.

Gretchen Golden operates a rooming house behind Symphony Hall. She continues her late husband's theatrical agency: booking acts on weekend gigs, and of course, she knows my dad. Not only is she my landlady, but also my agent. When she goes to her office, she gets me a job for Saturday night without my having to make the rounds. I am on my own and I love it, but not everything is so convenient for me, however. Boston does not allow overnight parking. Behind a seedy apartment building near my rooming house, I find a back alley used by the garbage collection trucks. Each night I jump the curb and park my car close to the building between garbage cans, rats, roaches and dead alley cats. Fortune shines on me as the car sits there unmolested, never towed away, waiting like the Bat Mobile for my weekend sorties.

On weekends, I work night clubs with the usual strips and dirty comics, and do my homework in a dressing room. Most of the clubs are just raunchy, smoke filled, glorified bar rooms. It is not the show business lifestyle I wanted; but there is always tomorrow, and there are some pleasant diversions when some of the girls on the show volunteer to help me with my homework. They think I'm cute, and for some strange reason they all know Dad. My education continues outside the class room and into the dressing room where I hear the gossip, and learn who is who in the Boston theatrical scene. Dressing room talk can be quite informative, revealing what agents to see and who to avoid. It's a never ending flow of information and advice – some helpful, some not.

All of the performers I work with have a part time job on the side and we all belong to the union AGVA (American Guild of Variety Artists). Being in the union doesn't get me any more work than I'm doing – working in beer joints on Saturday night – but like every one else, it helps maintain the illusion we all share that we are in show business. The waitress who hustles tips serving dinner at Howard Johnson's by day becomes a glamorous exotic dancer, worshiped by men – mostly sailors – at Izzy Ort's Golden Nugget by night. The shoe salesman who measures your foot at Feline's basement in the morning becomes a Las Vegas comic sensation at the Hangers Club in the evening. The more you drink, the funnier he gets.

One weekend, I met my fellow performers at the Olympia Diner where the acts usually assemble to be driven in one car to a show somewhere out of town. As usual it is a long trip to Connecticut where the night life abounds. The trip and the show go well until the return home when I hear a continuous "thump – thump" coming from under the wheel well. After stopping and inspecting the tire, I discover that at piece of tire has broken off one of my cheep retread tires – *sonamamitch!*

I cut off the offending piece of rubber and continue down the road until the thumping sound returns. We drive slowly all night, but the thumping sound continues to reasserts itself. As we stop and cut off each offending piece, each tire in turn is reduced to a bald facsimile of its former self. The incredible shrinking tires continue to shrivel up as we slowly make our way back to Boston, arriving just as the sun brings in a new day. After dropping off my irate passengers at the Olympia diner, I return the Bat Mobile to its secret cave in the back alley, there to await our next adventure. It occurs to me that new tires will cost me more than what I made from playing the date – *Jesus, Mary and Joseph! Maybe I should have stayed home.*

*

The Old Howard in Scolley Square is an old-time burlesque theater in the red light district of Boston. I'm booked there for two weeks and am delighted. We have a pit band, a chorus line, straight men and baggy pants rubes: naughty comedy the way your grandfather liked it. We crank out show after show and I'm there all day and night, either on stage or in my dressing room doing my homework. In a back alley across from the stage door is a clam and chip shop that keeps us nourished. The old timers on the show have a large steamer trunk with the traditional bottle of whiskey in it, while the ladies walk around half naked and think nothing of it. The theater is dirty, naughty, and smells like an old theater ought to smell. The audience consists of dirty old men who sit watching the show wearing silk gloves, pumping away on their love tools. I have mixed feelings – I love the business, I hate the business.

The circus comes to town and I'm getting excited. I want to visit the show but all is not right with *The Greatest Show on Earth*. The circus and the union are engaged in a labor dispute over unionizing the circus. Our union president, Jackie Bright, calls out the members to strike the circus and form picket lines at the entrances of the Boston Garden. Nobody shows up for picket line duty until the union offers a free lunch; then predictably every tap dancer, stripper and dirty comic in Boston becomes a political activist.

I am appalled and refuse to join the picket line, not even for the free roast beef sandwich. However, I do go to see what's going on and notice that all the strikers are people I know who know nothing about the circus. Someone there sees me and I am accused of being a scab for attending the circus performance

– how rude! People don't realize it at the time, but the large tented railroad circuses of the past are on their last legs. Although the circus suffers from economic woes, increasing costs and dwindling attendance, the union harassment is the final blow. *The Greatest Show on Earth* folds its tent for the last time later in July in Pittsburgh, and my childhood dream of performing under the big top folds with it – *sonamamitch!*

I am growing weary of my lifestyle: thirty five dollar Saturday night gigs in beer joints with strips, dirty comics, and drunks. Is this the show business that my mother warned me about? Am I following in my father's footsteps? *Jesus, Mary and Joseph!* There must be something better than this. College is on summer break and so one night I move out of my flat on Symphony Road, pack up the Bat Mobile, and drive off to Chicago for the summer and new horizons.

My mimmay called everyone a "sonamamich"

Mom (lower left) and her for sisters, Miriam, "Cookie," Anna and Flora

Nana with Uncle Donald in South Boston (1942)

*Dad, a musician of the big band era, was always
dapper and sober when he went to work*

Sixteen-year-old Terry appearing on WCAU T.V.'s
Candy Carnival *in Philadelphia (1955)*

Chapter III
From Minneapolis-St. Paul to Germany

The drive from Boston to Chicago takes about twenty hours. In the wee hours of the morning, I say goodbye to Boston and drive all night. The trip is tiring, but fame and fortune awaits; I press on, catching naps in the car at various rest areas along the way. In Chicago, I visit Ernie Young, an agent who produces a T.V. show called Super Circus. I would love to be on the show; however, all he has for me is a string of fair dates in Illinois in August, two months away. What to do until then? The other Chicago agents don't seem to be interested in me and I can't just hang around town waiting for a phone call. The local union office suggests that I try booking in Minneapolis, so off I go. After arriving in town, I check into the downtown YMCA then go to visit Benny Schwartz, local impresario and theatrical agent.

Benny is sitting in his chair, smoking a cigar as I enter his office and he beckons me to sit down. He must be hard of hearing, I'm thinking, because I notice that he is wearing an earphone with a wire going to a microphone in his shirt pocket. He holds the telephone up to the microphone, looks at me and says, "What's your name?"

"Terry O'Brien," I respond.

"What do you do?" says he.

"I'm a juggler," say I.

The conversation goes on about a minute with Benny asking questions and me responding. After a while Benny says, "Fine! I'll get back to you." He puts down the phone, looks at me and then says, "So what can I do for you, young man?" He had been talking all the while to someone on the phone, not to me. I feel stupid, so I take it from the top and do my tap dance again. The phone rings and he puts the receiver up to his pocket again. My ears perk up as I hear him say, "Why I have an act right here; I'll send him over." The Gay Nineties on Hennepin Avenue needs an act and I need a job.

Abe Perkins is a short, fat, cigar-chomping, no-nonsense nightclub manager. The establishment consists of two rooms, a lounge bar on one side, and a restaurant-bar with a stage on the other. There is a kitchen in the back and dressing rooms upstairs. Besides myself, the show consists of a line of four dancing girls, Nancy (singer), Teddy (Black tap dancer), Paris (stripper and female impersonator), and Lee (dirty comic and female impersonator). Backing the show is a four-piece band, led by bass player Bill Kelsey. The show is augmented by assorted busboys and bartenders who get on stage to do their thing. It's the bawdy Boston bar atmosphere all over again, but with a new twist – Paris the stripper and Lee the comic are men in drag and the clientele are mostly gay. The club is a beehive of activity both during the day and at night, when we do four shows to a crowd of rude and rowdy revelers.

On stage, Lee is not just a female impersonator, but a red-hot mamma with a foul mouth whose act is mostly trading insults with a constant stream of heckling from the audience. He's a big man and looks grotesque in the dressing room in his high stockings with garters, girdle, high heals, heavy makeup and wig lying on the table. He is the queen, the grand dame, the diva and a real bitch all wrapped up in one.

Paris, in contrast, is more sophisticated: not just female impersonator who strips, but a dancer with exotic tastes, a queer with class, a Mary with majesty, a pervert with poise, a deviate of distinction, the fairest of the fairies, the finest of fags, a fruit with finesse, not you're ordinary swish – in a nutshell, he is a lady. In the dressing room, Lee and Paris spend their time arguing about makeup, dresses, wigs and the like. Lee is course and crude while Paris is prim and proper. Paris considers himself a nymph, while Lee is just a whore. They tell stories about their experiences that would make the faint-hearted cringe and blush. It's just the same old vulgar dressing room talk I've overheard many times before.

I take it all in stride as I go through my nightly routine, all the while focusing my attention on Scarlet, one of the chorus girls. She, like another girl in the line, is underage for working in a nightclub. Fresh out of high school and dancing class, Scarlet endeavors to work her way through college as a hoofer. Her dream is to someday perform with the Rockettes in New York – *a noble aspiration.*

We crank out shows week after week in an atmosphere of noise, smoke and laughter, which tends to dull the brain. Lee packs in the crowds and the audience loves the show. Back stage, the various dramas of life go on, and at the end of our working night, we are all exhausted. Bill the band leader,

44

myself and a few of the girls like to go out to a late-night pizza place after the show. Scarlet is fun to have as a girlfriend – sort of. In spite of our seemingly party lifestyle, she remains religious and shy; my efforts to score with her go unrewarded – no cigar. No matter, I already have fair dates booked in Illinois and greener pastures await. After my engagement at the Gay Nineties with its raunchy, smoke-filled, night lifestyle concludes, I travel to the calmer environment of the county fair: fresh air and country girls.

County fairs in the Midwest are lots of fun. Besides the usual carnival midway rides, the cattle and agriculture exhibits, there is a grandstand show featuring circus acts and usually a celebrity headliner.

Most acts sleep in their vehicle behind the stage located inside the arena track where horse or car racing are presented during the day. Sweet smells of fresh cut hay fills the night air, while the sounds of farm animals emanate from barns and tents, lulling the tired performer to sleep. In the morning, the aroma of coffee and bacon floats through the air from the Methodist Church cook house concession where one can enjoy an 85 cent breakfast. My station wagon is laid out like a gypsy caravan with a mattress in the back and camping equipment stuffed in every corner. During the summer, my car is my house, transportation and my refuge – the lifestyle of the circus trouper. The stage show consists of a melange of acrobats, trapeze artists, slapstick-comedy teams, dancers and various kinds of animal performers – the likes of which were last seen on the vaudeville stage. With the decline of the theater and night clubs, performers found a refuge of sorts on the fair circuit or in the circus. At least they can make a living in the business while hoping for bigger and better things tomorrow. Television has changed the industry and affected all within. Fortunately, the country pumpkin fairs still survive and continue the old-style entertainment.

The tour goes well with relatively short jumps, easy shows and fun and games with the other performers; and once in a while, I get to practice my courting skills on town girls – *life is good.* As fall approaches and the fair dates wind down, I am faced with a decision. I can return to Boston to continue my education at Northeastern U. or transfer to a college in St. Paul and continue working at the Gay Nineties. I ponder the pro and con of each scenario. The long drive back to Boston does not appeal to me, and in St. Paul, they won't try to tow my car away. I've had enough of Boston so I decide to transfer to Hamline University in St. Paul, and continue working my way through college at the Gay Nineties. A new college environment is just what I need – a relaxed and friendly atmosphere in contrast to the cold, conservative atmosphere I had grown accustomed to in Boston. My nightlife of course is an entirely different story, but a gig is a gig and I need to work to go to school. The girls at college are pretty and friendly – most of them, except for the dogs, play the going-steady game. I'm back working nights at the Nineties and the word gets around the campus that I work in a naughty place where a good Methodist ought not to go. The students, though friendly, eye me with curiosity as if I don't belong in their world. Working one's way through college in a night club of ill repute is not politically correct on a Methodist campus. The first room I try to rent off campus is in the home of a minister who doesn't want me coming home at all hours of the night – *how rude!* Down the street I find Widow Mondale who already has a schoolteacher as a border and agrees to take me in. At last I can move out of the Y.M.C.A. in Minneapolis. I settle into the campus routine, and like at Northeastern U. in Boston, I play trombone and excel in German.

Fall arrives in Minnesota, and as the leaves begin to turn, there is a brisk coolness in the air, a bad omen of what is to come when winter arrives with a temperature colder than any cold I have experienced before. My contract at the Nineties comes to an end, and not only that, the whole show and band get replaced by the new craze in America – Calypso.[7] No problem, by now I have established a reputation with the agents in Minneapolis and I begin working club dates on weekends.

Package shows of magicians, singers, dancers and other novelty acts like myself pack ourselves into a car and travel to towns all over midwestern states. We perform at banquets and local festivals; so I get to see a lot of the country; but I'm still only making $35 per show plus gas – just enough to get by, but I'm on my own and enjoying life. I even send Dad some money just to show how successful I am in show business – I only do it once however. Meanwhile back at Hamline, I'm the top banana in the German class. My professor, Dr. Berg, likes me so much for my interest in the language that he even invites me over to his house for dinner. Dr. Berg suggests that I spend a year at a German university. Immediately, my imagination begins to engage as I ponder a new adventure. With my juggling act to support me, I'll become an international performer – why not? The wheels in my head are turning. Dr. Berg makes the arrangements for me to attend Phillipps University in Marburg, Germany. My thoughts are on intrigue and adventure as I make the long drive from St. Paul to Boston where Dad has me booked on a ship bound for Liverpool; from hence I will proceed by train, then ferry across the English Channel to Holland, then again by train to Germany.

Dad has a job in Boston playing piano for Miss Adrienne's school of the dance. It is not a great job for a musician, playing for dancing school recitals, but a gig is a gig. Being back in Boston is more pleasant, however, knowing that at last my ship has come in – even though my ship is nothing more than a Liverpool tramp steamer called the *H.M.S. Newfoundland*, which makes cargo stops in Halifax and St. Johns. The O'Briens once made the trip on such a ship when they came to America from Ireland, and now, I'm going back the other way. I ponder the philosophical relevance of it all. Nothing comes to mind except the image of Yanks boarding the vessel to cross the sea to Britain to fight our country's enemies. It is my first time crossing the Atlantic on a ship. My heart is filled with excitement and apprehension as I begin a new adventure. Dad knows all about sea voyages since he played in a band that performed on a cruise ship that traveled around South America before I was born. He tutors me on shipboard routine and etiquette – telling me also that if I need money while abroad, just write. However, I am determined to make it on my own with my juggling act – besides, I'm too proud to beg.

Departure day arrives and Dad comes to see me off, along with Arthur and his sister Betty, two dancers from Miss Adrienne's School of the Dance whom I have gotten to know through my father playing rehearsals at the school. We make our farewells, the visitors leave the ship and the gangplank is raised. As the tugboat comes alongside to tow us out into Boston harbor, I imagine the ship is about to join the wartime transatlantic convoy to run the gauntlet of German wolf pack U-boats laying in wait.

The next day, the ship arrives in Halifax harbor – busy with both fishing and ocean going vessels. While the ship unloads cargo on the wharf, passengers either go ashore to explore the town or watch the unloading procedure. As I wander around Halifax like a seaman on shore leave, it brings to mind the John Wayne movie *The Long Voyage Home*, which I had seen as a child but now seems all too real. The stevedores unload and take on cargo in the same way they have done so since the arrival of coal power and steam ships. The ever-present seagulls make their presence known as they fly about, screeching and looking for an opportunity to steal some food. Everywhere is the smell of fish and the crisp salt air.

Sounds of whistles from ships and toots from tugboats penetrate the ears. Two days in port is too much for me and I am eager to get underway. Finally, after a week on board, the crossing begins.

The ship plods through the rough seas, pitching and rolling as I lay in agony from seasickness on my rack in my cabin. I'm having second thoughts about the wisdom of all this traveling to a foreign country to attend a university – *Jesus, Mary, and Joseph!* After a day of torture, I gradually begin to feel better and get my sea legs. Then after the evening meal in the wardroom, the other passengers and I retire to the second-class passenger lounge to play bingo and drink Guinness. This is my first introduction to Guinness Stout, and I find it both bitter and refreshing. Brewed in Dublin, it is the life's blood of every Englishman and Irishman alike. The members of the crew are old salts, and tell tales of Atlantic convoy crossings during the Second World War with German U-Boats stalking them. We listen intently as we drink our Guinness and sing songs of the sea. By the time we are ready to retire, it begins to feel strangely enough like 1943, as if we have mysteriously passed through a time warp. We all retreat to the main deck and peer out into the open sea, watching for periscopes and torpedo wakes.

Filling up on stout, standing a grueling night watch, and searching for submarines can lull a fellow to sleep and we soon abandon our stations and retire to our staterooms. The day and night routine are the same for the five days crossing: eat, sleep, read, drink and look for German U-Boats. Fortunately, I manage not to get seasick again; but now the voyage becomes boring. On the last night of the crossing to Liverpool, I'm filled with anticipation and can't sleep. All night, I stay on the deck, as close to the bow as second class passengers are allowed – watching and listening. I know that I will regret getting no sleep the next day; however, so long as I can't sleep in bed, I might just as well be up on deck so I won't miss anything.

As we enter the channel to Liverpool, I hear the clang of buoys and see lights of ships passing by, making their way from the harbor, out to sea. My anticipation grows as I make out the outline of a city in the dark and smell the odor of burning coal – a smell that I remember from my childhood in Boston – the smell of the big city. Moving lights in the distance of ships in the harbor dance in the night sky. Other ships in the channel pass us by; but then two tugs approach as our ship slows to a stop. The tugboats come alongside to push us to the dock. Just as we tie up, the sun appears on the horizon and a strange feeling comes over me knowing that I am in Liverpool – *just like in the movies,* I'm thinking.

After breakfast, we prepare to disembark and a new adventure begins. I have a busy day ahead of me. With my trunks containing my personal belongings plus props and wardrobe of my unicycle-juggling act, I set out on the train for London and doze en route. I am overtired and overburdened by all my baggage, but of course I need my act to make a living while living in

Germany. The train arrives in London at Victoria Station, a magnificent monument to the age of steam where I struggle to change trains for Dover then take the ferry across the English Channel to Holland.

After arriving in the land of tulips, I'm back on the train, and on to Marburg, Germany. I feel so insecure and apprehensive – alone, with everything I own, in a foreign country where I intend to live, work and attend a university where a language is spoken that I barely understand. I feel ghastly unprepared for such a quest – *Jesus Mary and Joseph!* International travel can be difficult enough, but I am a poor foreign student and am doing it the hard way. I thought I knew adequate German, but reading and writing is an entirely different media from listening and speaking.

As the train passes from Holland into Germany, the conductor comes through and says something simple in German -"Fahrkarten bitte!" (Tickets please!) I don't know what he is saying, but I know what he wants. I listen to the chatter of the people on the train and wish I could understand. Strange, that after all the work to acquire a language, I don't understand it when it is spoken. The train ride seems endless as I peer through the window, watching the countryside pass by with the landscape still littered with war damage. My whole concept of Germany had been shaped by war movies as a child and I can't help thinking of spies on the train as I wait for the Gestapo to come through checking papers. So here I am at last in my spy trench coat, living a childhood fantasy – wondering why the war had to end so soon before I had a chance to participate.

By the time the train arrives in Marburg, I am half-awake and half-asleep as I hear on the speaker – "Marburg – Marburg, hier ist Marburg." I have arrived. Two university students who have been sent to meet me on the platform take me to a rented room on the top of a hill, overlooking the town. The students, like all German students, speak English and are eager to practice on me. They are from the World University Service whose role is to help foreign students get settled and enrolled in the university.

They are very helpful, but the room they have rented for me has no heat – not only that, but my bags will remain in customs for another week until they send me a letter to come and get them. Due to my own ignorance, things are already not going smoothly for me, but then I am here to learn and learn I must.

Marburg is an old university town, which was not bombed during the war and still has its ancient character. Mentally, one is thrust back in time to the middle ages. The university, like most of the town, was built before

Columbus discovered America. The whole environment enchants me, but I have trouble communicating at first and feel out of place and very insecure.

There is a market day in the town square on Saturday when farmers come into town wearing the traditional costume of the region. Some of the students look odd in their cord knickers, which I haven't seen since I wore them as a kid in South Boston. Complementing the local attire, an ancient castle sits on top of the hill, and throughout the town are cobblestone streets, old churches, back alleys and stone stairs that meander up and down. There is a distinctive old world atmosphere with all its charm.

We eat in the mensa,[8] the student cafeteria – the building is so old, it tilts. We get a complete meal, which costs only one mark (about 25 cents). The tuition for a semester is $50 – no problem, I can handle that. I go to classes, listen to lectures, but I don't understand much. I see little children in the street chattering away in German and think to myself, *How do they do that?* Learning to speak the language comes painfully slow and I tend to socialize with the other foreign students who like to practice their English on me.

We have a Fasching (Carnival) celebration and all us foreigners come dressed in the attire representing our native land. I come dressed in western wear: rawhide fringe jacket, jeans, boots with spurs and a cowboy hat. I go a bit overboard and carry a six shooter in a holster, which I had brought with me for barter. I do my cowboy unicycle-juggling act in the show and am a hit. One German student wants to buy the pistol, but he wants to know if it works. He, his friends and I go out behind city hall for a demonstration. I fire six shots in the air and everyone scatters and runs, leaving me puzzled as I stand alone with the smoking gun. I see him again the next day and trade the pistol for a camera. Weeks later, we meet again and he wants to show me his hand, which has bits of lead imbedded in the skin. He had been in the woods shooting and noticed that the cylinder was always loose. He holds it steady with one hand while firing the gun with the other. The bullet does not come out straight, but scrapes the side of the barrel and some of the lead shoots out sideways. He wants a discount – sorry, all sales are final.

At night, I enjoy strolling through the town, exploring all the nooks and crannies. Occasionally, I stay for hours outside a church listening to someone playing the pipe organ as I look at the stars and ponder the relevance of life in a different country. At the foreign student socials, I meet Walter, an American ex-G.I. of East Indian extraction who grew up in Boston. He studies art under the G.I. bill and floats around Europe, going to various universities. He is a bon vivant (doesn't work) who favors the Bohemian lifestyle and his looks are deceiving. He grows his hair long – conforming to the Sikh religion, but doesn't wear a turban. He has dark brown skin, but out of his mouth comes Boston street talk. He lives in the classic artist atelier (attic studio) where he paints, cooks and sleeps. I find myself at his flat quite often where we play chess and talk about girls. He likes to make curry dishes with hot sauce and I acquire a taste for it. He has an old van, a dog and a girlfiend, Gisela. We travel around Germany together and I learn the fine art of poor student survival. In each town we visit, we head for the university where we eat at the mensa and rent a cheap room in a student hotel. I don't exactly enjoy the European, poor student lifestyle, but I am determined to see it through.

Walter is a wheeler-dealer and has no problem attracting women. When he is out scouting for girls, he sets up an easel somewhere in town; then with his pallet in hand and his French beret on his head, he paints a landscape. Like a spider waiting for a fly, he waits. As he paints, a pretty girl buzzes by and stops to ponder his work. As she ponders the masterpiece being created, she is soon mesmerized and caught in a web of art enthusiasm. Eventually, he invites the girl to his flat to see his etchings and they retire to the spider's lair. I stand in amazement at his audacity, but it works. Walter introduces me to Ingeborg, a hairdresser whose father had been a Major in the S.S.[9] during the war. I invite her home to see my juggling props and unicycle in my rented room. I don't have any etchings, but have to make do with what I have. We enjoy amorous activity and I feel my horn getting stiff. Suddenly, I prematurely squirt in my pants – *sonamamitch!* I don't know what to do and decide to break it off and take her home.

As we kiss goodnight, I sense that she is disappointed. The next day at the hair salon where she works, I wait outside for her to appear at closing time. She never comes out, but rather sneaks out the back door to avoid me – I get the message, I'm a dud – Ganz nah, aber keine Zigarre.[10]

Walter and I sign up for a student bus trip to Berlin. We have a pleasant bus ride until we reach the border with East Germany and stop at a military checkpoint. Through the window I see East German soldiers, barbed wire, watch towers and police with dogs, checking vehicles. Although I am a bit apprehensive, I'm thinking – *wow, just like in the movies*! As the Vopos[11] come aboard and check our papers, I am in fantasy heaven. Quietly, but with mild apprehension, I sit in the back of the bus like Allan Ladd, waiting to show my papers. The Vopo scans my passport and glances at me with a cold stare. I give him my best grin and he departs from the bus. As we get under way again, I breathe a sigh of relief, like when going home to Boston after a visit with my relatives in Fall River. This Cold War stuff makes me nervous. Again, we go through the same routine as we enter Berlin, but now I am more relaxed, even blasé.

Berlin is divided into 4 zones by the Allies and is sill mostly in ruins – the devastation is almost everywhere. The bus continues through town to a youth hostel in the French zone, in an area that escaped the bombing during the war; there, we disembark. The next morning, Walter and I, wearing our classic spy trench coats, decide to visit the Russian zone, which is separate from East Germany. The Berlin subway system runs freely throughout the city and passes from one zone to another. The train is crowded with people, chatting and laughing, when suddenly the lights blink off then on again, marking the arrival into the Russian zone where they have a separate electrical system. An eerie silence suddenly grips the car, as we enter the first station in the Russian zone. As the train stops at the first East Berlin station, I sense tension among the passengers. They are all silently reading a newspaper as the cars stop and the doors open – *unbelievable!* It's an Orwellian scene as we exit the car while East German and Russian soldiers enter. I stand in awe, as I look around and see every other person wearing a uniform. I'm in another world and enjoying every minute of it.

The prices for things are marked the same as in West Berlin, but because of the deflated value of the East German Mark, we have already changed our currency from West to East at a rate of three to one so we can do some serious shopping. Although the quality of most goods is poor, much can be said for film, food, cameras and clothing, which interests us the most. We have picked the right day for taking pictures. The East German army will be parading down Stalin Allée to honor the Ambassador from Hungary. They come goose stepping with an oompah marching band, and I can't help thinking it must be 1942. It's not a good time to run out of film, but I do. Fortunately, an East German soldier standing next to me offers me a roll of film, which I accept as a gesture for good American-East German relations – nice chap – even if he is a Communist.

Later with some of our student group, we visit the museums and theaters, which features high quality exhibits and entertainment for a ridiculously low price and just right for a poor foreign student like myself. In our travels around the city, we meet Russian soldiers who want to trade souvenir logo pins.

For some reason, pin trading is a big thing to a Russian soldier, though not exactly my cup of tea. I think it is just a ploy to check us out but I indulge to make them happy. We explore the ruins of Berlin including the Reich Ministry, which are nothing more than a pile of rubble and the flooded tunnel leading to the Hitler bunker. We rummage through the shell of the Goebel propaganda ministry looking for souvenirs. I find a German army helmet, a machine gun and a potato masher grenade, all rusted beyond value. Later, we return to West Berlin to visit the Russian war monument – a huge structure with tanks and Russian soldiers guarding it. Walter wants me to sit on a Russian tank for a photo. Clown that I am, I comply by sitting on the gun barrel of the tank.

Russian soldiers are not amused and rush towards me, shouting something in Russian and gesturing with their rifles. They don't seem to be happy about my being on their tank. Walter takes the photo, I dismount and we walk briskly away, but not soon enough to avoid the West German police who intercept us and proceed to give me a tongue lashing about provoking the Russians and starting World War III. We make our apologies and gracefully depart the area.

The next day is a big day in my life: my 21st birthday and I'm in Berlin, Germany, at that. One of the students gives me a chocolate bar, which I put in my shirt pocket for consumption later, after which I take the subway to go to downtown Berlin and celebrate. By now I know Berlin pretty well, but even so, I take the wrong train, which leaves the city and takes me into East Germany. At the next stop, I realize my mistake as the train stops and the Vopos come aboard to check papers. Travel from East to West Berlin is allowed, but to enter East Germany, a special visa is required that I don't have. As they proceed through the train checking documents, I cower in a corner trying to make myself invisible – it doesn't work. I am exposed and asked for my papers. *What would Humphrey Bogart do now?* I'm thinking. I show my passport to the stone-faced Vopo who then says to me "aussteigen!" (get out). Suddenly, visions of a concentration camp flash through my mind as they take me off the train to a holding cell at the station where I have to answer a lot of questions. Fortunately, my German is good enough to convince them of my peaceful intentions even though they don't seem too happy with my presence. I get a tongue lashing for provoking them by not having the proper papers, and trying to start World War III. Then, I am escorted back on the train – *how rude!*

Like having gone to Confession at St Augustine's church in South Boston, I am relieved to have survived interrogation with the East German police, and reach into my pocket to enjoy my candy bar and celebrate my twenty-first birthday. To my chagrin, I discover that my candy bar has not only melted, but also stained my shirt in the process – *Jesus Mary and Joseph! Some twenty-first birthday* – I'm thinking as I struggle to eat my melted chocolate bar with my finger. The rest of the visit to Berlin is uneventful, likewise the bus trip back to Marburg. Strange that as the bus arrives and the students all depart to their different ways, I should think of Marburg as home, but I do. I find it interesting how one can adjust to his surroundings, and after time feel a sense of belonging.

I contact a theatrical agent in Frankfort and he books me in the Reinland Kabaret on Kaiser Strasse in Frankfort. My first paid engagement in Germany, and suddenly, I am elated. I pack my gear, board the train for Frankfort and am off to unknown adventures as a German cabaret performer. The Kabaret is the typical night club with a floor show that I had grown to love and hate in Boston, but now it's with a German accent. There is a band, an assortment of variety acts and I have my own dressing room. There is something about a dressing room that no matter in what country it is, it becomes the refuge of the vagabond troubadour – a familiar place – a safe heaven.

My uncle Bob, born in Germany and married to my mother's sister Miriam, has a cousin Heddy who lives in an apartment house in Frankfort. They welcome me to stay in the spare guest room on the top floor of the apartment house and it suits me fine, even though the mattress gives me a backache. Max, Heddy's husband, has a doctorate in mathematics and once was a college professor. While on the Russian front as an Army radio operator, however, he was wounded and remains paralyzed on one side. Max has trouble speaking and further demonstrates his disability as he checks the time on his wristwatch while holding a cup of tea, thus proceeding to pour the brew into his lap – I try not to laugh. Max and Heddy have three children younger than myself who are curious about their American cousin who entertains in a Kabaret. Together we enjoy pleasant family interaction while my German improves considerably.

The engagement ends and I return to Marburg. For some reason, however, I never get another booking of my act in Germany. My unicycle-juggling act does not seem to be up to European standards, and I am not the polished performer that I think I am – well, no matter. Dad continues to send money once in a while and I continue with the same university routine until soon it is time to return to the good old U.S.

By this time, I am stretching my Marks thin, hoping to have enough to travel back to Liverpool where Dad has me booked for a return to Boston on the *S.S. United States*. The sailing is still a few weeks away and I am faced with a lot of traveling and not enough money. *Will I survive? – Jesus, Mary and Joseph!* I have saved enough Marks just to make the trip, but neglect to compute the rate loss, converting into Pounds Sterling when I arrive in England. I check out of my room a day early, to save one day's rent and spend the night with all my gear in an abandoned house where I sleep uncomfortably on the floor.

The next morning after making several trips struggling with my luggage, I sit in the Bahnhof (railroad station), sipping my breakfast coffee while waiting impatiently for the train. A rather large clock on the wall ticks away while I stare at the hands, hoping it will make them move faster. Suddenly, the sound of a whistle announces the trains arrival and my departure from Marburg and from Germany. I have mixed feelings – I'm glad to leave, I'm sorry to leave, but leave I must, for further adventures await.

The return train ride through Germany and Holland seems altogether different from the first time I rode a year ago. Rather than dreaming about the future, my thoughts go back to all of the experiences I had in Germany and all the friends I am leaving behind. I take the ferry in Holland and arrive in Dover where the immigration officer wants to know how much money I have to enter the country. Since I only have a few Pounds Sterling he tells me that I don't have enough and must go back to Holland – *how rude!* What a way for a Brit to treat a Yank! Actually, I have just enough money to get to Liverpool, but the ship doesn't arrive for another week. Eventually, they relent and allow me to enter, since I do have my boarding pass; furthermore, they wish me "godspeed" – *Jesus, Mary and Joseph!* Still another train ride is needed to London where I change trains at Victoria Station then on again to Liverpool where I arrive tired, hungry and broke. How will I survive in Liverpool for a week with not a penny in my pocket? Juggling 3 balls on a street corner of Liverpool is an option, but only as a last resort. Here I am standing on the platform of the Liverpool railroad station with all of my worldly possessions, wondering what to do, when I spy a travelers aid notice on the wall. I check my bags at the left luggage window and find my way through the streets of Liverpool to the Travelers' Aid office. Actually, it isn't an office at all, but the home of an elderly lady who belongs to some sort of religious evangelistic society that stands on street corners to read the bible to passersby. The widow of Deacon Smith opens the door and stares at me as I explain my plight. She invites me into her parlor, and with a nice smile, she asks, "Would you like a cup of tea, love?"

"Indeed I would," say I, as I sit on the sofa and sip a proper English cup of tea. She is sympathetic and understanding as I spill my tale of hardship and woe. She has heard it all before, and sends me over to the Liverpool Seamen's Aid Mission, which is a refuge for old salts and other scurvy scum from tramp steamers and the docks of Liverpool. They take in lost souls like myself and provide a meal and a rack to sleep in. The evangelistic society pays for my stay, and of course, I have to promise to repay the society some day when I become rich and famous – I'm grateful. The question now is: how does one with no money spend a week in Liverpool? Good old Dad comes to the rescue with money in the mail, and not only do I have enough to get my luggage out of left luggage at the train station, but I can even take the overnight ferry to visit Dublin. Lady Deacon Smith can wait for her repayment until I'm back in the U.S.A.

The overnight ferry to Dublin, second class, is an unforgettable experience as if I haven't had enough unforgettable experiences. The second class area is nothing more than a compartment with a wooden bench and a bar. The ferry leaves early in the morning and arrives in Dublin just after dawn. My fellow passengers – Irish working men on their way home for a visit – and myself spend a sleepless night drinking Irish stout and singing Irish songs as we plod across the Irish Sea to Ireland. It is a scene right out of a movie though I can't remember which one. I am near collapse but thoroughly enjoying myself never the less. The sun begins to rise as the ferry enters the River Liffy and ties up at the wharf. Still groggy from a sleepless night sitting on a bench, I feel better after having breakfast in the first-class wardroom, after which I go ashore. As I walk along the dock to O'Connell Street, the heart of Dublin, a feeling of familiarity comes over me even though this is my first time in Ireland. I see familiar architecture, horses pulling wagons, fruit and vegetable carts, street musicians and everybody is Irish. It's South Boston all over again. The only difference that stands out is people riding bicycles. There is a student hotel on Harcourt Street next to Stevens Green in the university area where I check in and promptly fall asleep.

For the next couple of days I roam around town, seeing all the sights, tasting the food, and drinking the beer. Although I can only spend a few days visiting, I know that someday, like MacArthur, I shall return to Dublin to live, to love and to learn – this is the place I want to be; but in the meantime, another all-night and uncomfortable Irish Sea crossing awaits. For some reason, the overnight return trip to Liverpool seems pleasant enough, knowing that my refuge on a ship awaits in Liverpool. The morning sun rises as we enter the Liverpool harbor and through my blurry eyes, I make out *The United States*, tied up at the dock and awaiting my arrival. My ship has finally come in.

German fasching (carnival) with Ingeborg and other university students (1958)

Terry poses for a photo as Russian soldiers rush towards him

Chapter IV
From Minneapolis-St. Paul to France

There she floats in all her majesty, the *U.S.S. United States:* my refuge, my sanctuary. As I stroll up the gangplank, my personality suddenly changes from the stereotypically poor, struggling student, into a dashing playboy of the Western World. There's nothing like an ocean liner to boost one's moral and inflate one's ego. The trip back home now feels much different from the initial voyage to Europe, then filled with apprehension and fear of the unknown. Although the ship provides a more luxurious environment than the freighter *Newfoundland*, the routine is the same: eat, sleep, cruise for girls, followed by bingo and Irish stout in the passenger lounge, then finishing with the usual reconnaissance from the deck for German submarines.

All the while I was in Germany, things were happening at home. In order to continue his career as a musician, Dad had to leave town and work in hotels and resorts in Florida. Not a bad gig for a musician, except that he has a house and my mother and sister living in New England. Mom and Dad do the unthinkable – they sell the house in Swansea and move to Orlando, Florida. Little sister Sharon also does the unthinkable, and elopes with my former class mate – a Protestant from the top of the hill – *Jesus, Mary and Joseph!*

After the ship arrives in New York, I take my first airplane ride to Orlando. After playing the role of the poor student in Europe, I now feel a great sense of achievement as I look out through the window of the airplane, imagining what it must have been like for the B-17 bombers being attacked by German Messerschmidts. Soon reality overtakes me as we land in Orlando and Mom and Dad await my arrival. Dad is especially glad to see me with the five bottles of Irish whiskey that I brought back from Ireland.

Dad is playing in a band at the Cherry Plaza Hotel on Lake Eola, the swankiest place in town, but his old bad habits remain intact – Florida style. After coming home from the hotel in the wee hours of the morning, and much to the chagrin of his neighbors, Dad likes to mow the lawn in his underwear, thus perpetuating among his new neighbors the already bad reputation of the musician. Dad gives me his old car, and I'm off to Minnesota to resume where I had left off with my intellectual pursuits, but now things are different: although I'm reduced to skin and bones, I speak German.

*

At Hamline University again Dr. Berg, my German professor, is proud of me. Little does he know that I almost started World War III – not once, but twice. Things in Minnesota have changed during my absence, and yet everything is the same. Perhaps, I am the one who has changed. Now I'm a senior in college and still top banana in my German class. My romantic situation improves when I meet Sandy, a student nurse who seems to be attracted by my German language skills. She is blond, taller than me, wears glasses and a kerchief around her head. Outwardly she appears plain and shy, but in private, she is a serious student nurse and wants to teach me the uninhibited art of love making. Her interest in me startles me at first – it must be my newly acquired European sophistication that she finds charming or perhaps she likes the way I juggle.

Whatever it is, Sandy from South Dakota and I have the traditional American college romance. Aside from my academic and love life, I return to making a living at what I do best, doing my juggling act on club dates around Minnesota. And as before, I'm just scraping by and wondering if I can ever make it in life as a juggler – *will I succeed in show business – will I ever play the Palace?*

My French teacher, Miss McGee, is impressed with what a year in Germany had done for my German and proceeds to talk me into attending the Sorbonne in Paris, France. Now that I am a seasoned European traveler, the idea has some appeal. Being able to perform is like having a ticket to any country. One can always make a living there or, falling short of that, at least survive. Thus having survived Germany, I now set my sights on France for the coming fall semester. My summer tour of pumpkin fairs around the Midwest looks good, and I should have enough money to make it to France and book my act in some cabarets – *a piece of cake.* Now all I have to do is work on my French.

Graduating from college is a momentous occasion filled with both joy and sadness. I'm happy to be leaving school, but I'm sad to say goodbye to my girlfriend Sandy – parting is such sweet sorrow.

Never the less, it is almost time to get my show on the road. The show must go on and county fairs are my favorite place to be in the summer. Many of the performers are acts that I have worked with before on other shows. Although we all come together from different parts of the country to appear in a show, we feel a sense of comradeship like a family coming together. New friendships are made, and also old grudges rekindled. Of course there is no gossip like dressing room gossip – a place where someone not only has the inside story, but desperately wants to tell everyone. Perhaps it is the compulsion of the performer to continuously entertain to a captive audience.

During the breaks between fairs, I return to Minneapolis and resume a relationship with Scarlet, the dancer from the Gay Nineties who is religious and shy. Unlike Sandy, she is somewhat reserved or perhaps doesn't like me that well. In any case, she still hopes to go to New York some day and dance with the Rockettes – an elusive goal to be sure; however, a substitute opportunity does present itself to her.

Scarlet is offered a chorus line job, touring state fairs produced by the Barnes & Caruthers theatrical agency in Chicago – somewhat short of her goal, but such is life. I continue with my tour while Scarlet goes to Chicago to stay with her aunt while she rehearses the dance routines with the other girls at a local dance studio. Alas, I feel like I am in love again and count the days and the towns until I get a break and can visit my sweetheart in Chicago. Finally, somewhere in Illinois, I get a week off and an opportunity to dash to Chicago to visit Scarlet, and also to show my face at some theatrical agencies. Once in the city, I head for the usual place for cheap room and board, the University of Chicago campus. Scarlet is glad to see me – *likewise, I'm sure.*

I take my girl out for a night on the town by visiting Riverside Amusement Park where we are entertained by the traditional low key forms of entertainment: the tunnel of love and the parachute fall – not very exciting, but Scarlet is easy to please. We follow that by ride downtown on the elevated train to a downtown restaurant where we each get a steak dinner for only $1.09. Scarlet is not impressed, but then on a juggler's salary that's the best I can do. Scarlet is in a pensive mood and, in a moment of truth, spoils our fun by revealing that she is pregnant from her last boyfriend whom she hates, and she doesn't know what to do – *Jesus, Mary and Joseph!* I thought she was religious and shy. Although I'm curious to know the story, I don't ask. As a sympathetic gesture, I invite her to come home with me to Florida after the fair season – debonair cosmopolitan that I am. We agree to meet in St Louis at the railroad station on a certain date, after which we will drive together to Florida. There, she can have a cheap vacation and I can prepare for my trip to Paris. *Perhaps, my gracious offer might even earn me a girly treat* – I'm thinking.

With everything said and done, we part company. She goes off to the state fair dates and I go off to my pumpkin county fairs. I'm feeling mixed emotions: I'm sorry for her plight, but at the same time I'm glad to be going to Paris. As time passes, the turning of the leaves announces fall and the end of the fair season in the Midwest.

As prearranged, I arrive in the St. Louis train station only to hear my name announced on the loudspeaker that I have a phone call. Scarlet is on the phone and tells me that her last show date has been extended and she shall be late arriving by two days – *sonamamitch!* Reluctantly, I agree to wait until she arrives; but what shall I do for two days in St. Louis? I have always wanted to see the St. Louis Zoo. Now I have a reason to go and spend lots of time, which is exactly what I do. After spending two days at the zoo viewing the animals and two nights sleeping in my car, I know all the animals and they know me. By now, I've had it with the zoo and don't want to see another four-legged creature again – I'm sure that the animals feel the same about me. Scarlet finally arrives and we drive straight through to Florida, avoiding expensive restaurants by eating tuna fish sandwiches as we go. By the time we reach the Sunshine State, I don't want to ever eat tuna fish again. Mom and Dad have mixed feelings about Scarlet: Dad likes her – she's a dancer, Mom doesn't like her – she's a dancer – well, no matter. We enjoy going to the beach during the day and listening to the Jimmy O'Brien Orchestra, at the Cherry Plaza at night. Dad acts like a gentleman and Mom holds her tongue.

One night after my mother goes to sleep, Scarlet sneaks into my bedroom and gets into bed with me. I get my treat. Suddenly, Dad comes home from the hotel, and goes into his music room, puts on his tapes, lights up a cigarette and opens a bottle of his favorite beverage, P.M. Whiskey. Soon, he is in musician heaven. Scarlet, wanting to avoid embarrassment, tipsy toes out of my room and back to hers – after all, she is religious and shy. Although attracted to Scarlet, I am not willing to get involved in her personal problems involving another man. The next day, we put Scarlet on the train for Minneapolis and I begin preparing for my next adventure, the conquest of France.

*

After a routine flight from Orlando with bags and baggage, I'm back on the docks of New York where I board the *U.S.S. United States* – an old friend from a previous Atlantic crossing. Images of old Fred Astair movies cross my mind: shipboard romances, comedy and intrigue at sea. At any moment, the girl of my dreams may come walking through the hatch or descend the ladder or appear on deck, just like in the movies. My fantasies are reinforced with the unexpected appearance of Hollywood star Gary Cooper, whom I spy, walking along the deck. The other passengers gawk and take photos. Not wanting to appear as just another freaky fan, I watch Mr. Cooper from the corner of my eye, and after he passes, take a nice photograph of his back. The crossing of the Atlantic is routine: eat, sleep, cruise the ship looking for my true love at night in the lounge, bingo and drinking, followed by a vigil from the deck for submarine periscopes.

The ship's arrival in Le Havre fills me with anxiety. The ship now feels like home and I am about to leave a secure environment and enter not only an unknown world, but all in French. The train leaves Le Harvre for Paris with my luggage: props, unicycle and slack wire rigging, which looks like a hammock, but folds up into a trunk, and myself. I'm hoping to see some impresarios (theatrical agents) in Paris and get a few dates so I can survive. As the train passes though the French countryside, I'm wishing I had spent more time on French rather than fooling around with women. Suddenly, I feel stupid again as the train conductor comes through the car asking – "tickets (tee-kay), s'il vous plait" (tickets please). Alas, like in Germany, I don't understand him, but I know what he wants. My inability to understand French when I hear it frustrates me. The clickity-clack of the train soon dulls my brain and lulls me to asleep.

As I slowly drift away in slumber, I see visions of myself, a super spy with the American O.S.S., infiltrating Nazi occupied France on my way to Paris to rendezvous with the French resistance. Again, I am wearing the appropriate secret agent trench coat on my "mission." The train pulls into St Lazarre Station where I check my bags until I can fetch them later.

After walking out of the station, I am approached by a Frenchman who is lost and asks me for directions. Of course I can't help him; but it's nice to be asked in any case, even if I don't understand what he says. I respond in my best French that I just got off the boat; so he smiles and walks away. I make my way on the metro to the Sorbonne where I check in and stay in a cheap student hotel across the street. The city is wonderful and fascinating, filled with strange sights and noisy sounds. I thought I knew French, but like in Germany, I have no ear for the spoken language and have to suffer through the agony of non-communication and misunderstanding again.

The school finds me a room on Rue du Bac (Ferry Street) on the top floor of an apartment building where Madame Martin has a vacant room with a balcony overlooking L'Hôtel des Invalides and La Tour Eiffel (Napoleon's tomb and the Eiffel Tower.) This will be home for the next year, and so I feel comfortable and secure with Madame Martin who makes me a cup of tea every night and allows me to have visitors. The courtyard below the balcony is part of the cathedral down the street; the periodic ecclesiastical chanting of the monks below is charming.

After learning how to get around the city on the metro, I begin calling on impresarios, hoping to book my act. Being a new act in town, it takes quite some time before any of the agents offer me a job. In the meantime, I just play the role of the student in Paris and concentrate on learning French. I begin attending class and find myself socializing with foreign students like myself. Although from different countries, we all seem to share a common isolation from the French mainstream. Living in Paris is relatively inexpensive – the university costs $50 per semester, and my room rent is a dollar a day. I eat in one of several student restaurants around town for on a Franc per meal (20 cents). The food is not great, but there is enough and it satisfies. I have a student identity card that gets stamped when I buy a book of meal tickets. I'm assigned to dine at two student restaurants, one of them called Israëlit, which caters to Jewish students – they serve horsemeat every Monday. At first I'm squeamish, but gradually, I get used to it, and it doesn't taste half-bad.

One day while visiting my favorite pâtisserie (bakery) before going to class, I happen to meet Ursula, an attractive young German girl, and one of my classmates who, like many foreign girls attending the Sorbonne, lives with a French family and is employed by them as a nanny. She is surprised that I speak German. Like many other young, foreign girls, she's here to learn French and enjoy a story book, Parisian romance. But then, that is why I'm here also. We immediately strike up a friendship. From then on my German improves considerably, but not my French. Ursula is 19 with lovely brown hair and hazel eyes. Soon I find myself taking her to the St. Lazarre train station after classes. There, she takes the train to a Paris suburb where she lives with her French family. Of course, her French is better than mine. Aside from romance, there is another compulsive need – to earn a living.

The impresarios around Paris are not impressed with my act. I do manage to get a few cabaret dates, just enough to get by. Rickey is a Black man from Mississippi: an expatriate who came to France to study and liked it. He then married a French girl and stayed in the country. He is a musician who books bands and shows at the service clubs of American military bases around France. He books me on a two-week tour of service clubs, along with a French striptease dancer, a male (guitar playing) blues singer from New York and a Black female calypso-singer from Jamaica – the five of us are the whole show.

Together, we embark on a show business odyssey throughout France, travel together in a tiny French automobile with most of our props and wardrobe strapped to the rack on the roof of the car. Sammy, the singer, has a phobia about his guitar getting wet in the rain, so it has to be carried inside the car. We are packed in like sardines as we troop from base to base, stopping at night to sleep in an auberge (inn.) Fi Fi the dancer has a pretty face but that's all. She is flat and skinny, a most unusual aura for a strip tease dancer – I'm wondering how she makes a living. Since she speaks no English and the rest of us do, she either sits quietly, smiling, or gives me French lessons, which soon irritate my fellow passengers.

Occasionally, she tries to interact with our Anglo conversations, smiling and nodding, pretending to understand, but doesn't. Chantal the calypso singer, on the other hand, is an incessant talker who dominates the conversation when there is one, and talks continuously when there is not. The young service men that we perform to do not take our show seriously.

We get lots of hoots and hollers from hecklers in the audience – *how rude!* It's not until Fi Fi – the final number – removes her bra to reveal two tiny nipples that the audience reacts with enthusiasm and gusto.

Fi Fi's flat bosom always brings down the house. Our tour of France is exhausting – long jumps crammed into a sardine can, followed by entertaining a lynch mob of drunken soldiers. After our last show in Verdun, we drive all night in the rain back to Paris. Aside from the few Francs I was able to earn, the only good part of the tour was seeing the French countryside. I'm glad to be back in my pad in Paris again with Ursula. In spite of my relatively low expenses and the occasional club date, I still have trouble making ends meet and must ask dear old Dad to send me an occasional hand out. He really doesn't understand my situation and the most I ever get in a letter is a twenty-dollar bill.

Pierre, an impresario on the Avenue Des Champs Élysée, has a two-week stand for me at the Moulin Rouge in Brussels. My problems begin at the beginning. I need to take the train to Brussels from Gare de L'Est, (R. R. Station East), located on the northeast side of town. From the Left Bank where I live, transporting all my props, rigging and wardrobe poses a dilemma. I have too much to carry at one time, and I can't afford a taxi. The Metro station is a ten-minute walk from where I assemble all of my things on the sidewalk in front of my flat. My plan is to hopscotch my baggage, taking one load forward and depositing it on the sidewalk then returning for the second load and moving it past the first, to be deposited further on – a clumsy operation to be sure, but why spend money on a taxi? Thus slowly I work my way towards the Metro station Rue du Bac. People walking by glance at me curiously as I trudge with my loads ever closer to my goal et voilà! (there it is) – after an hour, I'm there. Maneuvering everything into the Metro station and onto the train while swimming with the flow of the crowd is a daunting, but not insurmountable, task. Unfortunately, the line I catch at Rue du bac does not go directly to Gar de L'est, thus requiring changing trains at Les Halle station. Navigating through tunnels and up and down stairs in the Paris Metro system while carrying costumes, wire rigging, and personal luggage is not for the faint of heart. Undaunted, I press on until I finally arrive at Gar de L'est where the train for Brussels awaits.

The club has sent someone to pick me up at the station. They arrive, take me, bag and baggage to the club, then later find me room in a cheap, theatrical hotel in a back alley, a short walk away. It is January, the weather is cold and damp, and the days are short and dreary. I am not enjoying Brussels and wish I were someplace else. The club Moulin Rouge is located in the center of town. While not in the same class as her sister club in Paris, the club features a band with a floorshow. The lounge is basically a men's club, where each table comes complete with female companion, waiting for a man to approach, sit down and buy her a drink; rather than chose a table, the man chooses the girl. First class musicians staff the band, typically found at all European Cabarets. Besides my juggling-wire act there is a troop of Flamenco dances from Spain, José, a roly-poly Mexican folk singer and Claudie, a French dancer who happens to live around the corner from me in Paris. From my dressing room behind the bandstand, I enjoy watching the Spanish girls in their dressing room on the other side, walking around bare breasted – they seldom bother to close the door. A caballero (gentleman) shouldn't be gawking at such things, but I do anyway. I wish I could speak Spanish and communicate, but I can't, so I must struggle along in French. We soon fall into a routine of cranking out two shows a night. Sometimes, André the band leader invites me to play the trombone for the dance set.. The only tune I know that they play is "Blue Moon." Typically, in show business all over the world, a camaraderie develops and the band thinks of me as a fellow musician. I even write my name on the dressing room wall along with all the other acts that have called it home – a longstanding tradition in show business. Working nights and sleeping most of the morning during winter in Europe, I never get to see the sun. I find myself up and about every day in late after noon, strolling around town after a late breakfast.

One day, as I am wandering around the cold, bleak streets of Brussels, a man wearing a pork pie hat grabs me by the arm and offers to take me away from all this, and run away with him to the sunny Côte d'Azure – *how rude!* In any case, I don't know where that is. Being propositioned by a dirty old man in Brussels takes me back at first, but I have learned to expect the unusual in Europe and gracefully disappear into the club where I feel secure in my dressing room. I'm not too keen on my lifestyle in Brussels; but I need the money and a gig is a gig. After the engagement is over, I return home to my flat in Paris to continue the poor student lifestyle of wine, cheese and my girl, Ursula. This time, however, I have enough money to take a taxi home. There's something about Paris that makes one fall in love, and I do – Vivre l'amour! Vivre Paris! Vivre La France!

In December, Pierre calls me to do a television show in Italy before Christmas. Thoughts of a warm gentle wind from the Mediterranean, scented by the aroma of pizza and spaghetti, cross my mind. Further pleasant thoughts occur after I book an overnight train ride through Switzerland to Turino on the legendary Orient Express, backdrop of many spy and murder novels from the past – my kind of train.

When the time comes to pack up and leave town, once again on the streets of Paris I give a repeat performance of hopscotching my baggage to the Metro station to avoid paying for a cab.

My compartment contains five other passengers besides myself. I eye each one of them suspiciously, fantasizing that one of them is a spy. During the night as we slumber in our pull-down sleeper racks, the train makes its way through the mountains of Switzerland. The motion of the train gently rocks me to sleep and I begin to dream of murder and mystery aboard the Orient Express. Alas, morning finds us traveling in Italy. As I awake and look out the window at the Italian landscape, I am very disappointed. Not only is the view cold, dark and depressing, but nobody was murdered during the night.

It's Saturday afternoon as we arrive in Turino. People from the television studio pick me up at the station and take me to the hotel Ligure – the baggage to be picked up later at customs. Fortunately, everyone in Turino seems to speak French, so we are able to communicate without much confusion. I enter the hotel dining room, eager for Italian food. The waiter must be reading my mind as he sets a large bowl of spaghetti in front of me. Shortly he returns to remove the empty plate and asks me what I would like to eat – I thought I just did, but no this is Italy and spaghetti is always served before the meal, not as a meal itself – what a revelation. I order the main course, which together with the spaghetti, is more than my poor, student stomach can tolerate – stupid me! I later vomit in the gents room. I may be in Italy, but my stomach is still in France.

The television show is on Sunday, so the studio people send someone to pick up my baggage at the railroad station on Sunday, the day of the show and the day when the customs office is closed, and my props and rigging cannot be retrieved – sans props, sans show, *sonamamitch!* The studio pays me my salary, makes apologies for the inconvenience and they put me on a train for Germany – Vecino, però no sigaro.[12]

I'm looking forward to spending Christmas with Uncle Bob's relatives, the Tashe family, in Frankfort before returning home to Paris. The overnight train ride is uneventful. It has been a few years since I was in Germany; however, I feel right at home and speak the language like a native. Max's daughter Hildegard has grown up since we last met. Now a lovely girl of sixteen, with blond hair, she and her twin brother Werner greet me with warm smiles at the train station. I enjoy a traditional German style Christmas for the second time in my life. Frankfort is white with snow and the traditional candles still decorate Christmas trees in the homes, rather than electric lights. In the city square the traditional winter carnival offers rides to children, and a visit downtown is a must. We enjoy the tradition, food and drink and Gemütlichkeit (feeling of well being.)

*

Another long train ride to Paris, then back to my flat from the station in a taxi. My Italian misadventure allows me some spending money, even to pay the back rent that I owe Mme. Martin, my landlady. My girlfriend Ursula and I resume our routine: attending class at the Sorbonne, taking long walks along the promenade of the Seine, sipping wine and eating bread and cheese at a sidewalk café, then retiring to my flat to play chess where I usually win the game and Ursula gives me a treat. April in Paris is miserably cold and wet. It is also time for me to get serious about my French language and prepare for my exam, which includes reciting a poem to the professor. Ursula tutors me as best she can; but as we roll into the month of May, springtime blossoms with a vengeance and one's thoughts turn to l'amour rather than language study. We take our exams and I give my recitation. I manage to pass, but Ursula gets a bon travail (good work) on her certificate while I don't – well, no matter, I have only to type the accolade on my certificate myself, and no one be the wiser – Proche, mais pas de cigare.[13]

Soon it is time to return to our respective countries and we feel the pain of lovers parting – our destiny awaits in the great unknown. We meet again at Gare de L'est. There, as she boards the train for Nürnberg, we have a tearful goodbye. My own departure is a bit more complicated, as I again play the leapfrog game with my baggage from my flat to Metro Rue Du Bac at the end of my street then on to Gare St. Lazarre, several miles away. From there, I have just enough franks to get to Le Havre where the S.S. United States awaits my arrival. Aboard the ship again I feel warm and secure, safe on my refuge – an American ship. I feel both the happiness of fulfillment and the pain of departure.

Bound for New York, the ship makes a stop over at Cobh,[14] Ireland. Since there is no pier to accommodate large ships, we anchor in the harbor where a ferry comes alongside to take on and disembark passengers. During the transfer, a trunk falls into the harbor and floats away. From the deck, I watch amused and amazed as a dinghy chases after the floating luggage, and plucks it out of the water. As I watch the fiasco, I entertain thoughts of my gear sinking out of sight – *Jesus, Mary and Joseph!*

As the ship steams out of Cobh harbor, I stare at the green hills and white washed stone houses. My mind wanders as I contemplate the beauty of it all. Slowly, as the sun sets in the west, we head out to sea and the Irish coast fades in the distance, my thoughts turn to my next adventure, the conquest of Ireland.

The Atlantic crossing is déjà vu[15]: eating, sleeping, girl watching and drinking in the passenger lounge at night, followed by a concerted effort to sight submarine schnorkels from the deck. Like my return from Germany, I arrive in New York broke and skin and bones, but now I speak French. Uncle Bob, who lives on Long Island, meets me at the pier and puts me on a flight to Orlando. Uncle Bob still speaks German, and much to my delight, my German has improved considerably while living in France, and I am able to out German Uncle Bob.

*

Back home again, Dad is still up to his old bad habits while Mom continues to chatter incessantly when she's happy and nag when she's not. Dad continues to drink all night and smoke cigarettes all day. Mom likes to smoke a cigarette once in a while too. Since Dad does not approve, she sneaks a smoke in the utility room attached to the house where the odor doesn't linger too long.

Dad of course is not fooled and hides Mom's cigarettes when he finds them. Mom, in retaliation, searches out Dad's stashed away whiskey bottles, and pours the devil's delight down the drain. Some of the clandestine places for hiding cigarettes and whiskey are very imaginative, but don't deter a determined Dad nor a super-sleuth Mom who never have a conversation, but rather an argument. My parents seem to enjoy being adversaries rather than a loving couple – no matter – I need a Florida vacation at any cost.

Most of my time is spent practicing my act in the backyard, still dreaming of becoming a circus star, a celebrity: admired by men, worshiped by women and idolized by kids. I'm also making plans to enroll in the University of Ireland in Dublin. Thoughts of Ireland fill my mind as I enjoy the Florida sun.

Terry with girlfriend Ursula in Paris (1958)

Chapter V
Shamrocks, Leprechauns
and Duffy Circus

Flying to New York to catch an ocean liner is becoming a pleasant past time. The *H.M.S. Queen Mary* will be making her last voyage before being retired and sold to Japan, and I am to be aboard to celebrate this momentous occasion. The *Mary* is more interesting than the *United States*, in that it has lots of little nooks and crannies to explore. Cozy lounges here and there make great places for a rendezvous. On this particular voyage, there are nannies going home to Ireland and England after having spent some time working in America, each one looking for a shipboard romance to write about in their diary.

Having more than one romance is the name of the game played by all. Of course, keeping them separate from each other on a ship requires stealth and cunning – a romantic cat and mouse game of hide and seek within hidden compartments and secret alcoves of the ship. Romance at sea fires the passion and nourishes the soul – providing, of course, one doesn't get seasick. For passengers, there is, of course, the usual beer drinking and bingo game at night in one of the many lounges, followed by the deck ritual of scanning the horizon for life rafts, oil slicks, ship debris and such.

The ship arrives in Cobh harbor, drops anchor, and awaits the ferry to take us to the mainland. Alas! like my last visit here, a piece of luggage is dropped into the harbor and must be plucked out of the briny deep – *Jesus Mary and Joseph!* – *a bad omen,* I'm thinking. Fortunately, I arrive on shore with baggage intact. There is a lingering odor of burning peat in the air, which first attracts the new to Ireland. There is no central heating in most homes, but a fireplace in every room, continuously fed with peat, found in abundance in Ireland. Another observation for the new comer is that like in Oklahoma, the

73

wind never stops blowing. Here I am, an American student, standing in Cobh, county Cork, on the same spot where my ancestors stood waiting for the ship to take them to America. Pondering that gives me a warm feeling of coming home.

From Cobh, I need to take the train to Cork City then change trains for Dublin. While awaiting the train, I spy Duffy circus posters on walls and in windows around the town. Of course, I just happen to have my act with me: slack-wire, unicycle, props and wardrobe, in anticipation of working theatre dates in Dublin. By the time the circus is scheduled to come to town, I'll be long gone; nevertheless, I'm wondering what it would be like to travel around Ireland with a circus. Unbeknownst to me, I'm destined to find out.

The train arrives at Euston station in Dublin. As I leave the station and walk onto the streets of Dublin, I sniff the air. The pungent odor of peat burning in every hearth in the city saturates the atmosphere. Contributing to the bouquet are thousands of draft horses that continue to make their rounds delivering freight and merchandise around town, thus giving Dublin a unique, though not necessarily unpleasant, Irish "aire." I make my way, bag and baggage, to Koinonia[16] House, a youth hostel for foreign students on Harcourt Street where I had once roomed. The house is a series of three old Georgian houses with walls knocked out between them to create one structure. Most of the students living there are East Indians, Afghans and Pakistanis, all studying at the Dublin Surgeons College. Although old and drafty, the hostel is adequate and cheap; not only that but it is only a block away from my new school, University College Dublin.

After getting adjusted to my new environment, I begin classes studying the Irish language then contact Johnny Darlys, a local impresario and former vaudeville dog act – one of the many Hungarians who during the Hungarian revolution fled to Ireland. Now, all I have to do is wait for a job to come in. In the meantime, Trinity College has a Gaelic class that I attend one day a week. I become the professor's best student and he never learns that am not enrolled at Trinity, but another university, U.C.D. Eating at their student cafeteria is not only convenient and cheap, but provides additional opportunities for meeting new people.

One day, Mr. Darlys rings me up and offers me a job on a Pantomime[17] at the Theatre Royal in Waterford with Jack Cruise (the Bob Hope of Ireland.) Jack has an office on Fleet Street where I go to pick up my contract and meet his attractive secretary Patricia who is typing away at her desk. She is a lovely 19-year-old with long black hair and hazel eyes. Not only does she type, but she also sings for Jack on his shows at the Theatre Royal in Dublin. I am struck by her beauty and immediately fall in love – again. I invite her out to lunch and she responds but is rather cool towards me. We engage in small talk and she reveals her dream of becoming a singing sensation in the theater. Little does she know that the theatres in Ireland, like in America before, are doomed to oblivion. Unfortunately, due to our conflicting schedules, we never perform on the same bill. Jack and his troupe of singers, novelty acts and teenage chorus girls from a dancing school in Dublin, tour the theatre circuit in Ireland. Much to my surprise and delight, Ireland is at least ten years behind America. While all the old theaters in America have succumbed to the wrecking ball, the old movie palaces with a Wurlitzer organ and a pit orchestra are still alive and well in Ireland, along with vaudeville, dance halls, and big bands, mostly because television has not yet arrived in the Emerald Isle and people still listen to radio.

I work Jack's dates and continue my old pastime of studying in the dressing room. All the while I am continuing my correspondence with Ursula who is working as a nanny for a family in London in an effort to learn English. London is so close and yet so far. Still the poor student, I'm not financially sound enough to go to see her. Although still in love with Ursula, I am nevertheless fascinated with Patricia. So far, I've managed to scrape by with the few club dates I get plus the money I get from Mom and Dad. As spring approaches, Mr. Darlys brings me out of the doldrums with an offer to tour Ireland with James Duffy and Sons Circus, "One Night and One Night Only."[18] Mr. Darlys, my Hungarian agent, wants to know what name I use for my act. "Why I use my own name," say I.

"That will never do – too many O'Briens," says he. "By the way, where are you from?"

"Boston," say I. From then on I am known in Ireland as The Great Boston.

(According to legend, for some obscure reason in 1875, John Duffy, a shoemaker in Dublin, began a circus. After his death in 1909, his widow Annie continued operating the show until her death in 1916. Her two sons John and James continued the business until they had a falling out and each went on the road with their own show in 1918. Imperial John, as he was called (he must have been a real sonamamitch), continued running the circus until his death in Cork in 1947 when his son John Jr. took over. Brother James married Selena Kayes – an English woman and daughter of William "Buff Bill" Kayes who operated his own circus before and after the First World War. James and Lena Duffy, together with their seven sons, continued the family tradition until James died in Cookstown, County Tyrone, in 1959. John Jr. then went out of business in 1960, leaving the James Duffy and Sons, with Lene and the seven boys at the helm, to carry on the family circus tradition in Ireland.) The show doesn't have a winter quarters of its own, but rents out a farmer's field in Clondalkin, outside of Dublin. The show is scheduled to open in early April in Athy, County Kildare, and so I begin to prepare myself to join the show a few days early so as to get situated in my wagon and be ready for the grand tour.

Not having a vehicle, and again low on funds, I work my way to O'Connel bridge where I catch a double decked bus to Clondalkin. Because of my load, I'm forced to make three trips from my flat on Harcourt Street to the bus at O'Connell Bridge then on to Clondalkin where I deposit everything I own in a wagon, which will be the home of the Great Boston for the next six months. Actually, I only have half a wagon: there being a partition in the middle, separating the wagon into two living quarters – the other living space being occupied by Peter "Paytr" Cullen, an elderly (50 something) trumpet player. The wagon that Paytr and I share is actually the front door wagon. It has the show's name in lights and a couple of collapsible panels, which serve as a main entrance of sorts. The wagon is lighted during show times and I manage to rig up an electric light bulb, which remains on as long as one of the two show's farm tractors is running. Also in my wagon are a bunk, a closet, a gas ring for cooking and a gaslight. The ceiling leaks whenever it rains and water runs down one of the four walls, depending upon which way the wagon happens to lean.

Ireland has dreadful weather in the spring: rain, drizzle, cloudy gray skies and penetrating cold. Having contracted the flu from my drafty flat in Dublin, the first night in my new home is miserable – no blankets and only seven shillings in my pocket, trying to sleep with three layers of clothing on to keep warm. The bed is very hard and I am unable to fully stretch out, as the width of the wagon is shorter than I am. I had always wanted to perform in the circus, but this is ridiculous. My dream has turned into nightmare – *Jesus, Mary and Joseph!* In the morning, I am rudely awakened by a jolt, which flings me out of my bunk. I open the top of the half door to discover that we are traveling down the road with a tractor towing my wagon, with two attached wagons trailing behind.

Sitting above the wagon hitch is the smiling face of Jimmy Mahoney (clown, magician, and general roustabout) riding shotgun while Jimmy Duffy (ringmaster) drives the tractor. Driving another tractor is Billy Duffy, pulling the pole wagon, canvas wagon and a caravan (house trailer). The show travels only in the morning to the next town: seldom more than 20 miles away, but crawling along at 10 miles per hour, it takes hours to get there.

Jimmy Mahoney and Johnny Duffy do the clowning on the show. Although his mother Lena fronts as boss of the show, Johnny, the eldest son, is the final authority. The clown routine is that of the straight man and rube, doing mostly talk gags and insulting each other.

"You have a face like the rock of Cashel," says Johnny to Jimmy. The crowd roars with laughter.

"Your mother wears Wellingtons," retorts Jimmy.

The crowd screams with delight. Later, Johnny rides the "bucking bicycle" into the ring. The rear wheel is offset on the axel, creating a deliberate up and down wobble.

"Would you be gettin off-o-me bookin boycycle now," demands Jimmy.

"Not a-t-all," retorts Johnny, "It's me bookin boycycle." The audience boils over in laughter.

Back and forth they go: "Get your hands off-o-me bookin boycycle now when you're told."

"Gimmee the bookin boycycle now – you ee-jit" (idiot).

They argue, they fight, the audience is now rolling in the aisles, finally, one of them emerges as the winner and rides off, bucking up and down, to a standing ovation.

Jimmy Mahoney and his wife also do an oriental magic act in which Jimmy hypnotizes her then suspends her on top of the tip of three daggers, standing upright from a support in the ground. The lady wears a harness with a slot just under her neck, hidden by a veil. The dagger has a steel pipe running through its center and into a frame along the ground – the length of her body. Jimmy slips the tip of the dagger into the slot as he holds her horizontal and voila! the lady is floating on the tips of three daggers. Jimmy paints his props one day, but by showtime they are not completely dry. During the performance, Jimmy goes though the usual routine of hypnotizing his assistant then placing her suspended on the three daggers. Because the paint is still sticky, the tip of the dagger becomes stuck in the slot of the harness. Consequently when it's time for Jimmy to lift his wife from the dagger, she can't be budged. Jimmy chants the magic words again, but to no avail. His wife opens one eye and mumbles, "What's wrong!"

Try as he may, the suspended assistant cannot be unstuck. One by one, the Duffys come over to give assistance – again, no success. The suspended woman continues to be stuck in suspense. Finally, all the members of the band come to give assistance. The whole mob surrounds the suspended assistant, picks her up and with the entire contraption dangling from the back of her neck, carries her out of the ring. The audience cracks up with laughter.

The band consists of Paytr (Peter) plus (brothers) Tommy, Albert, Arthur and Alfred Duffy. Since the Duffys are also the mainstays of the performance, there is continuous activity in the band wagon as the time comes for each of them to put his instrument down, change cloths behind the bandwagon, and come out into the ring to do his act. I am in a particularly bad spot in the program, because after the band plays for Arthur who precedes me with his trapeze act, they all change for the riding act, which follows me. I am left only with Paytr, playing the trumpet with one hand while beating the rhythm on the drum with the other. Paytr, the one man band, wears the same tuxedo every day and night of the entire season. He wears it not only playing trumpet in the band, but also during the build up and pull down of the tent. Paytr, still dressed in his tux, carries quarter poles on his shoulder is forever complaining about his bad heart and not being able to continue such strenuous work. As he strides, carrying the pole across a wooden platform (the Duffy version of a stage), he breaks into an impromptu tap dance, slapping his knee with his hand as he laughs and continues to lug the pole to the pole wagon. I don't know if Paytr sleeps in his tux, but I think he is able to stand it up in the closet without a hanger. Paytr is a likable old chap, but not very bright. The Duffys have a family gag of sending townspeople who have a complaint to the new man on the show – myself. Being wise to the ruse, I forward the disgruntled circus patron to Paytr, the designated complaint person wearing the tuxedo who always listens and tries to help. Poor Paytr never catches on to the gag.

Besides the Great Boston, there is the Great Hymas, acrobat from England, the Great Elanis, acrobats from Switzerland and assorted other "greats" and not so greats. Jimmy Duffy's two daughters, Ellen and Elena, do a table and chair contortion routine, and Tommy's wife, Gerty, tap dances to an Irish jig on a piece of plywood on the ground. Duffy wives, kids, girlfriends, horses, dogs and goats all perform doing a variety of low skill acts. Audiences are always enthusiastic and satisfied. All of the artists on the show are introduced in the ring by ringmaster Jimmy Duffy, as coming direct from some other country – a circus tradition. Our English acrobat and nice chap, Johnny Hymas, cannot be introduced to Irish audiences as being direct from London, lest some of the rowdy in the crowd do him some harm. He has no qualms about being direct from Belgium.

The one ring big top has two aluminum king poles. The Duffys use one or both of them in setting up the tent, depending on the size of the lot called the tober. Out from the center of the tent is a circle of wooden queen poles while side poles surround the outside. The ring curb is always placed around one of the king poles. Occasionally, we arrive in a town where our competitor, Fossett Circus, has preceded us. The Duffys are careful not to place our ring curb in the still visible outline in the turf left by the Fossett ring; otherwise, the show will be cursed with bad luck – even more so than the usual revolting developments.

In the morning, Tommy Duffy goes on ahead to mark the route for the show to follow, often stopping along the way to go fishing in a stream. Where there is a fork in the road or a turn to be made, Tommy takes a sod of grass and drops it accordingly, to mark the turn in the road. Road signs are few and far between, and Billy Duffy, coming up from behind, can't read anyway. A common problem along the rural roads of Ireland is a herd of sheep that pass over Tommy's sod markers. The difference between sheep dung and our low tech route markers are no longer discernable. We then have to stop our caravan, pick up sticks from the ground, and carefully probe each sheep pie in order to find the official Duffy Circus route marker.

Starting a lorry (truck) in the morning involves a procedure that I never witnessed before. Whenever a Duffy asks if anyone has a match to start the lorry, he isn't kidding. Only one tractor has a starter. Once running, it pulls a second tractor in order to jumpstart it. I stand in awe, watching the two tractors line up in front of the horse lorry and begin tugging. Then, in order to heat the intake air, a Duffy with a burning piece of cloth at the end of a stick runs alongside holding the flame over the carburetor until the engine starts.

Whenever something breaks down on the road, the Duffys check their pockets to see what they have to fix it with: a piece of string, a rubber band, a paper clip. I don't know how, but we will continue down the road making every town – except two. On the one occasion we can't set up the tent during a hurricane, on the other, only one man shows up to by a ticket. The Duffys return his money and the show moves on.

It rains every day during April, the first month of the tour as we make our way towards Donnegal where the weather begins to improve. Although the incessant rain has stopped, it remains chilly the rest of the season. We are forever stuck in the mud and have to use both tractors and everyone pushing to get the show off the tober. I cook for myself in my little wagon, and as we travel down the road, pots and pans hanging on my wall clatter and clang. My usual meal is spaghetti since it is the easiest thing to prepare, and of course tea. The show does not provide water, so in each town, we tip a little boy a shilling to go to a nearby house and beg some. Sometimes they return with the water, sometimes they don't.

There is no toilet on the show. The Duffys take to crouching behind walls and bushes. Myself, I use a little bottle I keep in the wagon; also, I fold a newspaper into a paper hat in which I make a deposit, then discretely toss it away. Arthur Duffy finds one of them one morning and compliments me on my tidiness.

Hotels in Ireland rent us a bath for a shilling. As for our laundry, we go the local convent, where for a few shillings the clothes are not only washed, but divinely dried, immaculately ironed, and heavenly folded by the ladies in black.

After the show is loaded up at night, we visit a local pub where we drink and sing Irish songs to the accompaniment of Paytr on the accordion. One night, however, I am the last one back to the tober, and I forget to close the gate behind me. In the morning, the eight horses – having been let loose during the night to graze – are gone. We find them peacefully grazing downtown at City Hall where they have eaten all the flowers surrounding the building. We round them up and leave town post haste.

All the while on tour, I continue to correspond with Ursula in London. I send her photos of me performing in the circus. She is not impressed, and I can understand why – rather than being engaged by a high class show, I have taken up with a band of traveling gypsies. This is certainly not the lifestyle I had envisioned the circus to be. Duffy Circus is show business in its most primitive form: no glitter, no glamour, no sparkle. The only asset is that I'm getting to see the country. By this time, I am not thinking much about the present as I am of the future. There must be something better in life than Duffy Circus, but where, when?

In Croom, Limerick County, a nice-looking young girl is hanging around the show and I feel attracted to her. I get acquainted with Marrie and invite her into my wagon after the show where we enjoy a Duffy Circus "one night and one night only." The next day we move to Limerick town for a two day stand where Marrie unexpectedly shows up with her girlfriend. Of course I am delighted to see her and we spend some free time exploring Limerick town. Although young looking, Marrie is very mature and tantalizing. Like a sailor at sea, months of living in a circus wagon can make a young man lonely and amorous. Later, while Jimmy Mahoney is doing his magic act, Marrie shows me a few tricks of her own in my wagon while her girlfriend waits outside. After we enjoy a cup of tea, I have to excuse myself to perform – The Great Boston must make his appearance to the lovely people of Limerick. After the show, the girls depart and promise to visit me again in tomorrow's town, Newmarket on Fergus.

The next day, we arrive in Newmarket, erect the tent and prepare for the show, but the girls fail to appear. Later that evening, I'm in my wagon dressing for the evening show when I hear a knock at the door. Expecting a pleasant surprise, I open the door to see two Gardaí na Síochána (Irish police) standing there. It seams that two girls from Croom ran away from home and were last seen hanging around Duffy Circus.

The Garda would like to search my wagon – *search indeed!* My wagon is only two steps long from the door to my bunk, and two steps wide from the gas ring on one side, to the closet on the other.

Nevertheless, the Garda enters and looks into the closet. "Níl aon ghirseach anseo,"[19] says he. "By the way," says he, "You know that in this country, the girls need to be seventeen to consent." – *Jesus, Mary and Joseph!* I don't know what to say, so I just stand there and give him my best grin. The Gardaí continue looking around the circus as I prepare for the evening performance. It's show time and the girls haven't shown up – I'm hoping they don't. Just as I begin my performance, the Gardaí enter the tent and stand in the main entrance like statues, watching me perform – *sonamamitch!* I'm a nervous wreck and can all but keep from dropping my balls or falling off the wire, but the show must go on. To a great round of applause, I finish my act, take a bow and depart the ring while the Gardaí exit through the main entrance. The Great Boston's reputation as a gentleman remains intact in Ireland.

From County Donegal, the show moves into Northern Ireland, or as some of the Irish say – British occupied Ireland. Crossing the border reminds me of crossing from West to East Germany. Armed border guards examine the circus, then allow us to proceed to Derry where we have a two-day stand. The I.R.A.(Irish Republican Army) is still active, and I am taken back to see all the police stations surrounded by sandbags and guns. During the Irish revolution, the Duffys were known to smuggle guns, hidden in the wagons, through the British lines. Of course the Duffys would never fly the Union Jack over the circus tent while in the North, even though the Irish tricolor always flew over the tent in the Republic. Nevertheless, the circus is a nonpolitical and international institution and we enjoy good business and good will throughout the tour. While drinking in a pub after the show one night, the Duffys recount to me one tale about the time their father played the town of Coalisland, County Tyrone.

(A little boy who was getting into mischief around the show was not so gently kicked off the tober. The boy went home and got his father who came back to the circus looking for a fight; the father in turn was thrown off the tober. The father then went to a local pub and rounded up his friends. Full of drink and looking for a donnybrook, they got the fracas that they wanted with the circus folk who drove them back to town where they proceeded to round up reinforcements. By then, of course, the town had turned into an ugly mood, and the Duffys knew that it would be wise to cancel the date and leave town. The townspeople, however, knowing that the show would have to pass through town in order to get to their next engagement, had gathered in the town square with assorted weapons, waiting for the circus to pass through. Realizing that they would have to fight their way through Coalisland, Mr. Duffy ordered two of the quarter poles to be lashed to the pole wagon so that they would protrude out on each side. Then, all of the circus personnel, with wooden stakes in hand, mounted the horses hitched to the wagons. At the command of "charge," Duffy's impromptu cavalry with horses galloping and wagons bouncing, led by Mr. Duffy commanding the pole wagon with its protruding quarter poles, managed to beat its way through the mob and gallop out of town from whence they never return.)

The season grinds on and on as we plod ever onward around the Emerald Isle. There is a noticeable change in the air as we enter the month of October – the wind stops blowing constantly and the leaves begin to change color. The circus season will soon be over and I must contemplate my future. A show business career in Ireland doesn't look lucrative. For some time I have contemplated flying an airplane in the military. Now that I am 25 years old, the maximum age for military service and flight school, the time has come for a decision and a commitment. On my salary of 20 punt ($60) per week, I have been able to save enough money for another Atlantic Crossing back to the States; not only that, but I have enough money to travel to Germany to visit my Parisian girlfriend Ursula, with whom I continue to correspond. By this time, she has returned home to Nürnberg after her sojourn in London. It has been more than a year since we have seen each other. My spirits soar as the days dwindle down to the end of the season and the closing of the show.

After the final performance in Lucan, County Dublin – the one hundred and eighty-fifth town – the show returns to Clondalkin, from whence I retrace my steps to Dublin; this time I take a cab and stay in a hotel with a hot bath. Back in Dublin town again, I pay a visit to Jack Cruise, hoping he might have a date for me and also to see his lovely singing secretary Patricia who still fascinates me. A dilemma arises – in a few weeks I plan to visit Ursula in Germany, and yet, there is something about Patricia that turns my head towards the Emerald Isle. Her beauty and singing charm holds me in a trance, in spite of my thoughts of Ursula. Which one of my loves to pursue – like trying to choose a restaurant for diner, do I want Chinese or Italian, Irish or German? I'm in a quandary, but then such is the game of life – decisions – decisions.

Even though my sights are set on Ursula, I don't know how she feels about marriage or leaving her country to go to America. Before any girl will have me I have to settle down and get a steady job – something with a stable element that appeals to women – military service. Something could go wrong with my plans, however. Maybe Ursula will reject me – then what? What I need is an alternate plan – a redundant girlfriend.

Jack is still producing theatre shows around the country and has been using his secretary, Patricia, as lead singer most of the time. I visit her in Dundalk where she is performing with Jack's troupe. Patricia is glad to see me again, but doesn't greet me with enthusiasm. Duffy Circus people are, of course, not on the same professional level with the Irish theatre crowd, so she remains aloof. Nevertheless, I'm glad to see her. As she sits in the dressing room powdering her nose, waiting to go on stage, something about her reminds me of my mother: she loves to talk – not necessarily an endearing attribute, but something I could live with if I had to. Patricia's next engagement is the Theatre Royal in Waterford where I had worked for Jack a year before. We travel by train together to Waterford where she gets off and I continue on to Cork and then Cobh to catch the ship to the U.S.A. via Le Havre. She still has this career thing and has yet to warm up to me. We kiss goodbye, but I don't tell her that I am off to Germany. She is still pondering my relevance in her life, but I have no time for that. There are oceans yet to be "swum" and mountains to be "clumb." Alas, another travel odyssey unfolds: the *United States* leaves Cobh, bound for Le Havre where it will tie up for a week before steaming on to New York. While the ship is in port, I intend to travel on by train to Gare St. Lazare in Paris, take the Metro to Gar de L'est where I take another train to Nürnberg and my sweetheart, Ursula. Alas! the things that the male of the species will do in order to find a mate. It all doesn't make sense and yet some mysterious force compels me to go on.

The train finally arrives in Nürnberg. Ursula meets me at the station and I am overjoyed to see her. Suddenly, all the effort to get here seems a noble and worthy endeavor. As we embrace, she surprises me by speaking English. All those months in London have done wonders for her language skills. She welcomes me to her home and I get to meet the whole family who are polite, but eye me suspiciously.

Her father is an interior decorator and wears a quaint Hitler mustache. The family is Germans who had lived in Czechoslovakia, and were later forced out by the Russians after the war. They make me feel uncomfortable when they speak to each other in Czech while in my presence. Although friendly but reserved, they are respectful and delight in showing me the town.

Ursula takes me to dine in an ancient castle now a restaurant, the Kaiserschloss (emperor's castle). And so, it is in an atmosphere of the age of chivalry, knights and ladies that she says, "Also ja, Ich werde dich heiraten."[20] A feeling of joy overwhelms me as we kiss over the dinner table within the walls of a medieval castle. As we take a romantic walk back to her home, we discuss our future life together. She is working as a reservation hostess for Lufthansa Airlines and enjoys her job while I am about to return to the States, get a real job in the military and become somebody. At the appropriate time, we will then get together for a wedding in Germany. Oddly enough, she asks me not to mention our engagement to anyone yet as she wants to break the news at the proper time and place. A ring, of course, will have to wait until I get home and get some money, and although her request puzzles me for the moment, I acquiesce nevertheless.

The next morning, Ursula's mother makes me a lunch to take with me, then Ursula puts me on the train for Paris. During the trip, I think nice thoughts about my future, eat my lunch and float on air – life is good.

From Nürnberg to Paris, then to Le Havre, ever onward towards my ship and old friend, the *S.S. United States*, which waits patiently for my arrival. Still another Atlantic crossing and I'm feeling like Barnacle Bill the sailor. No longer do I get seasick in rough weather, and by now, I know the ship inside out. Even the secret door that leads from second class – where I belong – to first class – where I prefer to lounge – is still there for me to use at my discretion. Of course, girl watching is still the favorite shipboard game, even though I do feel a bit reserved now that I am engaged – or so I think. In the evening, there is still bingo in the passenger lounge with drinking at the bar, followed by the customary assembly on deck to seek out enemy torpedo wakes and conning towers. My Atlantic "convoy" arrives safely in New York and the "troops" disembark for destinations unknown. As for myself, I'm on my way home to Mom and Dad in Florida where I intend to join the military and make something of myself. My romantic, roaming student days are over – *Jesus, Mary and Joseph!*

Duffy Circus in County Donegal (1961)

Chapter VI
Anchors Aweigh

Back in Florida again, I relish the security and comfort of being home with Mom and Dad – sort of. After resting up with the usual Florida things to do, like lounging on the beach and soaking up the sun, I apply for enlistment with the Air Force. They send me to Tampa on a bus with other aspiring candidates and we undergo testing for officer candidate school, but things are not going as planned and I flunk the test. They offer to take me as an enlisted man but I decline. All of my heroes in the war movies were officers, so I want to be an officer too. I realize my mistake right away. I never prepared myself for the exam so I go to plan B; I buy a book on Navy entrance exams and study to prepare myself for the Naval Aviation Candidate School.

Another problem arises – while in High School during the Korean War, I had been classified 4F by my draft board due to an old knee injury suffered while playing football. Actually, it didn't amount to more than a calcium deposit below the kneecap, but it looked ominous. Not being keen on going to Korea, I limped into the draft board office counting on my trick knee to do the trick. Mom's former boyfriend and member of the draft board – convinced of my handicap, much to my delight – decided that I wasn't fit for service. Now, of course, things have changed. Not only do I want to enlist in the military, I need a job. After weeks of study and preparation, I take the Navy exam and just pass, but I make it. Now comes a waiting period for my orders to report for duty in Pensacola.

Mom and I decide to take a non-stop bus ride to visit her sister Miriam near San Francisco. Husband, Uncle Bob, is the director of the National Cemetery there. Recalling the pleasant bus rides in Europe, I think that seeing the country by bus will be a lot of fun – at the least I can kill some time while waiting to report for Navy duty. By now I should know that, while travel plans are so easily done in one's mind, the reality of implementing them is frustrating and exhausting. I'm figuring that rather than stopping at night in a motel, we can just sleep in the bus and continue along the trip and save money at the same time.

My European student survival techniques still with me, we spend four sleepless days and nights on Greyhound buses. Not only are they hot and uncomfortable; but trying to sleep at night while traveling on a bus is not as easy as one thinks. When I'm awake, Mom talks incessantly, even when I try to read. I try to sleep and my brain doesn't want to turn off. As I look out the window while crossing the desert in Texas and Arizona, I seem to see Indians pursuing a stagecoach – I'm so tired can't sleep. My mental state is a blur of fantasy and reality all in one – I'm in never-never land. *Am I home, dreaming that I'm sleeping on a bus or am I sleeping on a bus dreaming that I'm home?* The trip grinds on and on. The smell of carbon monoxide invades my senses and the constant sound of the diesel engine numbs my mind.

Mom catches the flu from a Mexican fellow on the bus who sneezes constantly. Finally, we have to make a stop for the night to recuperate somewhere in Arizona. By the time the bus reaches San Francisco, Mom and I are reduced to zombies as we stagger off the bus to await the arrival of cousin Steve, who is to pick us up and take us home. We call the house and announce our arrival, but Steve falls asleep again after our phone call and is three hours late arriving at the bus station. Mom is furious while I am just in a trance. Eventually, we recover from the trip and enjoy a nice visit with my Aunty Miriam and Uncle Bob and my cousins. Mom chooses to return to Florida by air while I choose another long bus ride along the northern route so that I can see more of the country. Surprisingly, the return trip to Florida alone turns out to be a pleasant experience. During the trip, my thoughts are on Ursula. I haven't told Mom and Dad about Ursula yet since my life seems to be in turmoil at this point, there being too many unknowns which are yet to be resolved. Hopefully, when I return to Orlando, I will hear from the Navy as to when to report for duty and also from Ursula as to when she is coming to America. Ironically, there are two letters waiting for me when I get home. As the old adage goes – there is good news and there is bad news – first the good news.

The Navy has sent me orders to report for flight training in Pensacola, Florida. The bad news is a letter from Ursula that begins: "Terry, you are not going to like this letter" – I don't. She decides that giving up her country is too much for her and will marry the boy next door – I thought I had everything all figured out. All the nice thoughts of her, which I had carried around in my head, shatter like broken glass – I'm crushed.- *sonamamitch!*

*

Basic training at Navy Flight school is divided up into three parts: military, physical training and academics. The physical fitness part is a piece of cake; being in shape from lifting side poles on Duffy Circus I earn a merit badge. The military part, drilling, marching, inspections, etc., is designed to introduce a new lifestyle of togetherness and instill team spirit; that, along with nitpicking attention to detail, frustrate me, but I manage to adapt. Academics I find difficult since I have no prior knowledge of aviation in general and the lectures and books are in the technical language of aviation. Since I don't speak the language, I soon discover that I don't know my zenith from my azimuth.

The Navy wants us to work while under stress. They provide the stress; therefore, we are constantly stressed out. Of course the answer to stress is sleep, but we are only allowed 5 hours of it a night, enough to satisfy our basic needs while still maintaining the mental pressure. In the beginning, I feel stupid as I struggle with the daily routine. There is so much to learn and so little time to learn it; and all the while, I am haunted by thoughts of Ursula. Nevertheless, I study, I train, I persevere, and I survive. Gradually, the memory of Ursula fades out and Patricia fades in. Going from plan A to plan B, I begin corresponding with Patricia again – *what do I have to lose?* She picks up on it and my spirits soar. She wants to know why I haven't written to her in a long while, but then she never wrote either. Suddenly, my future looks bright although the pressure of basic training remains daunting.

My refuge is the Training Command Band under the direction of Chief Symington – a roly-poly musician who reminds me of bandleader Paul Whitman without the moustache. Band duty is great: we don't have to stand inspection during the Friday graduation ceremony and the Admiral sends us on concert tours around the country on Naval aircraft. We fly to West Virginia for Vice President Johnson and play at the Texas State Fair in Dallas. We also march in a parade in St. Petersburg, Florida, where Mom and Dad come to visit and cheer me on as I come marching down the street playing my trombone.

After three months of basic training, the big day arrives when I march onto the parade grounds with my graduation class to receive my commission as Ensign in the U.S. Navy Reserve. Ensign O'Brien gets his gold stripe and a cigar. There is one sour note, however, I graduate at the bottom of the class

– not exactly the goat at the bottom, but down in the cargo hold with the others who managed to squeak by. Now that I am at Saufley Field, I learn how to fly the Mentor, but continue playing in the band. The admiral sends the band to lead the Mardi Gras parade in New Orleans. Rather than fly, we get a special treat. The band will steam from Pensacola aboard the aircraft carrier *U.S.S. Lexington* across the Gulf of Mexico to New Orleans, where the ship will be put on public display for the occasion. The officer band members are billeted in officer country, located forward on the hangar deck. My cabin is so far forward that I can walk on the bulkhead and the one porthole looks down on the water rather than out. Being on a carrier fills my mind with thoughts of Navy battles of Midway and Coral Sea. It is night time as we cruise the Gulf of Mexico. On the forward starboard antiaircraft station I smoke my pipe and, in my reverie, scan the horizon looking for Japanese battleships.

All is quiet except for the sound of the waves and the wind – a childhood dream fulfilled – better late than never. As the sun rises, I rise from my rack and can see through the porthole that we are tied up at the dock in New Orleans and it's time for breakfast in the officers' wardroom. The band assembles on the flight deck to welcome aboard local dignitaries and the general public. Later, buses take the band to an assembly area where we form to lead the Mardi Gras Parade through downtown New Orleans and into the Vieux Carré.[21] We strut our stuff, marching along in front of the floats, adorned by costume-adorned revelers while thousands of people cheer and throw confetti at us. After the parade, we get tickets to a costume ball at the many arenas around the city that host the various "krewes"[22] participating in the parade.

That evening while strolling along Bourbon Street on my way to the ball, I ask a young lady dressed as Olive Oil for directions to the arena. It just so happens that she is also on her way there – and so together, Olive Oil and her sailor man make their way through the French Quarter to attend the ball. It's a sailor's delight: eating, drinking and dancing at a costume ball in New Orleans. Just as I am about to take Olive home – she lives not far away with her mother – it begins to rain. We run along the carnival-debris-cluttered streets getting soaked. By the time we reach her house, we are drenched. Her mother invites me in out of the rain to dry off and suggests that I take off my uniform so that she can iron it dry. In the meantime since I'm in my underwear, she says that I can wait in bed to keep warm and even take a nap – *sounds like a "wiener" to me* – I comply. Olive in the meantime has taken off her wet cloths and decides to wait in bed with me while her mother irons

90

my trousers in the kitchen. Here we are, Olive and I, a girl I have just met, fooling around in bed with no clothes on, while her mother in the next room might walk in on us any minute – *Jesus, Mary and Joseph.* Before things get out of hand, Olive's mother calls out that my laundry is done so I immediately spring out of bed and retreat to the kitchen where I dress back into my uniform, now nicely dry and pressed. I thank Olive and her mother for being so kind and swagger back to my ship along the back alleys and streets of the French Quarter. It begins to rain again so I duck into the French Market not far from where my ship (*The Lady Lex*) is birthed, both to get out of the rain and to enjoy a beignet (doughnut). Although delicious, the beignet is notorious for its coating of white powdered sugar. At the slightest ill-timed breath, the powder disburses to transfer itself to ones clothing. Taking a bite on the inhale is the way to eat a beignet. To sneeze while biting, which I do, is to invite a cloud of white powder to emerge, enveloping the entire body, which it does. Thus my soggy naval winter blues appear to have a fine coat of snow on top of the rain. A dreadful sight I must be, as I stagger past the Marine sentry and up the gangway of the *Lady Lex*. After a great week enjoying Louisiana Creole cooking, marching in parades during the day and partying at night, the ship gets underway in the wee hours of the morning, returning to Pensacola – home from another dangerous mission.

Back at Saufley Field, it is back to the business of learning to fly. Never having flown an airplane before, I find I find it a daunting task and wonder if I can ever learn. Understanding all the various components of flying is one thing, but then putting it all together into a comprehensive and organized train of thought is something else; I am overwhelmed, but I press on. The months pass by slowly as I accumulate flying hours and the ability to control an airplane grows. One basic problem to be overcome by all student pilots is to develop the ability to concentrate on many things at once, rather than focusing on one thing. This ability can only come with time and practice. In the meantime, the smell of hydraulic fuel begins to nauseate me; nevertheless, I gradually acquire the skill of flying, and eventually the day arrives when I make my first solo. At the Officers' Club, my instructor cuts my necktie in half with a pair of scissors – the standard first solo ceremony. The aroma of sweet success (cigar smoke) fills the air.

Olive Oil of New Orleans has been keeping in touch with me all this time; but my thoughts are on Patricia. I write to her for the last time and graciously end our relationship – not that we ever had one.

Christmas leave is coming up and so I begin to make plans to go to visit

Patricia in Dublin. Another travel odyssey begins to take shape and my problems begin at the beginning. At Operations in Pensacola, I sign up for a hop to Washington, D. C., where I can take a bus to McGuire A.F.B. in New Jersey and, from there, a MATS[23] hop to Minden Hall, England. However, the crew of the *Lexington* have most of the flights out of Pensacola booked, and I get bumped off. At the last moment, however, someone gets sick and I'm given his seat. Relieved, I begin the flight to New York and then to Washington, from where I take a train to Baltimore and, finally, a bus to McGuire in New Jersey.

Actually, the trip would be much easier to get off in New York and, from there, take a bus direct to McGuire, but poor planning seems to be my fate in life so I do it the hard way. Arriving the day before Christmas, and with no flights going my way, the base shuts down for the holiday – *sonamamitch*. What am I going to do until after Christmas? A little side trip to visit relatives where I can kill time is just what I need.

Mom's sister Cookie lives in Connecticut with Uncle Joe, the black sheep son-in-law of the family. Mimmay dislikes him even more than my Dad because he likes to gamble.[24] I always liked Uncle Joe, because during the war, he was a side gunner in a B-17 bomber, and in my youth he would take me fishing. The bus takes me to the Port Authority in New York where I transfer to New Haven and arrive at my aunt's home, exhausted and with no one at home. Their kindly neighbor takes me in to await the arrival of Cookie and Joe and I promptly fall asleep in a chair. Eventually, my relatives come home and suddenly my fatigue evaporates. We have a nice Christmas family gathering, and for the moment, all is right with the world, except that I have ahead of me a grueling task of getting to England and then Ireland just to see a woman who may not give a fig for me. I don't reveal my intentions to my aunt and uncle, since they wouldn't understand. I bid them adieu, and am off again on my quest, like a knight from King Arthur's court, Sir Terence, filled with a new breath of hope and inspiration, and mounted on his noble steed charging blindly into adversity, retracing his trail to McGuire A.F.B. for a military hop.

Upon arrival, I check in at operations and begin the long wait for a flight. There are many others like myself waiting for a flight and it is usually on a first come, first serve basis. Some bumping by senior officers does occur I soon discover, adding more frustration to my already tight schedule. By late afternoon, I'm about to fall into a stupor, when suddenly, I have a stroke of luck – well, sort of. There is a flight going right away to Rhein/Mein Airport in Frankfort. It is not exactly where I want to go; however, it is close enough – *once in Europe I can wing it from there.* The flight departs for Frankfort, Germany, and I sleep all the way. Upon arrival, I discover that I have to wait another day for a flight to England. In spite of my best laid plans, nothing seems to be going right for me.

Being in Germany again jolts my memory, and suddenly, suppressed images of Ursula come to mind and emotion overwhelms me. Now boiling with rage, I ring her up on the phone and her father answers. I find it rather amusing that he is shocked and surprised at my call, and as expected, he tells me that she is not there. Undaunted, I hang up and send her a telegram that I am on my way to see her, and I take the next night train to Nürnberg. The night is bitter cold and it is snowing in Germany. I sit on the train contemplating what I will say to Ursula. Peace of mind demands a confrontation with my former love.

Even though I realize the futility of my actions, I haven't a clue what I shall say to her, but I must say something – I must see her again. Strangely enough, I began a trip in Florida to see Patricia in Dublin, and am now on my way to Nürnberg to see Ursula. Is some mysterious force at work, controlling my will – *am I under a spell unable to resist?*

As the train rocks me gently, I doze, confused and stressed out. The snow-covered countryside, barely visible in the moonless sky, passes by as I look out the window. Just after midnight, the train arrives at the Haupt Bahnhof (main railway station) in Nürnberg.

The hour is late and the temperature is cold. With hardly anyone at the station, an unfriendly atmosphere prevails as a handful of passengers disembark and walk along the platform towards the main concourse. A few people stare at me as I walk along the platform in my Navy winter blues with gold Ensign epaulets and white cover with a golden eagle emblem. The station is almost deserted except for two men I spy standing at the passenger exit gate. Right away, I recognize the Hitler style moustache of Ursula's father. As I approach them, the father greets me and introduces me to Ursula's new fiancé. Numb with fatigue and cold, I stumble with my German. They respect my uniform and are scrupulously polite; however, the message is clear: Ursula has made her choice and I might as well get out of town – *how rude!* Instinctively, I offer my hand as a beau geste (noble gesture). Then as they turn to leave, I stand there stunned, not knowing whether to laugh or cry. Still smarting from the encounter, I pick up my bag and walk across the street to the Allied Military Hotel where I check in. The German clerk is surprised that I speak German since most American servicemen don't. Although tired, my heart is in agony and I can't sleep. The hotel bar is still open; there I try to drown my sorrow in German beer. In the morning, I will be on my way again to Frankfort, but for the moment, I put down my thoughts in a letter to Ursula. By now it is past 2 a.m. and I feel compelled to go for a walk. The city is empty and cold as snow continues to fall. As I walk the streets of Nürnberg, my breath turns to steam while the snow on the ground crunches under my feet. I trudge aimlessly along the quiet streets of the city, and yet, I know where I'm going. I find myself on the street where Ursula lives, looking up to the top floor and the darkened window of her bedroom in her family's apartment – the same room where I had slept during happier times. I walk over to the building and deposit the letter in her mailbox.

The next morning, I'm on the train for Frankfort, sleeping all the way. As the train arrives at the station, I awake with a start. *Where am I; where am I going; what was I doing? Yes, I remember, I'm in Germany, on my way to Ireland to see my girlfriend Patricia – it's all coming back to me now.* At Rein/Main, there is a hop going to Mindenhall, England. They take my bags and send them on ahead on an earlier flight already booked up that apparently has plenty of cargo space. Finally the time arrives for me to depart when I learn that I have been bumped off the flight by a senior officer – *sonamamitch.* I start to panic; my bags are already in England, and I'm still stuck here in Germany. The sergeant in charge knows just what to do; he bumps an enlisted man off the flight and I'm on my way to England. I feel a sense of relief as we cross the English Channel, but Dublin is still a long way to travel. No problem – I've done it all before so I know that I can do it again. This time, however, I decide to do it the easy way: from Heathrow Airport, I catch an Air Lingus flight to Dublin.

While flying across the Irish Sea, I'm surprised to meet Tommy Duffy who is just as surprised to see me, and in uniform at that. He had been in London on business and is returning home. After arrival in Dublin, Tommy and I have a jar of Guinness at the airport lounge and enjoy a nice chat. Patricia is singing on the Jack Cruise show at the Olympia Theatre and Tommy tells me that Jack will never let her go, but wishes me luck with my romance never the less.

(The Olympia theatre on Dame street opposite Dublin Castle has occupied that site since 1879, when it first opened as the Dan Lowry theatre.) Old and decrepit, it still has a charm that only old theatres can have. The bus stops in front of the theatre where I exit; then I proceed down the cobblestone back alley to the stage entrance. Patricia is sitting in her dressing room as I walk in and at long last I embrace my dream girl. The show is still going on and it's time for the cast to take their bows. Jack suggests for a gag that I go out and take a bow too – and so I do. The audience doesn't know who I am, but I get a big hand in any case. It's just a musty old theatre in Dublin, but to me I'm in paradise and whatever obstacles I had to overcome to get here was worth it – or so it seems. After the show, Patricia takes me to Croyden Hotel where Jack had called ahead to get me a special rate. She accompanies me to my room where we relax and embrace. Patricia seems particularly warm and friendly as she lies down on the bed to offer me a treat.

Suddenly, there is a knock on the door. It's the concierge who informs me that I only paid for one person and that my guest will have to leave – *sonamamitch!* I want to punch him out but don't want to embarrass Pat, so we leave. Beagnach, ach níl aon tadóg dom[25] – never mind, I still have a week to spend in Dublin with my girl and there's still plenty of time for love.

The week seems to fly by. Patricia is busy performing at the theatre and enjoys showing me around to her friends – it must be the uniform I'm thinking. She still dreams of performing in London and becoming a star in the theatre. Apparently, she's looking for a wimpy, stay at home husband who will do the ironing while she is taking bows on the stage and sells records. I think she is foolish and wonder how I could fit into such a scheme. I know not what fate has in store for us together; I only know that I want her. It is a dilemma that will have to be played out. On New Year's Eve, we go dancing at the Metropole Ballroom on O'Connell Street. I seem to be dancing on air as we waltz around the ballroom. At midnight the band plays "Auld Lang Syne" and we kiss in the New Year – it's 1963. Alas, duty calls, and love will have to wait. Like the sailor in story and song, I bid Patricia and Ireland *Slán agabh,!*[26] then fly back to London where I then catch a train to Mindenhall – from there to await a hop to McGuire and back to square one – the Naval Air Station at Pensacola, Florida.

Back at the base, I have mixed feelings – I'm glad to be back – I hate coming back. Our basic flight training in the Mentor concludes and the class divides into two groups. The guys in the top half of the class goes to jet training in Mississippi, and we not-so smarts at the bottom go to propeller school located at Whiting Field. No problem – all my childhood movie heroes flew props. The new airplane that I learn to fly is a Trojan, which not only serves for training purposes, but also is used as a fighter-bomber in many countries in the world. It carries two .50-caliber machine guns in pods and six rockets under the wings and also one 500-lb. bomb under the belly. My new flying machine intimidates me at first; but gradually, I get the feel of the beast and become quite fond of it once I know what I'm doing.

After weeks of dual instruction, I solo again then practice aerobatic maneuvers over the Gulf of Mexico. Some of my fellow student flyers think this is fun; but I find myself thinking that I would rather be drinking beer in the officers' club. To make my practice sessions more enjoyable, I fantasize that there is a Jap Zero on my tail, and I'm trying to shake him. Now I'm behind him and I squeeze the trigger on my stick – my machine guns are not armed – and splash one Zero. Although I'm a good pilot in the air, my landings are above average, I am but a fair student in the classroom on the ground. Since I have a tendency to learn slowly, time is not on my side. The Navy gives you the books today and wants you to know it yesterday. Before I learn one subject, we are already onto something else. I am increasingly frustrated and my brain is dead. In one week's time, I have five exams scheduled, which is stressing me out. After failing radio instrument navigation,[27] they let me take the test again, but raise the passing score for the second go at it. My score is higher than before, but nevertheless lower then the second standard for passing – I am suffering from mental fatigue. That in itself is not so bad. However, this is peacetime and the Navy doesn't need lots of pilots. Most significant, however, is the fact that I am in the bottom third of the class. Bluntly, they invite me to leave – *sonamamitch!*

Ensign O'Brien aboard the U.S.S. Lexington CVT-16 (1962)

With girlfriend Patricia in Dublin (1963)

Chapter VII
The Washington Connection

The Navy knows that I speak German, so I am transferred to the National Security Agency, located outside Washington, at Fort Meade, Maryland. For a while I am feeling crushed, but I try to think of Patricia and brighter things to come in a new job and a new environment. Arriving at my first duty station, Navy Security Group at the National Security Agency, I am told nothing about my new job, because I don't have a need to know, and I need a *TOP SECRET CRYPTO* clearance, which will take about a year. At first I think they must be kidding, but alas, it is true. During the interim, they put me in charge of the mess with a crew of cooks and dishwashers. On Fridays, I inspect the barracks and do various assigned chores while awaiting my clearance. Gradually, I adjust to my new lifestyle in Washington, and continue to correspond with Patricia in Dublin – trying to coax her to come to America. She, of course, is still singing around Ireland and focusing on stardom someday – a noble aspiration, but not a practical one since theatres are doomed to the wrecking ball. Marrying me would be a much better choice. Not being satisfied with my dull and boring lifestyle, I join the Fort Meade Flying Club, and enroll in a German course at the University of Maryland.

While attending German literature class, and quite by chance, I happen to meet my old friend Walter from Marburg, now working at the university as an art history professor. All this time he has been studying at several universities in Europe, and is now married to Regina, a big German woman with a Doctorate in Chemistry. Although married with three children who speak English and German, Walter has not changed his carefree lifestyle and plays the skirt-chasing game as usual. Regina knows that he enjoys other women and, while disapproving, tolerates it never the less. "Men have different needs than women," says she, rationalizing his behavior. Poor Regina, plump and unattractive, but with a brilliant mind, is resigned to her fate of being the cook, maid and babysitter, while Walter lives his fantasy of perpetual youth – still and always the university student prince, now turned professor. Walter and I see the sights of Washington together and cruse for chicks at the favorite places where the foreign nannies like to hang out. Regina, of course, knows what we're up to but doesn't make a fuss, at least not while I'm around.

Having learned how to fly an airplane in Pensacola, I acquire a taste for flying that won't go away. The flying club at Tifton airstrip at Fort Meade welcomes me as a new member and I proceed to work on a private pilot license in a Cessna 150, a reliable and inexpensive airplane that is easy to fly. Flying again satisfies my ego and helps me to get over having been washed out of Navy Flight School. Flying crosscountry is particularly enjoyable as I visit the various airports in the Maryland and Virginia area. The day arrives when I am scheduled to fly into Baltimore Friendship Airport for my private pilot exam and check ride. After filing a flight plan, I take off from Tifton, after which Approach Control inserts me into a landing sequence, followed by the control tower, which clears me to land between incoming passenger flights. With some apprehension, I press on, but my nerves of steel carry me through, and I land and taxi to the examiner's office without incident. Although I am a nervous wreck by this time, I pass the exam and the check ride with the examiner – *so far, so good,* I'm thinking. Now with my brand new Private Pilot's license, I take off again for the return trip to Tifton. After arrival, however, I fail to close my flight plan as required by regulations, and while I'm drinking beer and smoking a cigar at the Officers' club, a radio search for me is underway. The flying club officers know where I am and so the search is called off; nevertheless, they are peeved with me. My flight falls short of perfection, and all I can do is give them my best grin – no matter, I now have my private license and have achieved one goal with others to come.

One Sunday, I'm walking along Baltimore Street – the entertainment district of Baltimore – and look at the marquee of a burlesque house. Low and behold I read: Now appearing, Serrie – The Dutch Doll. I haven't seen her since we played a gig together in Western Massachusetts where she was arrested for speeding. We were working a club called the River Boat – just over the New York State line. Serrie, myself and Tony the dirty comic were driving to Pittsfield in her yellow Pontiac as the Highway Patrol passed us going in the other direction. She is driving over the limit and knows it. As the trooper passes, he glances at us and she suspects that he will be turning around, and will soon be after her. She pulls over to the side of the road and suggests that I drive. I comply, but her ploy doesn't work, for soon after, the trooper comes up from behind and with his lights flashing he pulls me over. The Dutch Doll tries to act innocent, but the officer is not sympathetic. We follow the trooper to the station where she pays a fine for speeding .

Years have past since then, with Sierre still working the few burlesque houses that still exist – ever yet bumping and grinding to audiences of dirty old men and other strange people. She is surprised to see me again, and in uniform, as we talk about the good old days. Time has not been kind to her, and I feel sorry for her plight. Still a single stripper in her fifties, she carries on her trade in the old theaters that still haven't succumbed to the wrecking ball. The industry has changed. All the old time exotic dancers are gone, having been replaced by the go-go girls who no longer dance, but just wiggle in the nude in the bars that line Baltimore Street. They don't dance with class, not like Serrie -The Dutch Doll.

*

The unthinkable happens. President Kennedy is assassinated and Washington, D. C., is in turmoil. We all continue to carry on with our daily routine, but in a somber atmosphere as the country mourns. The body of President Kennedy is placed in the Rotunda of the Capitol Building where I go to pay my respects, along with thousand of others. The time is early evening and the line stretches for miles as I approach to stand alongside a group of college students from Philadelphia. The line is moving torturously slow and the hours drag by. As the line slowly moves people begin to chat, and by the time I arrive at the Rotunda, Margaret and I have become old friends and, by now, my "wait mate." Passing through the Rotunda, I stop at the casket, salute the fallen President, then continue through and out the Capitol Building with Margaret and the rest of the crowd. The experience is very moving and somber.

However, Margaret has now discovered that she has lost the group that she had come with, and doesn't know what to do. It is now way past midnight, and not only has she lost her group, but also missed the train to Philadelphia. Now I'm stuck with her and I don't know what to do either – *Jesus, Mary and Joseph!*

Suddenly it occurs me to call my friend Walter, and he agrees to put her up for the night. We drive to his place in Silver Spring where she meets Regina, their kids and Walter's Doberman that likes to bite people it doesn't know. Bewildered and apprehensive, poor Margaret, whom I had just met the day before, has adopted me as a stray cat adopts a master, and she is depending on me to solve her problem. Regina gives her a spare room for the night; and not wanting to just dump her on Walter, I remain and sleep in the attic with the dog. The next morning, I take her to the train station to buy a ticket home, and she calls her father. The train doesn't leave until the afternoon, however, leaving me to entertain her for the early part of the day. Although young and pretty, I'm nevertheless wishing I could get rid of her; but noblesse oblige (protocol demands) so I do my duty and put her on the train for Philadelphia. Later, she writes to me, and I answer; but I don't want to pursue a romance with her and gracefully bow out.

For hours, I stand on the sidewalk on a street in Washington, waiting to see the funeral procession of President Kennedy. The Kennedy family walks behind the caisson pulled by white horses. Little do I know, but two of the same horses will pull my marriage carriage for my military wedding.

All this, of course, is yet to come, but at the moment, I am caught up in the trauma and emotion of the moment. Uncle Bob has been transferred to Arlington Cemetery where he now resides and is in charge of the Kennedy burial.

All this time while in Washington, I have been writing to Patricia, and although she returns the mail, her letters are becoming less amorous and just friendly and polite. Something drastic must be done.

Determined to get a commitment from Patricia, I take a week leave to drive to McGuire, and from there catch a hop to Mindelhall Air Base in England then fly to Dublin for my rendezvous. As usual, the list is long with people waiting for a free ride to many destinations and I have wait my turn. Fortune shines – or so it seems. There is a flight going right away to Labrador, then on to Iceland. Labrador is on the way, and with some luck I can catch the next bound flight to England. Sounds good, but there is a catch. The plane is full, except for an open slot for a courier officer, needed to volunteer to accompany several bags of secret documents to Labrador – just my kind of job. As soon as I volunteer, they hand me a .45-caliber pistol and two large duffle bags, which I have to guard as they are loaded into the cargo belly of the airplane – leaving me the last person to board. The flight is long but I am relieved to finally be on my way to see my dream girl. The airplane arrives in Labrador during a snowstorm and it is freezing cold. I am the first one to deplane and take up my post at the cargo hatch waiting for someone to unload the cargo and relieve me of my charge. After the last passenger departs, I find myself alone, waiting under the airplane and wondering – *will I ever get to Ireland?*

Just as I am about to turn into a block if ice, a vehicle comes to pick me and the cargo up, and delivers me to the Officers' club where, by a warm fire, I thaw out while sipping whiskey and dreaming of shamrocks, Leprechauns and Patricia. The next morning, the snowstorm has ended and there is a bleak, but beautiful, white atmosphere about Labrador – a nice place to visit, but I wouldn't want to live there.

Fortune shines on me, as there is a flight out to Prestwick, Scotland, not exactly Ireland but close enough. I breathe a sigh of relief as the airplane takes off and I doze as we cross the Atlantic.

The landing strip in Prestwick is rather small and a road with commercial traffic passes across the runway. As I watch out the window, it is a strange sight to see automobile traffic lined up at a crossing gate, waiting for the aircraft to land on the runway. After landing, I get a ride to the Officer Quarters, an old-castle-type manor – a lovely place to spend the night. Sitting in an overstuffed chair while sipping scotch whiskey by the hearth conjures up memories of war movies, of British airmen waiting for the return of Spitfires after a dogfight during a German air raid. Like in the movies, after sipping my whiskey, I stand and toss the empty glass into the fire – a tribute to the pilots who never return. From Prestwick, I take a taxi to the airport in Glasgow and book a flight on Air Lingus to Dublin. Patricia knows that I am coming; but I don't know what to expect.

After arriving in Dublin, I call her to announce my arrival. She apologizes for not greeting me at the airport – she has a headache. This has a bad ring to it, and I sense that all is not right between us. After taking the bus to downtown Dublin, I stop to buy some flowers then take another bus again to Mourne Road in the borough of Drimnagh where she lives. She answers the door and greets me with a smile as she takes the flowers. Her mother is glad to see me and makes me a breakfast of rashers, eggs and tea. After a while of small talk, Pat offers to take me to a hotel in her new car. We are driving along to town and I'm feeling apprehensive. Suddenly, like a clown getting a pie in the face, she lets me have it. "You shouldn't have come," says she. "I don't want to marry you so you might just as well go back home." She goes on further to explain, "I'm theatre and you're circus; it would never work." I can only sit there in shock, not able to respond to the words that I don't want to hear. She then drops me off at the hotel, and without a kiss goodbye, drives off. Stunned, I stand on the street corner, wondering what to do next – *Jesus,*

Mary and Joseph! There is only one week's leave left until I must return to Mindenhal for a hop to New Jersey. There is now no reason for me to remain in Dublin. Patricia is leaving town also with Jack Cruise and his troupe to perform at the Savoy Theatre in Limerick. Since I also have to travel to Limerick to catch a flight to London from Shannon Airport, I decide to travel there also, visit the theatre and watch the show. As I watch Patricia perform on the stage, I'm hurting all over. Also on the program are other old friends from my show business days in Ireland. Surely I must say goodbye to them before I leave.

Backstage after the show I make my appearance in the dressing rooms. Everyone in the show knows about the breakup of our romance and offers sympathy. Patricia invites me into her dressing room, but is ice cold as she asks me to zip up her dress. I notice that she still has the makeup case that I had bought her for Christmas. I want to talk to her, but can't get her alone. She shoos me out, and so I leave the building, going outside to the stage door entrance where I wait for her to emerge alone. The back alley stage entrance has one overhead lightbulb, which in the fog blowing up from the river Shannon casts an eerie glow, as I in my trench coat stand there shivering in the mist, like a private detective in an old black and white movie. The door opens and Pat emerges; but she is with Jack who stands there stoically. She tells me that she has nothing to say and that I should leave her alone. Jack never says a word as the two of them stomp off across the street to Jack's car while I stand there in agony, watching them disappear into the fog – *how rude!*

The next day, I fly out of Shannon to London, check in at the American Military Hotel by Hyde Park and stroll around London brooding, and thinking bad thoughts. It's early spring, cold with drizzling rain and the famous London fog – reminiscent of Sherlock Holmes movies, which I loved as a child. As I wander about Soho, I'm wondering if I should join the French Foreign Legion to forget. Returning to Mindenhall, I await a hop to McGuire at the officers' club where I sip my whiskey by the fireplace then toss the empty glass into the fire.

*

My lifestyle in Washington is not very exciting. Other than my naval duties at Naval Security Group, while awaiting my security clearance, I continue to fly with the Tifton Flying Club, attend German classes at the University of Maryland and begin to practice my juggling act again in the post field house.

One day, I visit Irving Klein, a cigar-smoking theatrical agent in Baltimore where I hope to get a few weekend engagements to supplement my meager Ensign income. It takes time to establish myself with the local agents, but eventually, I start getting a few weekend club dates and it feels good to be back in show business again. The money isn't much but it helps maintain my ego and morale. Most of the jobs are banquet shows in Baltimore hotels, and I begin to establish a reputation as a local act. Engagements are slow in coming, so I drive to New York to visit my union, AGVA, and try to get some work out of the Big Apple. Instead of work, the union office gives me a list of agents, which I could have gotten from the yellow pages, causing me to wonder why I have been paying dues all these years. *Yes – by golly, I remember – so that I can fantasize that I'm in show business!* Just to be sure that I get the proper respect, I wear my uniform, as I make the rounds visiting agents. I may not get any jobs, but at least they won't throw me out the door. Unfortunately, I get lots of respect but no jobs.

The Palace Theater, the Mecca of Vaudeville, is closed and abandoned; but one theatrical agency still survives in an office in the building. Benny Swartz, who wears an old baggy suit with a gold watch and chain, sits puffing on a cigar while dropping ashes on his vest. He still gets a few dates in a few small towns in Pennsylvania, and I manage to score a few weekend dates with him. The dates are small banquet, low budget shows that most of the New York acts won't bother with because of the distance involved. My location, however, makes it ideal for me, but operating as a single juggler is a hard act to sell. What I really need is a girl in the act, someone that the audience would enjoy watching besides myself. As I drive back to Fort Mead, I ponder where to find someone interested enough in show business and in me to become a juggler's assistant.

At the officers' club where I occasionally eat breakfast, I spy a nice looking blond-headed girl who works as a cashier every Sunday. Liz is twenty-one years old, attends the University of Maryland and her father is an Army "bird" Colonel. Each Sunday, I make it a point to have breakfast and have a chat with her while paying my bill. Eventually, I invite her to go bowling one night on the base and from then on we are constant companions. Liz, however, is not as interested in show business as she is in having a man. She takes me home to meet her mother who takes a liking to me right away, while her father, the Colonel, is not impressed with a Naval Ensign who can juggle, but merely tolerates me. Now I am beginning to feel uncomfortable with this situation, while at the same time, I don't seem to be able to resist the magic charm of Liz. During this time my clearance comes through and I am able to begin the job that I was sent here to do in the first place.

The East German Navy has been assigned to me. My job is to listen to the voice transmissions of radio operators, translate the messages into English then write an intelligence report as to what they are up to. The only problem I have with the job is that I don't know anything about the East German Navy. Bits of information come my way, but I am never given an overall briefing about my subject of interest. Apparently I don't have a need to know or nobody cares much about them anyway – I'm on my own to learn as I go.

One of the first things I learn in Washington is the bureaucratic routine: look busy, shuffle papers around, tell someone where you are going when you leave your desk, drink lots of coffee, keep one eye on the clock and learn to sleep with your eyes open while apparently reading a document. Monday morning always brings the same question from co-workers; "Did you have a nice weekend?" and the same old reply, "It was all right." When not listening to intelligence traffic on tapes, there is the same piped-in music to listen to all day, which after a while tends to dull the senses and puts one to sleep. As I decipher then translate the German codes, I write a report, which is sent to a higher authority who edits it, and then returns it to me for rewrite. After meeting his approval, it is sent further along the chain of command where it is further edited and returned to me again for rewrite. By the time the report is finally accepted, it is no longer the same report that I originally wrote, but a completely different document, not written by me alone, but by several individuals – each one making changes and contributions. My final act is to stamp the document TOP SECRET.

Some of my other duties involve courier runs to the CIA and the Pentagon, which I thoroughly enjoy since it gets me out of the office routine that I have begun to dread. Looking busy in the office environment is not my cup of tea. We are all expected to look busy until fifteen minutes before quitting time. As the second hand of the clock hits the number twelve, an uncanny phenomena occurs as thousands of agency personnel simultaneously raise their heads and put down their pencils. Where there was silence and order there is now pandemonium as analysts, mathematicians, linguists, spooks, secret agents, sleeper agents, double agents and moles put away their work, and line up at the door – counting the minutes until the final second, when suddenly, a flood of humanity gushes forth out of the building and onto the parking lot, creating a traffic jam of biblical proportions. Amazingly, every bar surrounding Fort Meade is full within thirty minutes – on Fridays, fifteen.

CLOSE, BUT NO CIGAR

The boring lifestyle of the office routine is brightened my new love, Liz, with whom I rendezvous as much as I can. One day, however, I call her to hear her tell me that she can't see me any more. After bringing her home late the night before, we had a treat on the couch of her living room while her parents slept upstairs. Apparently her mother found incriminating evidence of an amorous nature on the couch the next morning, and confronted Liz. Not only do the parents not approve of illicit love going on in their house while they sleep, her father, the Colonel, threatens to have me shipped out to Alaska if he ever sees me again. For a while I am apprehensive until my dilemma concludes when the whole family is transferred to Ethiopia; coincidentally, I'm promoted to Lieutenant J.G. – *Jesus, Mary and Joseph!*

*

Since I can't join the French Foreign Legion to forget, I join the Baltimore Irish Cultural Society instead, hoping that there I will find my true love. She is not there, but Navy Chief O'Connor is. I thought that I was the only one in the Navy at the Irish club in Baltimore, but there he is – Chief John J. O'Connor – in his chief's uniform, bedecked with ribbons from World War II and Korea. He tells me about how he had been in the Philippines during the war, was captured by the Japanese, endured the Death March of Bataan and imprisoned until freed by General MacArthur. He tells a good story and I am a good listener. He has his wife Bessie with him who seems bored as if she has heard it all a hundred times before.

The Chief is well known around Baltimore and spends a lot of time in pubs where, says he, he recruits young men for the Navy – strange place for recruiting; but perhaps he is on to something there.

Occasionally I accompany the Chief on his rounds of pubs around Baltimore and make several observations. It seems that every bartender in town knows the Chief, and they greet us with a smile.

Another observation I make is that he never buys a drink; but rather talks to all the patrons at the pub until they are all buying the Chief a drink. Being active in the Catholic Church, he is involved in selling church raffle tickets, which he does very effectively at each bar we attend. Who can say no to a Navy Chief, survivor of Bataan and Corregador? I see a lot of drinking, and wheeling and dealing going on, but no recruiting. As the drink continues to flow, the stories get even better and donations to the church begin to mount. Initially, I suspect it must be a scam until he takes me to meet the Monsignor of the Catholic Church of Baltimore, who greets us warmly and accepts money for the church raffle – a traditional Irish Catholic thing. We also visit the Baltimore Chief of Police, the Boxing Commissioner of Maryland and the Baltimore Navy recruiting office where each time we are greeted warmly and the Chief is treated like an old friend. The Chief also manages to sell raffle tickets as he visits each of his acquaintances of high profile. He is the master of blarney, and I am really impressed – *hail to the Chief!* During Christmas, the Chief arranges for a party at an orphanage run by the church and recruits me to perform my juggling act and to dress as Santa Claus. I oblige and we get our picture on the front page of the Baltimore Sun – also arranged by the Chief. My Commanding Officer at Fort Mead is impressed. "I didn't know that Lieutenant O'Brien is so community-service minded" says he, "and who is this Chief O'Connor?"

My show business sideline feeds the Chief's creativity and imagination; thus he endeavors to produce a show featuring all Irish talent. I help him along by putting him in contact with some acts I know in Philadelphia who give ethnic-Irish-style performances. He has in mind to use the church community hall and sell tickets himself at the pubs around town, thus making a killing, which he will split with the church – a magnanimous gesture indeed. He hires tap-dancing twins, an Irish comedian from Philly, a piano player from Baltimore who has broken his arm and plays piano with his arm in a sling, a singing bartender from Mat Kane's Irish Pub in Washington and, of course, the Great Boston – direct from Duffy Circus.

Mat Kane not only contributes his bartender, but also buys an ad in the program and puts my poster of Duffy Circus on the ceiling of his Pub. After leaving Mat Kane's Irish Pub late one night, rather than drive him all the way home to Baltimore (he doesn't drive), I opt to have him put up at the Navy barracks at Fort Meade. It is after midnight and all the sailors are asleep. I wake up the Master at Arms, who gets dressed and I introduce him to Chief O'Connor, survivor of Bataan and Corregador. The Master at Arms, a First Class Petty Officer, is not too happy with us; but he does his duty and finds the Chief a bunk.

The next morning, the Chief has breakfast in the mess hall, and afterwards I bring him home to Baltimore. The Chief's visit is noted in the station log, and on Monday morning, the C.O. is again asking, "Who is this Chief O'Connor?"

It's show time but the advance sale of tickets hasn't gone well, probably because the Chief has elected to do it all himself. Although only five people show up at the door, the show must go on and it does. All the while we are hoping that the crowd is late, but forthcoming – it's not and it isn't. The show bombs, nobody gets paid and everyone is angry – *jail to the Chief!* We had planned to visit a few pubs after the show to celebrate our hit show. Rather than let a good celebration go to waste, we go out on the town to celebrate our flop. During the course of events, I overdo it with my celebrating and eventually vomit and have a slight fainting spell on the sidewalk outside of Bernie Lee's Irish Pub.

Feeling for my well-being, the Chief makes a blunder and calls my duty station to report the incident. Although I appreciate his concern, informing my superiors is not recommended, and any Chief should know better. Inevitably, I am called on the carpet to explain to the C.O. why I was falling-down drunk on the streets of Baltimore, and, "Who in Hell is this Chief O'Connor?" I explain the best I can, and give the Captain my best grin. He warns me about drinking with old Chiefs; and then I am dismissed to carry on about my duties – *Jesus, Mary and Joseph!*

Chief O'Connor continues to intrude into my life by again asking a favor of me. He has been promoted to Master Chief, and since he doesn't drive a car, wants me to drive to the Naval Academy at Annapolis to retrieve his new uniform, which he had left there at the tailor to have his new stripes put on. Not only that, but he has arranged for me to meet the Commander of the Naval Reserve in Baltimore, and as guests of the Commander, we are invited to inspect the crew aboard a Destroyer. I forgive him for getting me into hot water, and after fetching his uniform at Annapolis, we proceed to the Destroyer inspection in Baltimore. Preceding a tour of the ship, we inspect the sailors standing at attention on deck. Protocol demands that I follow the commanding officer with the Chief behind myself; however, I am surprised that he precedes me in the inspection, and doesn't seem to remember that chiefs follow officers. The ship's commander doesn't say anything and neither do I. Something else bothers me about Chief O'Connor – he doesn't wear his ribbons in the correct order, and never seems to carry his I.D. card.

*

Meanwhile, back at the office, I'm playing a dangerous game, dating two girls in my office at the same time. Alternating between the two, I invite Vicky and Jackie to my apartment to see my juggling clubs and play chess – I still don't have any etchings. We play music, drink, and cook and fool around. Sometimes I even juggle to keep them entertained. Keeping the two of them from finding out about each other is an intrigue at the highest level –

not for the faint of heart, but then secrecy, suspense and intrigue is what
N.S.A. is all about. They are friends and apparently don't mind playing the
game. However, the bomb is ticking and I wonder how long I can go on before
one of them plants it under my car. My dilemma is solved when Jackie gets
transferred to Berlin. Vicky invites me to a spook party in a Georgetown
apartment where four girls from the agency live. Most of the guests are
agency analysts and cryptologists, plus several agency Marine guards. While
dancing with Vicky, I spy one of the residents of the apartment, a tall girl with
dark hair and oriental eyes who smiles at me. Her name is Camille. She had
invited Vicky who then brought me along, and now something magic seems
to pass between us. Not wanting to be rude, I stay with Vicky, but
surreptitiously get Camille's phone number. Later, I invite Camille to our
office picnic. Tension arises as Vicky sees Camille make her entrance to the
picnic grounds; but then with the situation apparent, she gracefully bows out.
From then on, Camille becomes my secret agent "double O one."

*

One day I read in Amusement Business Magazine, that the Clyde Beatty,
Cole Bros. Circus will be playing in Philadelphia for a week and that they
only have two wire acts for their three-ring wire display. A bright idea forms
in my head: the circus might need an additional wire act to complete the 3 ring
display in Philly – being one of their biggest dates of the season. Since it is
only a ten-day engagement, I could take a short leave from the Navy and play
the date – that is if they hire me. When the show plays Annapolis, I invite
Camille to come along with me to see the show. Clyde Beatty, famous animal
trainer, radio and movie star, had already departed the show a few days
before, after giving his last performance on a Sunday afternoon in
Wilmington, Delaware. He was suffering from cancer and needed to return
home to California for treatment. Taking his place in the steel arena is
Clyde's former cat boy (assistant), Red Hartnet, who gives a credible
performance. After seeing the show, I make my move. As Camille waits in my
vehicle, I walk over to the silver Air Stream trailer of the circus owner, Frank
McCloskey, and knock on his door. Frank, an old time rough and tough circus
man, opens the door and stares at me while chomping on a big cigar.
Immediately, I go into my tap dance by introducing myself and showing
photos and old contracts by well-known agents in the business, hoping to
impress him with my rather modest reputation. While looking at me as he

puffs, he ponders my words at the mention of Duffy Circus, then raises his eyebrows in interest. He takes my phone number and tells me he will think about it and get back to me. Several days later, the phone rings and Frank offers me the Philly date at $200 per week. I am overjoyed – *that is more money a week than I make in the Navy.* Camille and I break out the wine and celebrate. In the weeks to come, I put in for leave, convert my new Volkswagen bus into a camper, and practice – practice – practice.

The day arrives when I'm off to Philadelphia to perform in a large American three-ring circus. My childhood dream has come true and I'm all excited as I cross over the bridge from Camden, New Jersey, and see the big top along with the Amusements of America Carnival set up on the Philadelphia side of the river at the football stadium parking lot. After driving onto the lot, I make my way to the backyard, where the performers have their trailers, and park at the end of the line next to a nearby fire hydrant that supplies the show's water and also serves as the elephants' shower. At the ticket and office wagon, I report to Frank and meet Edna Antes, widow of Bill Antes – prominent circus press agent of the gone-by railroad circus days. She is Frank's secretary/office manager, loyal confidant and a nice lady – always formal and correct who keeps an eye on the money and pays the show personnel every Friday. It is said about her on the lot that, when she dies, she won't be going to Heaven or Hell, but to Frank McCloskey.

Still lacking an assistant in my wire act, Tommy Clark, superintendent of props and rigging, assigns me Ophelia from Portugal who doesn't speak English. She is a single lady who works as a show girl and makes "cherry pie,"[28] cleaning the boss's trailer. I brief Ophelia as to when to hand me my props while I'm performing on the wire. Although not expressing herself well in English, she knows through experience what to do. The band master, "Boom Boom" Browning also needs to be briefed on what I will be doing in ring three where I have been assigned for the three-ring wire display. Boom Boom got his nickname from playing the big bass drum for Merle Evans, bandmaster of the Ringling Circus.

It's show time and the tent is filled with thousands of people. Although, I've done the act a thousand times over, I am still slightly nervous as I wait for my turn behind the sidewall while the show ensues.

Soon it's time for the wire display. The clowns do their walk around gags while the wire riggings are being set up for our display: in ring one Señor Muños who also closes the show by being shot out of a cannon, Ma Ho Pin (half Chinese and half German) who performs in the center ring with Herbert (husband and assistant) taking her cape and handing it back after the act. The ringmaster blows the whistle, the clowns retire and the band strikes up the music for the display as I, along with the others performers, enter our appropriate ring. I am overjoyed to be fulfilling a childhood fantasy; however, I need to keep my mind on my job so I can get through this gracefully. I am ever mindful of the juggler's curse – *Thou shalt not drop thy balls.* Lurking behind seat wagons and side wall are clowns and other performers curious enough to check out the new act on the show.

Ophelia first hands me my devil sticks, which I manipulate with dexterous legerdemain. Then she tosses me one at a time eight plastic flowerpots, each one of which I place on my foot and kick up onto my head, forming a stack of pots – onto which I kick up a ball which settles on the top pot – all this while balanced on a slack wire on one foot. The plastic pots are those I had bought at a magic shop behind the Moulin Rouge in Paris many years ago. As each pot lands on the stack on my head, Boom Boom gives me a rim shot with his drums telling me that the band is watching my act. We time the display so that we all take a bow together. Nobody says anything, but I get lots of smiles from the other performers. The clowns, of course, are very interested in me and give me all kinds of advice and suggestions for my act – everything from soup to nuts: I should do something with my hair, I should wear makeup, my wardrobe needs something. After the show at night the barbecues come out in the backyard, and the aroma of smoked chicken and ribs entwines with that of horses, elephants, lions and tigers, sawdust and hay. It all blends together in a delightful way that says "circus." During the night, I sleep soundly in my camper, lulled to slumber by the occasional grunt of some mysterious animal. In the morning, I am pleasantly awakened to the odor of coffee and bacon coming from the cook tent. A flag is raised on the tent when the meal is ready to serve. Performers, managers, clowns, sideshow people and working men all have their assigned table. It's not the same as good old Navy chow; but it is much better than the home cooking of The Great Boston.

Camille and her girlfriend come by for a visit and I show them around. She is taken in by all the glitter and glamour that only the circus can provide, and from then on, she is my constant companion. My fantasy week with the circus flies by, and soon it is time for me to go back to the real world of espionage, spies and military intelligence. Frank asks me if I want to stay on the show, but I have to remind him again that I am in the Navy, on liberty, and must return to my base. He tells me to contact him when I get out and so I shall. In the meantime, I have my duty to perform and return to Fort Meade while the circus moves on to the next town. Back at my desk again in Washington, I am greeted by the same old question: "Did you have a nice leave" – to which I give the standard answer – "It was all right."

*

Camille has a hobby of jumping out of airplanes with a parachute. One fateful day, she lands in a tree and has to be rescued. After a stunt like that, I decide that I need her in my act as a juggler's assistant. A seamstress in Baltimore makes Camille wardrobe for the act, and I teach her the routine. After some practice in the post field house – voila! a star is born. Our club date business begins to pick up as we work weekends in Pennsylvania, Maryland and Virginia. Although the work seems plentiful enough, we are still not making a profit – all the money going into the act for new props, costumes and photos. Still the joy of the road and being in show business is fulfillment enough for both of us.

Chapter VIII
Intrigue, Espionage and Marriage

Christmas is approaching and the agency is looking for volunteers to help plan and participate in their annual Christmas party. Each year, the agency rents the arena of the University of Maryland, and puts on a circus-type show to entertain the agency personnel. I step forward and offer my services to Karl Yenser, Director of Personnel Services, who is in charge of the event. My new additional duties are a welcome diversion: organizing the show, buses for invited handicapped children, food collections for the poor, and a million other details. I am most ably assisted by Ned Clark, a Marine veteran who keeps a helmet with a bullet hole in it where he was shot by a Jap sniper in Iwo Jima during the war. I think that the bullet must have grazed his head because he has an obsession to dress up like famous Ringling clown Emmett Kelly at any opportunity, and of course the Christmas party is one. Ned calls himself "Uncle Ned" whenever he is in his clown costume.

Karl has been working with Washington theatrical agent, "Tiny" Meeker, a big man who in the past had supplied musicians for the performance. Karl wants to save money by having the First Army Band of Fort Meade play the show. Tiny, of course, doesn't take kindly to not hiring local professional musicians, and so complains to the Musicians' Union. The complaint reaches the politicians and becomes a political issue about big Government taking away jobs from struggling musicians. Karl is peeved with Tiny and asks me to find another agent. Since Tiny never gave me a job in the past, I am happy to recommend Ervin Klein of Baltimore, my regular agent who at least gives me some work – even though it's on an irregular basis. Karl is forced to hire local musicians, but Tiny is out.

The day of the party arrives as the personnel of the National Security Agency all arrive in costume at University of Maryland Arena: I come dressed as a gorilla, Uncle Ned comes as circus clown Emmett Kelly, complete with a Weary Willy[29] clown doll, Camille comes dressed as a circus clown and Chief O'Connor comes as himself – complete with his medals still in disarray. Although not connected to the Agency in any way and not wanting to miss out on anything, Chief O'Connor volunteers to assist me in collecting the donations of canned goods for the poor. The Chief is a get-involved type of guy who likes rubbing elbows with higher ups. Although he is seemingly helpful at times, I sometimes feel uncomfortable with him nevertheless.

Through Erv Klein, Karl has booked a standard circus type show: La Norma (trapeze act) – formerly on the Ringling show, Tibor Alexander (dog act) – unknown to me at the time, he will become my agent some day, Kongo, the Killer Ape who makes the children laugh as he cavorts around the arena harassing his stooge wife planted in the audience and André Schweitzer with his wife René who perform on the wire and also do a hand-balancing act. Local musicians back the show, which goes over well and is enjoyed by all. The big brass is there at the performance, and I see nothing but smiling faces. Karl's boss, a bird colonel, is so pleased that he wants to introduce me and my assistants, Ned and the Chief, to our N.S.A. Commanding Officer, General Pat Carter. Like Curly, Larry and Moe, the Colonel leads the gorilla, the clown and the Chief to the General, who extends his hand to shake my simian extremity.

"General sir, I'd like you to meet the people responsible for this wonderful event," says the Colonel. We chat a bit and then I further introduce Ned, veteran of Iwo Jima, and Chief O'Connor, survivor of Bataan and Corregador. The General is impressed as he chats with Ned and the Chief about the good old days with General MacArthur in the Philippines.

After the event, Camille and I celebrate the conclusion of a job well done at the Tai Tung, our favorite restaurant in Washington's Chinatown. Camille is proud of me – *likewise I'm sure*. After a good Chinese dinner, the Lieutenant lights up a cigar.

I introduce Camille to Walter, my artist friend who all this time has been teaching at the university. Camille and I are both amazed that she already knows him from when she was a student at Ohio State where Walter was teaching art classes. Walter's contract is up at Maryland and he is packing to return to Boston to teach at the Boston Art College. Walter, a do-it-yourself-type person, acquires a truck frame from a junkyard and intends to build himself a carry-all trailer for the move rather than spend lots of money. The trailer, like my first car, looks good, but isn't. We spend all night emptying out his house in Silver Spring, Maryland, and loading all his belongings into the makeshift carry-all, while Regina cleans up behind us. Finally, the traveling heap is ready for the road and proceeds along, pulled by Walter's car containing the wife and kids. It isn't long before the axle of the trailer snaps and the caravan comes to a screeching halt. Walter is forced to spend money on a U Haul. Regina, upset by the farce, cries while the kids sleep as we spend the rest of the night in the street, transferring the load from one trailer to the other. As the sun begins to rise, the transfer is complete and Walter departs for Boston while I return to the base, mentally tired and physically exhausted – *sonamamitch!*

*

As fate would have it, Karl has decided that my exploits on the circus would be an interesting story for the Agency news magazine. Again, I become the center of attention as my cover is blown and everyone at the National Security Agency is reading about me. Karl's game, of course, is to get me transferred to his department so that we can begin working on his pet project: that of bringing the circus to Fort Meade with me promoting it. With my help, Karl contacts the Clyde Beatty Cole Brothers Circus and makes a deal. The sponsor is technically the Fort Meade Teen Club and they will benefit, but Karl and I will have all the fun of playing circus. The show sends us window cards and I am assigned a sailor to drive me in a staff car around the Fort Meade area where I put up posters and window cards on anything that doesn't move. Usually, merchants won't bother putting up a window card unless they get a free ticket to the circus. Not having tickets to pass out is not a problem, however, since no one refuses a Naval Officer in a staff car with a sailor chauffeur. Not only do I put up circus advertising all around Fort Mead, but at all four entrances of the Agency. Marine guards eye me with suspicion as I go about my duty. Even so, like Tom Sawyer using his pals to paint his fence, I manage to recruit some of the guards to help put posters up for me.

To attract attention and create interest, Uncle Ned roams around the halls of the Agency wearing his Emmett Kelly clown costume while wearing his I.D. badge around his neck – confounding the Marine guards scattered thoughout the labyrinth of the building who have never before seen a circus clown roaming around the National Security Agency. They stare at him incredulously – could this be some sort of foreign enemy spy? No! It's just

Uncle Ned with lead in his head, the Marine who always wanted to be a clown. Marine guards are not supposed to smile but Uncle Ned rates a huge grin.

The First Army Marching Band is assigned along with Uncle Ned and myself to visit all the schools in the area to drum up business for the circus. We attack our objective with gusto, saturating the area with posters, and visiting public areas with the band and the clown – until on circus day, the Big Top stands proudly, flags flying on the old airstrip behind the new bowling alley at Fort Meade, awaiting throngs of people and buses filled with children. The tent is filled, and circus owner Frank is impressed.

As Frank and I puff on our cigars, he says "Nice job, Terry" – *ain't it the truth! – ain't it the truth!* and again offers me a job when I get out of the service. Karl, also pleased at the outcome of the circus, has me doing a host of other projects in his department: the annual United Fund Drive and organizing military parades and retirement ceremonies while Camille and I continue to perform club dates mostly in Pennsylvania on weekends, making just enough money to pay expenses and have a good time.

*

I awake late one morning and fetch the morning paper, the *Baltimore Sun*. As I read while drinking my coffee, I suddenly gag and spill coffee on myself as I focus in on the headlines: "BOGUS CHIEF EXPOSED AS IMPOSTER AFTER FALL." I can't believe my eyes; the Chief had fallen down drunk after coming out of a pub and was taken to the hospital where they checked with the Navy and discovered the truth – he is not in the Navy and not married to Bessie. Although living together, he mysteriously managed to fool his "wife" about being in the Navy. The "Chief" is an imposter – *Jesus, Mary, and Joseph!* Suddenly, I'm called on the carpet again to explain. The F.B.I. wants to know if he might be a Russian spy, the General wants to know if he got into the Agency (he didn't), and my C.O. still wants to know – "Who is this O'Connor guy?" I'm getting phone calls at home and at work from Washington, Baltimore and Philadelphia. Trying to explain is a major undertaking and I'm wondering if I should pack my bags and get ready to be shipped out. Apparently, the Chief had fooled a long list of people, including myself, so I don't feel too stupid. Camille is with me through thick and thin and I find great comfort in her as things gradually cool down and I am no longer the center of attention. Life goes on as Camille and I continue our regular routine: working club dates, flying together around Washington and Maryland, attending the Irish Club functions and cracking codes at the Agency – Camille's job is in an area so sensitive, that to this day she still won't talk about it.

Camille is now more than just a slack wire assistant – rather my confidant and significant other. On St. Valentine's Day while eating at our favorite Chinese restaurant, Tai Tung, I ask Camille for her hand and put a twenty-dollar engagement ring from the Post Exchange on her finger. We choose a date for a wedding, but finances are low. Fortune shines on us, however, as Uncle Bob comes to the rescue. As assistant Director of Arlington Cemetery, he arranges a wedding for us at the cemetery chapel with a reception at the Officers' Club at Fort Myer, including the "Marriage Carriage" pulled by two white horses normally used for high-ranking funerals. Needing a Naval-officer type with sword for a military-style wedding, I recruit Lieutenant Kleinman, a nice Jewish fellow to be my best man while Camille gets her pal from college days, Patty, to play the role of bride's maid. Mom and Dad show up for the wedding while sister Sharon is still in Japan with her husband Cliff, now a captain in the Army. Camille is "Queen for a Day," as we walk down the aisle among friends and relatives. I'm a nervous wreck as Father Mulhern, the army padré, officiates; nevertheless, I maintain my military bearing. After the ceremony, we sit in our horse-drawn carriage on our way to the grand reception at the Officers' Club where we dance to Dad playing the piano. Dad is on leave from working the Breakers Hotel in Palm Beach where Mom is along with him. He suggests that since the house in Orlando is vacant we should go there for a honeymoon and save a lot on money. I think it is a great idea, but Camille is underwhelmed. We decide that this will be a token honeymoon, the real one to come when we are more established and secure.

Unknown to us, that won't be for another 35 years, till we enjoy a real honeymoon – a Caribbean cruise. Our first home is a mobile trailer in a trailer park where we begin to enjoy married life and continue our work routine at the Agency and our club dates on weekends.

One day at the office, I get a call from Father Mulhern who tells me that my marriage is not legal since he had neglected to have us sign some papers, and we have to do the wedding ceremony again – *Jesus, Mary and Joseph!* Father Mulhern then calls Father Kelly at Fort Meade and arranges another wedding ceremony for us at the post chapel at Fort Meade where we rush to during our lunch hour. Father Kelly is on the phone saying "Hello, give me dispensations please." Camille who is not Catholic wonders if he is calling

God. The word comes back from whence such things come, and with Father Kelly's mother as a witness, we are married once again. With just enough time to kiss the bride, we both rush back to our individual offices, where as usual, I am met with the standard greeting – "Did you have a nice lunch?" to which I give the standard reply, "It was all right." Upon leaving work to go home that afternoon, Camille and I watch, as an unmanned car begins to coast down an incline at the Agency parking lot. For some unknown reason, the car's brake had disengaged – and here it comes, crashing right into Camille's car – *sonamamitch!* We thought we had dispensation from above, but now Camille is not so sure.

During Christmas, we work a sports show in Lake Carmel, New York, where we spend the first night bundled up in sleeping bags inside our V.W. bus. We are working with chimpanzee star J. Fred Muggs, who began his showbiz career on the N.B.C. *Today Show* with Dave Garroway. Although portraying a male chimp, she is actually a female, owned by three former N.B.C. pages, Buddy, Roy and Jerry. They brought Muggs into the studio one day as a gag. J. Fred was discovered and became a star. "The Muggs Guys,"[30] as we call them, become our very good friends and they invite us to stay at their home for Christmas in Mahwah, New Jersey. They have an engagement at the New York Dog Show and we come along with them in the Muggs Mobile, a former bread delivery van rearranged for special use – to transport and house a chimp. Camille and I enjoy the dog show, see the show at Radio City Music Hall where my father once took me as a child and go ice skating at Rockefeller Plaza – these are good times.

Camille and I do a celebrity "roast" banquet show at the Waldorf Astoria for Hugh Heffner – owner of Playboy Magazine. We enter the hotel through the service entrance into the kitchen where there is a beehive of activity by cooks, bus boys and waiters – none of whom speak English. We are offered a cup of coffee, but Camille spies a roach and declines the offer. We take the elevator once ridden by Bing Crosby and Dad, up to the ballroom made famous by the Guy Lombardo Orchestra on New Year's Eve. The show turns out to be a burlesque-style performance with strips and dirty comics whose job it is to poke fun at Hugh Heffner sitting stoically with a slight smile as he takes verbal pies in the face. We do our act, take our bows, and then after the show, pack up and take the elevator back down to the kitchen where I need a cup of coffee – roach or no roach.

On New Year's Eve, we are booked in a beachfront hotel in Atlantic City where a room for the night has been included in the deal. It is an early show where we have to pack and run over to the 500 Club for a late evening show. It is the same club where Martin and Lewis formed their comedy team many years ago. Jerry Lewis once said that the dressing room was nothing but a nail on the wall and he wasn't kidding. After setting my rig and props for the performance, I go outside for a breath of fresh air and am surprised to see a limo pull up, and what appears to be a General get out. Automatically I salute, but upon closer inspection, I see that it is none other than stand-up comedian George Jessel who has just come back from entertaining the troops in Vietnam and is still wearing his U.S.O. uniform. George, of course, is the headliner on the show. The club is a dimly lit, smoky and noisy place, filled with throngs of people.

George thinks we are a nice couple and remarks at how tall Camille is. She accepts the compliment, but remarks on how short he is. I suggest that we eat something after the show, but Camille has spotted a roach and will have nothing to do with it. We do hang around the club, however, and celebrate the new year (1967) with George Jessel.

The Allentown Theater in Allentown, Pennsylvania, is a former movie palace that has been restored to its former grandeur. They are having Vaudeville revival night and I get a contract for the date. The show is headlined with Vegas Carr, once an exotic dancer of some renown – along with several vaudeville acts including a pit band and myself. The house is full with an enthusiastic audience. Camille and I have a lovely dressing room, which thrusts us back in time to the good old days of another show business era – the wonderful world of vaudeville. Everything about it is new, clean and first class – Camille is impressed. In contrast, we work the Troc Theater in Philadelphia's Chinatown, which has seen better days. There, we work with strippers: Blaze Star, Candy Kane, Pussy Willow, Bunny Buns, Cupcakes La Fleure (The French Maid), Kitty O'Kelly (The Irish Lassie with the Classy Chassie) and the usual dirty comics. The theater is old, dirty and raunchy with strange and unusual people in the audience reminiscent of my Boston days. Camille is not impressed, but a gig is a gig.

Meanwhile, back at the day job, a notice floats around the Agency looking for volunteers to sign up for a tour of Vietnam. Although they say that it is lovely this time of year, I decline the offer and decide to stay in Washington. It is considered a good military career move to go to Vietnam, providing of course that you come back alive; but I have a good thing going for me now with my part-time entertainment business and, of course, my wife and assistant Camille with whom I can't seem to get along without. My time in the military is growing short, however, and soon I will have to make a decision on whether to stay in the Navy and go to sea or get released from active duty and stay in the reserves. Not knowing what to do frustrates me; perhaps I will get a sign from the heavens.

The telephone rings one night while Camille and I are in bed. It is none other than Frank McCloskey who wants to sign me up for the 1967 season on his circus. I tell him that I'll consider it and get back to him. Camille is enthusiastic about a traveling adventure with a circus and agrees to retire from her job at the Agency, and becomes a full time slack wire assistant – a brave and noble decision on her part. Now with our future in focus, I am released from active duty, Camille quits her job at the Agency and we run away and join the circus – *Jesus, Mary and Joseph!*

Uncle Ned, Bessie, "Chief" O'Connor and Camille
N.S.A. Christmas Party (1965)

Cinderella and Prince Charming (1966)

Chapter IX
We Run Away and Join the Circus

Suddenly I'm faced with a multitude of problems – we need a truck and a trailer to replace two cars and a mobile home, and time is running short. We can't buy the truck and trailer needed for the road until we sell the equipment that we have, don't need, and can't use. We are in a quandary until brother-in-law Cliff – still in the Army and now stationed in Baltimore with sister Sharon and two daughters Lisa and Lydia – buys my V.W. bus. Camille's brother Jeff then pitches in to buy her car; and last but not least, our trailer park manager offers to buy our mobile home. With just a few weeks to spare, we purchase a two ton truck, a Concord travel trailer and we are off to Florida to join the circus in Deland. Just in time for rehearsals, we pull into the circus winter quarters – the old fairgrounds across from the Deland train depot.

(Frank, the owner of the show, had once been the general manager of the Greatest Show on Earth until he was fired by executive director Michael Burke, in what is known in the industry as the "St. Paul Massacre," after Michael discovers that duplicate tickets were being sold from the ticket wagons. On that fateful day in August, 1955, Frank, along with assistants Walter Kernan and Willis Lawson, were dismissed – at the behest of show owner, John Ringling North, for allowing graft and corruption to infest the show. Mr. Reynolds, our General Superintendent, and Tommy Clark, our prop boss, along with 30 others of the Ringling prop crew walked off the job. Frank was replaced by Art Concello, former trapeze artist who later was a partner with Frank with the Clyde Beatty Circus, but later had a falling out in a dispute over whether the show should play in arenas or continue under canvas. Clyde Beatty, of course, had sold his show to Frank, but continued to work until his bout with cancer forced him to retire. Frank's new co-owner is now Jerry Collins, former member of the Florida State Legislature and owner of the Sarasota dog racing track.) We will not see much of Jerry until catastrophe strikes the show.

(Arnold Maley, circus treasurer, along with Floyd King, the show's General Agent, owned the King Brothers Circus. In 1955, it was the largest motorized show ever seen in this country; but it was too big to sustain itself economically, and went bankrupt in spectacular fashion in 1956 with trucks and wagons abandoned – lying on roadsides all over America. Ironically, it's also the last year that the Clyde Beatty Circus travels by railroad and the Ringling Bros & Barnum and Bailey Circus performs under canvas.) Arnold keeps the money in dresser drawers and shoe boxes under his bed, lest anyone try to rob the safe in the office wagon, and enjoys confounding local bill collectors by paying them off with a paper bag filled with coins and crumpled up wads of bills. This is the stuff of circus history and legend. The circus isn't just a job, and it's more than a lifestyle – it is a culture.

Camille and I are filled with joy and anticipation as we drive on to the circus winter quarters pulling our travel trailer, and begin preparations for the 1967 season and a new lifestyle. The quarters are already bustling with activity: performers are practicing, equipment is being repaired and repainted, trucks and wagons are being moved about. Everyone is warm and friendly and makes us feel at home.

Besides our act, Camille must perform with the other girls in the aerial ballet while suspended on ladders from the canvas big top, easier said than done – first she has to learn the fine art of acrobatics in the air. Camille hangs by her ankle like a shank of beef, while below, Carlos, a Spanish juggler, teaches her the routine, which comes painfully slow. Camille has to learn what every weight lifter knows – a body in motion will continue in motion, thus decreasing the apparent weight. This phenomena, simply called timing, is a skill acquired only through practice and lots of Bengay. The skill comes slowly – painfully – burn by burn – ache by ache, until one day an aerialist is born. Camille is a bit self-conscious of Carlos looking up her crotch as she dangles over his head; however, being looked at in the circus is the name of the game.

After several weeks, the show is ready and departs from warm Florida, to the cold country of the North and the season opening at the Long Island Commack Arena. It is early spring in New York as the show arrives during a snow storm, and many vehicles need an elephant tow to reach the trailer parking area next to the building – an elephant tow costs five dollars. In spite of the adverse weather, the show sets up in the arena and rehearsals begin.

The Great Segrera is practicing doing a handstand from his balancing trapeze one morning and accidentally falls to the ground – breaking both his arms. He is out of the show and spends a few days in a hospital. Although we express concern for Segrera, such accidents are considered part of the circus routine, and so the show must go on – and so it does. Snow removal vehicles are hired to clear the parking lot to accommodate the crowds of people, filling the arena for the opening show of the season.

Camille learns that the girls' dressing room is the social center and communications hub of the circus. Within days, everyone in the circus will know everything said there in confidence. Young children who accompany the mothers in the dressing room can't be trusted not to repeat what they hear. The news and gossip flow like beer from a tap at an Irish pub. In clown alley, the gossip leans towards the sky-is-falling type, whereby the clowns delight in getting the show all stirred up over nothing. To them, this is the ultimate gag – like kids who like to ring fire alarms just to watch the excitement of the fire engines arriving – reflections of my own undisciplined childhood.

Two performances are scheduled every day and so a normal daily routine is established. The performers double as ushers before the show until the first act then we all disappear to get ready, each for his turn in the show. We all hate the job of ushering people to their seats, because patrons who don't like their seat want to argue with the usher about it. No day goes by without a hassle or complaint with members of the audience who will soon be laughing and applauding us as we perform.

The parking lot for the arena slopes up a slight incline where parked at the top is a garbage truck. A taxi arrives at the parking lot and out of the cab steps Segrera who is returning from the hospital with both arms in casts, sticking out in front of him – shades of the Frankenstein monster. Just as Segrera emerges from the cab, we see an unmanned garbage truck begin to move and roll down the incline toward the trailers. We stand there spellbound, watching the truck increase its momentum, heading right for Segrera's trailer. As he stands there motionless, watching the drama unfold, the truck slams into his trailer and punches it through the brick wall of the Commack Arena – *Jesus, Mary, and Joseph!* I'm tempted to laugh since it reminds me of a cartoon; however, poor Segrera appears to be in a trance and walks around with his arms extended – reminding me of a scene from the movie *Night of the Living Dead.*

After the show a few nights later, from our trailer we hear shouting outside in several languages, which all seem to mean one thing, "Fire!" Local kids have torched the hay stored in a pile by the menagerie – a Commack tradition so I am told. Between the water truck and all of us helping with buckets of water, we manage, with a minimum loss of hay, to put out the fire – *holy smoke!* With such events a common occurrence on a circus, it is no wonder that many people become superstitious and carry some sort of good luck charm to ward off misfortune. Some people are more superstitious than others – to the point of being eccentric. Herbie Webber, a former wirewalker on the show, had to wear the same lucky wire walking shoes at each performance, otherwise he might fall. As the shoes aged and wore out, he would re-sew them up after each performance, until over the years, he had recreated a completely new pair of shoes several times over. Eventually, the shoes bore no resemblance to their original self, but rather look like two small bags, woven from spaghetti noodles. For many years until even after he died, it was a joke around the circus industry – and still is. Other types of strange but interesting behavior emerge from circus performers in one way or another.

Mike is a two-faced clown. When he is in a good mood his clown makeup is impeccable. Using large false eyelashes, sparkling glitter and beautiful wardrobe, he makes a stunning appearance. Otherwise when having a bad day, he wears his old, rainy day costume, and just enough makeup to pass as a clown.

When Mike is in a bad mood, everyone sees the revenge of the clown written all over him. We all seem to have our own way of getting even with the world. When I am in a bad mood, I wear regular argyle socks rather than the matching color ones that fit each costume – revenge of the juggler. My off days, however, are known only to slack wire assistant Camille who scolds me for wearing the wrong color socks. I do, however, wear a St. Patrick medal around my neck for good luck.

The show finishes the Commack Arena engagement and opens under canvas in Virginia, thus beginning a grueling seasonal tour of one-day stands throughout the eastern half of the United States. Being in a different town every day presents an urge for personal needs to be addressed – spawning its own underground economy. There seems to be someone on the show to provide whatever service is required.

Tweety the clown (alias Kenney) is not only the show's mailman, but delivers the newspaper and the show news and gossip all at the same time. He drives a Winnebago motor home, in which his elderly mother travels with him. She is infirm and we hardly ever see her, but Kenney is devoted to her and we all admire him for that. Johnny, an acrobat from Hungary, is the carpenter and welder who repairs performers' trailers when they need attention. His repair work consists mostly of the chairs for the grandstand (the long side), which have to be folded and loaded each night then unfolded and set up again each morning. Johnny's brother Harry operates a pie car (snack bar) for the working men on the show from his trailer. It is not a lucrative business, however, since most of the men don't have any money.

Harry keeps a tab on those who owe, but on Fridays after they get paid, some of them blow the show without paying their bill. Occasionally, Bobby the "elephant boy" stops by with an elephant for a sandwich. Through the trailer window, Bobby passes the money and receives a sandwich. The elephant, standing by and watching, then passes her trunk through the window for her sandwich – Harry reluctantly obliges. An elephant's trunk in one's trailer gets whatever it wants, because an elephant never forgets.

Bobby's business is appreciated but, "Next time, don't bring your pachyderm," says Harry.

Other services are available: trailer cleaning by Ophelia, sewing and costume repair by Rita, Kilowatt provides a gypsy box for the trailers to plug their electric cables into while Charley "the water man" delivers water. Charley doesn't bother to flush the hydrant while filling up the water truck and usually delivers the water with a red tint. Mike the clown who follows the alternate lifestyle is a hair dresser, barber, and for those so inclined, serves as a male prostitute – by appointment only. Other services are provided along the road: Billy Rogers, trained parrot act who visits all the shows selling costume fabrics and decorations, and Banjo, an old crony of Frank's from the Ringling days, who organizes poker games for entertainment in the concession tent. Frank gets a cut when Banjo wins, so I am told.

Helpful circus fans appear on the lot in certain towns near where they live: Doctor Fitzpatrick from Atlanta who makes the rounds giving impromptu medical exams and writes a prescription. The doctor is always in when Old Fitz visits the lot. In the Washington area, lawyer Frank Ball is always willing to dispense legal advice, providing you let him add you to his circus photography collection from which we always get a copy. Around Miami, Johnny Cannole deals in truck and trailers for show people, which can be financed through his brother's bank in Altoona, Pennsylvannia, while Father Sullivan, the circus priest from Boston, visits all the shows frequently – saying Mass in the tent, listening to people's problems and bringing us news from other shows. There is even someone who teaches school to the circus kids through the Calvert Correspondence School in Baltimore.

Clown Jimmy James and I double as press representatives of the show: giving interviews, posing for photo ops and making appearances on local radio and television shows, arranged by the head of the media/press department, Colonel Roy Zinzer, former Army Colonel who fought under General MacArthur on the Pacific Islands. Knowing of my military background, the Colonel calls on me frequently to "volunteer" for a *Romper Room* television show or a local news interview. There is no cherry pie for this type of work, but the Colonel does take me out to lunch afterwards. While the show is in Philadelphia, the Colonel books me on the Mike Douglas T.V. show. In the studio lounge just behind the set, the guests on the show await their turn while watching a monitor of the show. While there, we meet Christine Jorgensen – the first American transvestite – and strike up a conversation. She had once been a man in the Army and is now a woman and a very nice person.

Each of us, in turn, go out when called, and perform for the cameras with a studio band. After the act, Mike comes over, and we chat on camera. Mike seems very friendly on camera; but as we break for a commercial, he totally ignores us as if we are not there. The cameras come back on and he resumes his interest in our act and in us. I find his on and off attention amusing while thinking that national television exposure will help my career; but nothing ever comes of it. After the telecast, we stroll around Chinatown, and notice that the old Troc Theater has been turned into a Chinese theater – now, only the ghosts of its former glory remain. Although curious about the place and its new venue, we don't have time to visit, and so return to the circus lot after our fifteen minutes of fame on television where we resume our circus routine.

During the course of a typical one day stand, two performances are given, around which our lives revolve. After the evening meal and just before the evening performance, the cookhouse begins to pack up and load so that, by the time the show is over, they are on their way to the next town. On days with short jumps, the cook tent is sometimes re-erected before the performance is over in the previous town.

While the evening performance ensues, the show is being packed, loaded and sent on its way to tomorrow's town. After the performance as the audience leaves the Big Top, only the sideshow, souvenir and food stands remain to collect that last dollar from happy and satisfied patrons. The show then travels from fifty to one hundred miles (sometimes more) to the next town. Performers have a choice, we can drive at night and arise late the next morning or get up early in the morning, then drive to the next town.

Camille and I choose to drive at night when traffic is lighter then, after pulling onto the next lot, relax. We sip our whiskey and retire for the night. Some people say that, "concessions move the show" – not so for it is whiskey, lifeblood of the circus – provider of energy, stamina and drive, from which flows the power to survive, endure and perform – it also puts one to sleep at night.

In our three ring wire display are, from Germany, Rudy with wife Gerda, myself in the center and daughter Dagmar in ring number one. Rudy does a drunken act on the wire – tormenting his wife while she tries to perform. He then performs on the wire in inebriated fashion – to the delight of the audience. Rudy chooses to stay over on the lot and get up early in the morning, so that at night, he can practice his act (the drunken part).

Bandmaster Chuck drives the ticket and office wagon, and manages to stop at a watering hole along the route every night, but nevertheless arrives safely, early in the morning. Not only does Chuck conduct the band, but plays the calliope in the sideshow where the strange, odd and unusual people are exhibited. The so-called freaks are usually just people with a physical deformity who choose to exploit their handicap and make a living from it. Other types of sideshow performers are normal in appearance, but do freaky things: eating fire, swallowing swords, walking on glass or driving nails up ones' nostrils. Frances Durand (sword swallower) does one better by swallowing a neon tube that lights up in his throat, which can be seen from the outside. One day, the tube implodes in his throat, and he is rushed to the hospital where hundreds of pieces of glass have to be surgically removed – causing Frances much distress. Betty Broadbent (tattoo lady) has her entire body covered with body art. If that were not eccentric enough, she lives in a station wagon, and collects plants as a hobby from all over the country, keeping her growing collection with her. By the end of the season, her collection of plants has grown into a forest within her car – so thick that one can no longer distinguish the driver from the trees. The rest of the sideshow consists of Bo Bo the Rubber Man (contortionist), Scotty (bagpiper), Andy (fire eater), Princess Ann (midget), and of course, the side show isn't over until the fat lady (Baby Wilma) sings – and so she does.

Finding workers for the circus is difficult, but not impossible. The show recruits roustabouts from the Salvation Army and other missions. They are homeless men, dependent on alcohol, usually with a tragic story in their lives – the losers of society. The circus offers them a romantic adventure, an escape of sorts, with room and board. Rex (elephant trainer) runs the blue room – a makeshift bar set up inside the elephant wagon after the elephants are unloaded, to accommodate the thirsty after a busy day working in the circus. The workers sit inside, drinking beer and watching black and white television, unmindful of an elephant stench that must be smelled to be believed. Rex, like Harry, also has a problem with workers blowing the show without paying their tab.

Each morning, the Big Top is erected and the seat wagons are brought inside the tent and set up. My cherry pie is working with the seat wagon crew – erecting seats in the morning and dismantling them at night. When road ready, the seven seat wagons carry an assortment of equipment – mostly props and rigging. Orlando, an acrobat who works with us, never seems to pay attention to the backside of the wagon where the prop men place my rigging to be later loaded and, on several occasions, folds up my rigging along with the seats – *sonamamitch!* The show then has to provide me with new rigging – much to the displeasure of the management. You could have the Rock of Gibraltar for a prop on the Beatty show, and in three months time it would be nothing but a bottle of sand.

The cookhouse feeds almost 200 people, three meals a day. The most frequently served meal is hot dogs and beans because it is the easiest and fastest to prepare. Having grown up in bean town, I have developed a taste for the little brown things, but not so with others. Jimmy, a young dwarf clown, hates them, and every time he walks in to the cookhouse and sees franks and beans, he walks out. We like to tease him by telling him that the reason he is so short is because he doesn't eat his beans. One night on the road and unknown to the truck driver, the cook tent falls out of the wagon and onto the road. Upon discovering the missing tent, the crew backtracks, thinking it will be lying on the side of the road. Mysteriously, however, the tent is not to be found, causing meals to be consumed in the open air until a replacement tent arrives. It is a common practice while eating in the cook tent to toss out residue coffee or tea from one's cup onto the grass. We are so accustomed to that, that when dining out in a restaurant, without thinking, I pour out the left over coffee onto the floor – *poor Camille can't take me anywhere.*

Clown Shorty Hinkle has been on the Clyde Beatty Circus since the show traveled by rail. He is neither a midget nor a dwarf, but a small man who makes up for his shortness of size with additional digits – he has six fingers and six toes, and while sitting next to people talking, likes to tap people on the knee for emphasis. He also has another quirk, he likes to sleep in a lady's nightgown. Shorty thinks that no one in the sleeper sees him putting on his sleep attire under the covers, but they do. He drives the band sleeper, number 34, and has extensions on the pedals to reach his short limbs. Shorty doesn't slow down for railroad tracks so the sleeping musicians sometimes get bounced around, even tossed from their bunks.

Newspapers are on the floor around the urinal just in case someone is relieving himself just as Shorty hits the tracks. Taking wide turns is not part of Shorty's driving technique. In the middle of the night he drives through towns like Godzilla, taking out stop signs, lamp posts and mail boxes while making a turn. One night outside of Wilmington, he stops for gas. After filling up, he then drives out of the station – taking the fuel pump with him. The fire department and the police arrive, and throughout the bedlam going on outside, the musicians sleep on undisturbed – *Jesus, Mary, and Joseph!* Shorty may be a small man, but he messes up big time. The next day, trombone player Bob Gray replaces Shorty as a driver. Coincidentally, Bob's father, also a musician, use to play with my father in the thirties and forties in bands around New England. Its pouring down rain one night as Bob pulls the band sleeper onto the lot in the wee hours of the morning. Bob has to make an emergency comfort stop so he ducks under the sleeper to relieve himself and to get out of the rain. Unknowingly, he squats under the piss funnel, and while he is going below, someone above is going too, and poor Bob takes a shower in the rain – *sonamamitch!*

The show plays Cincinnati for two days after hard rains had hit the area and Frank has to hire two Caterpillar tractors to haul the show on to a muddy lot. Ferry Forst (magician from Austria) has twin daughters, Bridget and Jutta[31] who leave their muddy but expensive boots outside their trailer where my dog Mike (a Brittany Spaniel) finds and eats them. Ferry is put out with us for a few days over the dog that everyone on the show likes except him. Mike the dog had joined the show in New Hampshire after being picked up by the concession guys after he wandered onto the lot one day. After being passed around to different keepers, Mike finds his way to me and becomes my pal.

As we walk around the circus, the former keepers continue to say, "Hi, Mike," to the dog, thus giving the impression to people who don't know me that they are addressing me, and that my name is Mike.[32] Mike the dog likes to bury bones under our trailer, which he then tries to dig up again in the next town, not understanding why it's not there today when he buried it there yesterday. One morning in Virginia, we let him out in the morning, leaving the screen closed but the door open. In a few minutes Mike the dog jumps into the trailer – right through the screen. Outside the door is Big Sid the elephant who uses our trailer for a good scratch, shaking us out of bed in the process. Big Sid, leader of the herd, is a movie star, having performed in the film JUMBO, and is my favorite elephant. I don't mind if she scratches on my trailer, but not while I'm sleeping – *how rude!* Mike the dog is with us most of the season until he is run over by a car in Georgia.

Dagmar (wirewalker from Germany) marries Niño (juggler from Portugal) and for a while seem to make a happy couple. This is not a marriage made in Heaven as Niño turns out to be a spouse abuser, and one day roughs up Dagmar in a dispute about coffee. Dagmar goes home crying to her father, there upon Rudy takes a water bucket as a weapon, and chases Niño around the Big Top – occasionally putting dents in it with Niño's head. The marriage is dissolved and Dagmar returns to her father's trailer. Father Sullivan, who happens to be on the lot, tries to console her while Niño, who is despondent, drinks a bottle of Exlax to end it all. The ambulance comes to take him away, but all he gets for his trouble is a big purge. The next day, he is back on the lot and the show goes on.

Later in the season, nerves are on edge and tempers short. Niño and Lothar (acrobat who does a one-finger stand) have a knock-down, drag-out on the track during the come in over an ushering dispute. Johnny Pugh, assistant manager, steps in, and the fight is over. Until he died, Johnny's father, "Digger" Pugh (London theatrical producer), would recruit and send over dancing girls to the circus. Johnny himself came over as a trampoline act and stayed on the show and is now assistant to manager Frank Orman.

The show comes to Trumbull, Connecticut, one night, and as we approach the lot, we find it barricaded and surrounded by police. They tell us that the circus has been cancelled and to get out of town. Paying for police protection is normal procedure; but the local authorities had upped the ante to something outrageous, and the show refused to pay. The show gets the day off, and we all park at the Ralph Emerson circus-themed park, not far from the location where we were to show. Ralph, a circus fan friend of Frank's, calls his place a museum, but it is nothing more than a junk yard of old wrecked and retired circus equipment that shows have thrown away. Although open to the public no one ever goes there. We find it a quaint refuge for our show, even though we find Ralph's fantasyland of circus junk amusing.

With nothing to do on a day off, Rex and I spend the time drinking scotch and telling stories. In the meanwhile his charge of elephants have gotten loose, and are wandering around the lot. Loose elephants tend to get into mischief so I volunteer to lead them back to their stake line – grabbing one by the ear, I coax her along and the others follow. Rex in the meantime goes into his trailer, gets his shotgun, and fires it into air. The elephants spook, and I find myself running in front of a herd of charging elephants – *Jesus, Mary and Joseph!* Rex thinks its funny for he likes to do outrageous things, but I am not amused. The show carries eleven elephants under Rex's charge that not only perform, but also work pushing and pulling to get tents up and to move vehicles out of the mud.

While the show is in Pensacola, Eva his wife is home giving birth to a daughter. Rex invites the band out to a fine restaurant to celebrate, and everything is on him. However, after the party is all over and out, Rex goes to each guest to borrow money to pay the bill for his party.

The musicians are not amused. Rex takes the girls swimming whenever the show plays close to water. Sometimes the elephants like the water so much that they refuse to come out; then Rex, with an ankus[33] clenched in his teeth, has to swim out to them and round them up. Just for a gag, Rex has been known to walk into a bar for a drink with an elephant in tow, much to the surprise of the patrons inside – the bartenders are not amused. From this escapade a legend is born, and a joke circulates around the circus industry. (One day, Rex and his elephant walk into this bar and says to the bartender, "Give my buddy and me a beer." The bartender looks at the two of them and says "Hey, pal, we don't allow animals in here – take that ugly, smelly creature outside"; to which Rex responds, "Well, if my friend can't drink in here, then neither shall I – we're leaving." The bartender then turns to Rex and says, "I wasn't talking to you, I was talking to the elephant.")

Rita from Columbia, the show's seamstress and costume maker, with husband Little Mike do a perch act with Rita on the ground supporting a long pole on her shoulder and Mike performing on top. Like Shorty Hinkle, they have been on the show since the railroad days. Mike was once the under stander, but after being attacked by their own German Shepard dog, he had not been able to hold the weight of the pole on his shoulder. During hard times, Mike was once forced to visit a farmer's field near the circus winter quarters, and shoot a cow, which he butchered then ate for several weeks thereafter – *holy cow!* Along with Rita and Mike, the women on the show like to hold a flea market and sell off to others on the show unwanted accumulations. One day as we are pulling on to the lot, we notice Rita and adopted daughter Alba standing among all their belongings. Behind us is Rex's wife Eva who loves flea markets and stops to rummage through the pile. While Eva is rummaging, she notices that both women are crying, and asks why. Rita explains that during the night their trailer was demolished in a road accident, and so everything they own was removed from the wreck, and is now here in a pile. Little Mike drives like Shorty Hinkle. Not only do they have small stature in common, but they are both accident prone. Eva is embarrassed to no end, and sheepishly departs from the scene. The show helps arrange for new travel accommodations, and Rita and Mike are soon back on the show and in business again.

Accidents seem to plaque the circus. In Virginia, the first day under canvas, Ronny, the transportation boss and chauffeur for Frank, runs over a workingman who is sleeping under the truck – killing him in the process. Schweitzer the rigger being in a drunken stupor and needing to relieve himself, gets out of his bunk in the sleeper wagon one night, and opens the door to walk outside – failing to realize that the sleeper is traveling to the next town. He takes one small step for a man and one giant leap out the door, taking a buster on the highway. The next day, he arrives on the lot, bruised and hurt. Instead of getting sympathy, Edna gives him a lecture for being drunk and stupid. "Donniker"[34] Mike was once a Greyhound Bus driver, but that was then and this is now. Outside of Toledo, Mike drives a truck into a ditch that then requires two wreckers to pull it out. The police take him to jail for drunk driving causing newly appointed assistant manager Bob Gray to get a paper bag filled with money from Mr. Maley who always issues crumpled up money in paper bags, and buys back Mike from the authorities. Frank, however, is not happy that Bob pays the fine, because he knows that they have to let Mike go eventually – so why pay out good money – *holy Toledo!*

The most notable event of the season happens in Auburn, New York. A storm has been brewing all day, and the sky is turning black. Sensing danger, Johnny Pugh orders precautionary measures to be taken. After finishing my performance, I dress for cherry pie – folding up the seat wagons – and from the rear of the tent, enjoy the rest of the show. As the audience watches the show, loose canvas is flopping up and down outside while the big top crew ties down the tent with extra lines and stakes. The sky blackens and the animals grow restless as the band plays and the performance proceeds.

As the Hungarian teeterboard display ensues, lightning strikes nearby and thunder drowns out the band. People nervously begin to leave the big top a few at a time. Just as the Hungarians finish their act and leave the rings, there is a loud rumble like a train – the unmistakable sound of a tornado. The big top rises as the big sucker-upper in the sky hits the big top, and all the stakes holding the tent down pop out of the ground. Simultaneously the lights go out, the band stops playing, and the audience rises to its feet.

There is pandemonium as the big top then comes down on audience and performer alike. A center pole crashes down through the drums, slicing through the bandstand, knocking the sousaphone player backward off the stand as musicians scatter like chickens. Cries and screams are drowned out by the roar of the wind, a torrent of rain and the crash of thunder. Hundreds of people are trapped under the canvas and the rain is coming down like Niagara Falls – *Jesus, Mary and Joseph!* Fearing that people could be injured and drowning under the canvas, I take out my knife like Tarzan of the Apes attacking a giant crocodile, and slice open the canvas to release people from their entombment. The menagerie tent is flattened and the elephants stampede. Electric power is out in Auburn, the town is flooded and 85 people in the tent are injured. Soon, help arrives: the police, the Fire Department, the Red Cross, the National Guard and the Civil Air Patrol. Red and blue lights are flashing, lions are roaring; elephants are trumpeting; lightning is flashing; and thunder is clapping. Cecil B. De Mille could not have staged a better catastrophe – I almost want to applaud. In the meantime, Camille is cowering in the trailer, watching from the window as events outside unfold. We spend all night cleaning up the mess, and at the crack of dawn, make a hasty withdrawal out of town. For the next three days in Buffalo, we side wall the show until last year's canvas is shipped in from winter quarters, and co-owner Jerry Collins shows up to treat us to a barbecue. Like the show, the barbecue must go on – and so it does.

The season grinds on and on, from the Easter Opening in Commack, Long Island, until the November closing in Orlando, Florida, with mostly one (occasionally two) day stands. By autumn, we seem to be functioning like robots. Not only are we physically tired, but also brain dead. Our small city that moves by night always seems to be the same and yet each day we are in a different location or a different state.

The very nature of constant travel where the environment is both the same and yet different causes confusion in one's mind. People are associated with a certain town and may go unnoticed if they appear on the lot in a different town. By the end of the season we have trouble remembering names and faces – and that's not all – the clowns do a safe-cracking gag, dressed in prisoner-striped suits, and it finishes with Batman and Robin coming out of the safe to chase them down the track. One early morning in Mississippi, Camille and I get out of bed, and get ready to travel to the next town – the show, of course, has already left the night before. Half asleep, I peer out the window and notice that the clowns are practicing their safe cracking gag in their costumes where the big top had been the night before. I find it strange, but take no notice of it until we are driving off the lot when it dawns on me that the "clowns" are actually a Mississippi chain gang, forced to clean up the lot after the circus. Camille teases me about my mental lapse, but the worst is yet to come.

Camille and I are invited to a party organized by some circus fans. Lots of local people whom I don't know are there, and we are all having a good time. After a few drinks, my eye catches a lovely shape across a crowded room. I find myself staring at the outlines of a lovely nymph from behind – my eyes fixed on her derriere, peeling off her clothes in my mind. I stand there in a trance, enjoying my fantasy until the girl turns around and suddenly reveals herself to be Camille. Immediately, the fantasy image crumbles – *I must be losing my mind – why that's no nymph, that's my wife! – Jesus, Mary and Joseph!*

Camille discovers one day that she can't stand the smell of coffee, and later after a visit to a local doctor, learns that she is pregnant. Later during the season, the girls on the show throw her a surprise baby shower in the big top between shows, right next to the bandstand – utilizing elephant tubs for tables.

The setting for a baby shower was somewhat unusual but Camille is delighted nevertheless. We are happy to be expecting a baby, and so now Camille and I begin to contemplate the problems of raising a child while traveling down the road with a circus. My own feelings are that Mother Nature will take care of everything so there is nothing to worry about.

Family member visits to the circus can cause problems. While playing Fall River during our first season, we make the mistake of pulling on the lot after a long drive late at night.

Early in the morning, we are rudely awakened by a knock on the door. There stands Dad's sister, Madeline (the scrapper), rough and tough, and ready for her favorite pastime – arguing. The aroma of her cheap perfume brings back memories of her hugs and sloppy kisses that I had to endure as a child. Of course she doesn't realize that we drove all night and need to sleep in the morning – *How can I shoo her away?* Reluctantly, we invite her in, and put on a pot of coffee. Camille sits there listening to family talk while pretending to be interested when suddenly there is another knock on the door. Standing there with a great big smile is Dad's other sister Helen whose husband ran off and left her years ago. Like a queen bee, she buzzes around aloof from the cares and concerns of her siblings. Tension rises when Helen enters the trailer and sees sister Madeline – they haven't spoken to each other in years. We try to carry on a pleasant conversation with one aunt sitting in the front and one sitting in the back of the trailer.

Suddenly, there is a knock on the door, and standing there is Dad's sister May (the chatterbox) who likes to dress funny, and always wares an Aunt Jemima bandana on her head. It's suddenly getting hot and stuffy as Auntie May enters into the trailer of doom. My stomach is turning, wondering what's going to happen. Camille carries on with chitchat as the three sisters glare at each other while acting nonchalant – still festering old wounds from ancient family squabbles. There is another knock on the door and in comes Cousin Sheila who while in high school ran away from mother Helen, and went to live with Auntie Peg – herself at moment on her way to see the show with daughter Colleen. Just before an explosion occurs, Camille announces that we have to go to work; and like the clown car gag where thirty clowns tumble out of a Volkswagen, our trailer regurgitates all my relatives. Fortunately, the show is fairly liberal about ducats (free tickets) for guests of show personnel so I dutifully hand out a ticket to each family member, insuring that they will say nice things about me. During pull down that night, the circus workers are attacked by an unruly gang of local toughs, and a "hey, rube!"[35] ensues. The circus wins the day with an elephant charge, sending the mob scattering in all directions – *Jesus, Mary and Joseph!*

By mid October, we approach the end of the circus season and begin the Florida tour. All of us on the show sense a change in the weather, signaling that there will soon be an end to this madness, and we can all go home. There is a tradition on the circus to copy another performer's act on the last show of the season. In our wire display, Rudy staggers into the ring (dressed in a tuxedo), with flowers to give to Gerda who is dancing on the wire. As Rudy staggers into ring three, I am mimicking him in ring two.

As Rudy performs, he is keeping one eye on me, and I can see that he is cracking up. Dagmar in ring one is laughing all the while as the battle of the drunks ensues. Rudy tries to out drunk me, but it is no contest – I've been practicing too. Other performers are watching the fun from behind seat wagons, while the audience gets a good laugh and the display gets the biggest applause of the season.

Mom and Dad invite us to park our trailer in their backyard and stay with them until we go out again in the spring. It's only for a few months, and think of all the money we will save. I can tolerate Mom and Dad, but what about Camille? Camille is weary, but will give it a try. Our stay will just be until the season starts again – just enough time not to wear out our welcome, nor get on Camille's nerves.

Chapter X
North and South of the Border

We are relaxing with Mom and Dad in Orlando, and content to be collecting unemployment from the state. Each year before we come to Orlando, the advance agent for the circus visits the unemployment office and deposits a pile of free tickets to the circus so that those people won't hassle us to try to find a job on the off season. Switching from constant go to inertia takes some adjusting, and we need the rest.

While Camille is around, Dad acts like a perfect gentleman and Mom tries to control her tongue. It is not utopia; but for the few months we have off, it is convenient and cheap. Camille is not overjoyed, but tolerates the situation, keeping herself busy designing and sewing our wardrobe for the next season.

Frank is throwing the annual end-of-the-season party at his home in Winter Park and we are invited. The affair is usually for the upper management who live in the central Florida area and we are delighted to attend a dress-up party where the ladies get to paint up their face and show off their jewels.

Camille buys a new dress for the occasion and is the belle of the ball. The party is in an annex of the main house, which has a bar, swimming pool, a sauna bath and a pool table. I'm impressed at the extravagance and apparent wealth. Evidently, there is money to be made in the circus business – I'm thinking. Frank's wife Brenda greets us with "Terry darling!" and "Camille darling!" Like the Gabor sisters, she likes to call everyone darling. All the men drink whiskey while smoking a cigar and talking about the good old days of the big railroad circuses, the daily circus parades and glamorous shows of the past. The advantage of truck shows over railroad shows, showing in arenas rather than in a tent and which towns have the highest grosses and the best lots are discussed and debated between sips, puffs and nibbles. The women concentrate on who did what to whom, and each question begins with, "Darling, did you hear…?"

Performers on other shows are dissected, inspected and hung out to dry by both sexes. As the evening wears on the smoke gets thicker, the noise gets louder and the stories get better. Mr. MacGarity, Frank's lawyer, tells me that I'm standing in the company office – "Some office!" I exclaim, "what makes it an office?" Mac explains that all the business calls are made from a telephone on a table in the corner, thus making the room a business expense for tax purposes. I wish I could talk him into buying an airplane as a business expense; but he already has a yacht and a condo on the beach.

Besides the Clyde Beatty Circus, Frank also own two smaller circuses: King Brothers, managed by Bob Coules, and Sells Gray, managed by Willy Story, both of which work the smaller towns. Frank sees a need to rotate the performers between his shows in order to keep the show fresh for the repeat business in every town. After three seasons on the Clyde Beatty Circus, Frank offers us a $50 per week raise and sends us to the smaller and less stressful King Brothers Circus for the 1970 season. Camille, now carrying a baby, needs a more serene environment for her delicate condition than the Clyde Beatty Circus can provide.

*

In the late '50s and early '60s, the Circus Hall of Fame in Sarasota was a must see for tourists coming to Florida. Managed by retired Army Colonel Naramore, the attraction was a living museum of the circus: featuring retired circus wagons, a puppet show, snack bar, various exhibits of circus paraphernalia, and a circus performance given four times a day.

During the off season, it is a convenient place for a circus performer to work and just about every act in the business has played there at one time or another. Unexpectedly, I get a phone call from an agent who wants to book me there for the winter off-season, until it's time to go out on the road again in the spring. Camille, who is beginning to show her pregnancy, declines to go, preferring instead to stay at home with Mom and Dad in Orlando for the relatively short time that I will be gone.

Appearing on the show with me in the building are Regalito the house clown who together with his family does assorted comedy routines, Carmen[36] (trapeze) with husband Larry assisting, and outside, Evy and brother Toby[37] (high wire), children of former Ringling headliner "The Great Arturo." Also in the outside courtyard surrounded by circus wagons is the Frank Simpson caged panther act.

Long-term trailer parking is difficult to find in Sarasota during the winter so I make arrangements with my former wire display comrade Rudy to park at his ranch outside of town in Myakka, and commute to work from there. Rudy has a large spread with cattle, but continues to live in his trailer until he can build himself a log cabin. Daughter Dagmar lives in her own room, which Rudy built for her in the barn.

Without my slack wire assistant, I'm lost. Needing a girl to hand me my props, I ask Evy to assist me and she obliges. After a week of shows, it is payday and I give Evy, a tip of ten dollars. Papa Arturo (The Great), however, is miffed and demands a bigger tip; so I give her another ten, and she is back in the act until she finally gets bored with it all and quits altogether. Regalito, from Mexico, sends his daughter to assist me and she won't accept money – *good show!* Regalito likes to clown around during my act by hanging his laundry up to dry on my slack wire – among other things. Some clowns will do anything for a laugh – *how Rude!* In any case, I can hardly complain that he is making a stooge out of me since his daughter is working for me for nothing.

We perform every day, week after week, then after work, I drive home to my trailer at Rudy's ranch where he and wife Gerda have their nightly barbecue going, and Rudy[38] continues to practice his act (the drunk part) while he tells me of his adventures as a sailor in the German Navy during the war when he got a medal for sinking a Russian torpedo boat.

*

Spring arrives and so it is time again for circuses to come to life and begin their annual migration around the country, bringing joy and happiness to the children of America. Camille and I report for duty with the King Brothers Circus, which opens the season in Ft. Pearce, then continues to tour Florida while sister circus Clyde Beatty goes north only to return to play Florida in the Fall.

Although smaller than Clyde Beatty Circus, King Brothers has elephants, camels and bears, a trained leopard, and the standard jugglers, trapeze artists, acrobats and clowns. Although lacking a sideshow, the show has all the atmosphere of a circus, and most of the equipment, although old, is freshly painted with a sparkle that attracts young and old alike. The show has a five-piece band: organ, drums and two trumpets and baritone played by bandmaster Carl Stevens. The group provides a phonic atmosphere of circus rather than a symphony of sound; nevertheless, the audiences are pleased and satisfied with the show. Camille is a real trooper and works in the show while pregnant and wearing her newly created pregnant wardrobe, which does a great job of hiding her condition.

Chef Doris runs the cook house and turns out good meals most of the time and hardly ever serves hotdogs and beans. Of course, we can still eat in our trailers if we don't like the menu of the day, and then there are the barbecues at night on a two day stand when at night after the show, we enjoy flipping ribs and chicken on the charcoal fire while the men sip Old Granddad and smoke a cigar.

The circus heads south, slowly working its way towards Key West, then after a two day stand in Miami, Camille decides to return to Orlando to await the arrival of our new trooper, expected in about a month. Camille travels home while I continue the tour with my new and not-so-lovely slack wire assistant Whitey, the prop boy who has bad teeth, unkempt hair and usually dirty coveralls – not an attribute to my performance, but necessary none the less. Show manager big Bob Couls and wife Mary Joe continue to pay me my full salary even without my lovely assistant while Camille stays with Mom and Dad, sewing wardrobe while awaiting the arrival of the stork.

We have lots of kids on the show, most of whom belong to Harry Rawls, concession manager. His kids delight in hustling popcorn and cotton candy – not just because they are helping their dad; but for a child to be a concessionaire on a circus is to achieve social status and monetary reward. Traveling on a show is a great education for kids since they get to see so many places that other children only read about.

Children on the road do their school work from the Calvert School of Baltimore, which specializes in correspondence education.

From Key West, the circus slowly makes its way north then turns west into Alabama. Camille has been off the show for about a month when one day a policeman comes on the lot to inform me that I am a proud father of a boy. Everyone on the show is delighted and I walk around passing out cigars. It will be another month before my father delivers Camille to the show in Dalton, Georgia, along with my new son Eoin who at the tender age of one month has opted to run away and join the circus with his mom and dad.

A new baby in the trailer requires some readjustment, scheduling our child raising routine around the performances, and now we travel during the day rather than at night. Soon everyone on the show is volunteering for babysitting duty while we perform during the show, and Eoin has lots of uncles and aunties to pamper him. Eoin gradually becomes aware of his world – and what a world it is: clowns, horses, elephants, camels and dogs, a big canvas tent, people wearing strange costumes with dingle dangles that glitter and the sound of music coming from the big tent – "Lions and tigers and bears, Oh my!" Then, there is the constant travel in the "chicken coop," our pet name for the trailer, as we do our one-day stands. There are only two days to think about in the circus: today's town and tomorrow's town. For Eoin, it's time to eat, time to sleep, playtime, travel time and show time. Being a new parent gives one additional motivation to persevere, to achieve and to endure.

We have a new Brittany spaniel, which we name Mike the Dog II, after the one we owned on Clyde Beatty Circus The dog is fine with kids and nice to have around; however, he has this thing about birds. From the moment we let him out in the morning, he goes bird hunting – forgetting to come back until we have to go searching for him. Doesn't he realize that we have to get to the next town – *apparently not.* In Kansas, we can no longer wait and leave him behind, only to return to pick him up on the lot where he sits waiting for us. In Nebraska, we retrieve him from the pound. In Illinois, he is delivered to us by the police. In Altoona, the dog catcher cites me for "dog on the loose," and I have to go to court where the Judge dismisses the case. Mike the Dog has to be kept hidden while the bears perform, lest the bruins take off after the dog, which happens occasionally when we are in a rush, and have other things on our mind.

The show's electrician, "Hard Times," has a Boston terrier with a strange obsession – it is in love with a camel. The dog follows the camel everywhere, and when the beast lies down, the dog embraces its head, sticks his noodle in the camels ear and humps away – all the while the dromedary lies still, smiling with a silly grin on its face – *how droll!* The dog is almost on the right track – at least the camel is a female. If we had a side show, we could bill them as the worlds strangest couple.

Elephants can sometimes cause problems. There is a short jump to the next town so we decide to go to see a movie in town after the evening performance, and leave the next morning. As we drive away from the lot, we see Jimmy (elephant boy) trying to load up Ola the elephant into the wagon. "Get in the house, Ola," says he in a commanding voice. Ola ignores him. We leave Jimmy to his charge, wish him luck and drive away to enjoy a night away from the circus. Upon returning to the lot several hours later, Jimmy is still talking to Ola. "Ola, get in the house," says he in a pleading voice, but Ola won't respond.

Okie the elephant trainer from Oklahoma who is already in the next town has to be summoned to return and coax Ola into the house, which he does. Poor Jimmy takes a lot of kidding on the show after that. The elephants are not keen on riding in wagons since big top boss George[39], the driver, once passed under a bridge too low, and pealed off the roof – destroying the wagon and dumping the elephants onto the highway. The accident shook up the girls but they were otherwise unharmed.

We have a busy routine while traveling under the Big Top. Before pulling on the lot in the next town, we try to find a shopping center where we can do a laundry and go shopping. Although we eat in the cookhouse, which saves us time and expense, we still have to shop for the other necessities of family life.

On the lot, we have to prepare for two performances besides other chores: truck and trailer maintenance, wardrobe repair, and of course tending our son Eoin. As we travel around the country, we dream of owning our own home someday and Camille assembles things that she would like to see in our dream house. It doesn't take long before the trailer is bulging at the seams with paraphernalia for our future home that we pick up on the road during a season.

By summer, the circus has made its way through the South into Pennsylvania and upper New York State, and by July, we find ourselves in Maine. The show is usually off the beaten track and we find ourselves in lovely little towns that we never knew existed – where the arrival of the circus in town is a major event. Along our tour of the country, we discover many historical locations and local attractions that we had only heard about but never thought of visiting, such as the Jack Daniels distillery – no free samples – and Mammoth Cave where my mother once told me that she had gone on her honeymoon.

We visit countless battlefields and visit every zoo we can find. I'm enjoying being a dad, and we try to make the most of our traveling lifestyle by showing little Eoin everything that a young boy should see. He is still too young to understand, of course; however, we are hoping that everything he sees will leave some lasting impression.

Life on the circus is not all roses, however, as we do experience some close calls – one night in Knoxville when the canvas truck begins traveling down an incline with no driver in it. We are in the chicken coop when we hear the shouting of warnings to get out of the way of the truck. Not knowing what is happening, Camille grabs sleeping Eoin from his crib, just as the runaway truck whizzes by, hitting a tree. Camille is unsettled by it all while Eoin sleeps away unfazed.

In Ponca City, Oklahoma, we are visited again by our second tornado encounter. Big Bob the manager sees black clouds gathering on the horizon, and stops the show sending all the patrons out of the tent, and peaking the canvas down around the center poles. Anything loose is gathered and stored as we prepare for the worst. Again the sound of the freight train, black clouds and unbelievable wind occurs as we all duck under trucks. Mercifully, the tornado spares the circus and passes us by, but the show cannot go on because the audience has fled. Eoin sleeps on as if nothing has happened. Peace and tranquility return as the circus continues its tour of Oklahoma and Texas.

A tragic event does occur on the show in Ohio when eighteen-year-old Billy (roustabout) goes swimming at a local quarry and drowns. Many of us from the show are also swimming there, and so I assist in removing the body from the water. For several days, we are all saddened by the event, but the show must go on, and it does; regrettably, the grim reaper makes another appearance as the end of the season approaches. Just a few weeks from closing, manager Big Bob discovers that he has cancer and leaves the show only to die a few weeks later. Frank sends "Red" White, former side show manager, to boss the show to the end of the season and bring it home – none too soon as our bodies and minds have had enough travel and adventure for a while. My brain must be going to sleep as I discoverer one day after taking the baby in his carriage to the ticket wagon where Mary Jo, the paymaster, is making out the payroll. After returning to the chicken coop with our salary, Camille asks in dismay, "Where is the baby?"- *oops!* I left the baby at the office wagon – *no problem,* he's still there; but I know I need a vacation.

Trying to continue in the Naval Reserve and travel with the circus requires better juggling than I am capable of. I arrange ahead of time to do my two weeks active duty on the off time at some Naval facility along our route and continue doing correspondence courses – somehow managing to retain my status as a reserve Naval Officer. My efforts do go rewarded, and I am eventually promoted to Lieutenant. During my travels with the circus, I continue to fly airplanes, trying to maintain my proficiency by renting an airplane at various airports around the country – hoping to someday fly for an airline. Although I now possess a Commercial Pilots' license and instrument rating attained at Orlando's Herndon Airport during the off season, I find my self too old (33) for an entry-level position with a airline – *sonamamitch!* Alas, I shall have to be content with giving airplane rides to fellow circus troopers as we travel around the country, and set up close to an airport – the boys in the band are my best customers.

*

The one-day stands of the tented circus are wearing us down. Although Eoin doesn't seam to mind a bit, his poor mom and dad need a change. With the death of Big Bob, we don't sign up for another tour with King Brothers, and never hear from Frank about it. Camille and I decide that it is time to move up in the business so we negotiate an indoor Shrine Circus tour with Edmond, Oklahoma, producer, Howard Suesz. The tour doesn't begin until the spring, however, and for the winter months, we have booked a tour in Mexico with Circo Atayde Hermanos.[40] We expect a grueling trip, driving to Mexico with the chicken coop and the dog, but the smell of adventure is in the air and we look forward to a new quest. The drive to Brownsville, Texas, is hot and boring. We have played Texas before; but for some unknown reason, the trip to Mexico seems endless in our two-ton, non-air-conditioned truck – straining as it pulls our thirty-foot trailer along the flat and arid landscape. Eoin and Mike the Dog sleep most of the way while I drive and Camille navigates.

It takes a few days travel, and upon reaching the border, we find other circus acts there waiting to cross: Tibby Alexander (dog act), the Keppo family (acrobats), Rock Smith (flying act) and Ma Ho Pin (wire walker) with whom I had worked many years ago on Clyde Beatty Circus. The Mexican government does not make it easy for Americans coming into their country to work. We all plan our arrival on Friday afternoon and meet at the office of the Atayde lawyer whose job it is to take us through immigration.

The paperwork is redundant and frustrating. I suspect that behind the foot dragging and nitpicking, there is a political agenda against Americans working in Mexico. Perhaps, they are giving us a taste of our own bureaucratic buffoonery against Mexicans.

Hungarian Tibby Alexander and Gypsy wife Irene have a problem of having more dogs than is permitted to enter the country. He needs special permission for an adjustment in number – even then, he is in big trouble if any of his dogs have puppies and increase the dog count. We seem to be making progress when suddenly at four o'clock, immigration shuts down and everyone goes home, telling us to return on Monday – *Madre Mia!* There we are with the rest of the American circus acts, parked on the street for the weekend, waiting for our papers so that we can cross the border. Not to worry, the house trailers have all the necessities of life, and I tend to think of the experience as an adventure, something to be enjoyed and talked about later over a glass of tequila. Not only that, but we now can spend our time exploring Matamoras and even watch a bullfight. Monday arrives and we finally get underway to Mexico City after having to stop along the way at three more checkpoints. I thought that the drive from Florida to Texas was tedious and boring – after leaving Matamoras the elevation continues to increase as we climb the Sierra Madre Oriental Mountains, heading south. Because of the high altitude, our truck can barely put out forty miles an hour and my foot hurts from holding the gas pedal flat on the floor of the truck. The desolation of the desert landscape while beautiful is nevertheless, foreboding – conjuring up visions of old desert prospectors crawling on their hands and knees, crying "agua"(water). Always interested in our environment, we notice distinct changes in the character of the cactus as we travel from one area to another. Periodically, we come upon the strange sight of children standing on the side of the road begging at the trucks passing by. A child standing by the highway in the middle of nowhere – *must be a mirage* – I'm thinking, but no, Camille sees them too.

As we crawl like a snail along the mountain ridge, we notice that at each sharp turn there is a trail of debris from previous accidents. Apparently Mexican truck drivers never heard of Newton's law of motion – a speeding truck traveling in a straight line will continue in a straight line regardless of the bend in the road. Another of Newton's laws is demonstrated by Sr. Muños, otherwise known as Captain Astronaught, the man shot from a cannon. He is driving his cannon towing a house trailer along the same stretch of highway to Mexico City to perform with Circo Atayde. While descending a steep grade, the brakes on the cannon begin to heat up. Before long, a fire erupts from the brakes as Captain Astronaught pulls over to the side of the road and attempts to put out the fire. Stored in a compartment above the wheel well on fire, are dynamite caps used to provide a "KA-BOOM" as he is slung from the cannon. As the Muños family duck behind some rocks, the dynamite ignites with the resulting explosion, sending the cannon down one side of the mountain and the trailer down the other – for every action, there is an equal and opposite reaction.

Eventually, we arrive in Mexico City and make our way to the Arena de Mexico, next to the municipal parking ramp where the show trailers are parked near the backstage entrance to the arena. Other performers already parked there call the place "The Black Hole of Calcutta." There is a constant cacophony of noise, day and night, from Mexicans parking their cars and honking their horns. Not only do the horns honk but they also play tunes. Traffic jams in Mexico City are a nightmare of sounds assaulting the ear, and car crashes at intersections with traffic lights are a common occurrence – Mexican drivers don't seem to mind busting a red light. A wrecked car may sit at a corner intersection with a policeman standing guard for days before it is carted away. Disturbingly, I see a dog struck and killed by a car as onlookers burst out in laughter – like in the circus when a Mexican clown drops his trousers, and the audience goes bananas – some sort of Mexican thing. During the winter months, the city suffers from atmospheric inversion. That occurs when the air at high altitudes is warmer than the air below, thus preventing the air surrounding the city to rise and clear. Exhaust gasses emitted from countless automobiles saturates the city air causing a burning sensation in the eyes and lungs. That, plus the constant din of honking traffic, curtails our long walks around the city and forces us to seek refuge in the Chicken Coop, parked in the Black Hole of Calcutta. Outside the arena is a strange and alien world with a different culture and language that I don't feel comfortable with. However, inside the arena is the circus: a world within itself, international in spirit and in substance, a familiar and comforting world, a colony of fellow artists in the middle of a foreign country. Mexicans have a different lifestyle than Americans; but they love the circus, and we pack them in.

The Atayde Brothers, Andrés and Aurelio, present everything that a large circus should present: tigers, elephants, camels, jugglers, acrobats, aerialists, clowns and even a pigeon trainer from Germany who has a nasty habit of spanking his pigeons when they don't perform properly – as if the bird is suppose to know. Those of us in the show do not take kindly to him.

Camille has been contracted to perform with the girls in the aerial ballet. However, Mexican girls are small people and Camille stands out like the jolly green giant, causing her to be cut from the number – much to her relief, as she didn't want to do it anyway. In any case, we enjoy being on the show and love the applause. With my limited Spanish, I do interviews on Mexican T.V. talk shows and give out lots of autographs. I'm feeling good about myself – not that I have reached the pinnacle of my profession; but that I have gone to a country that has lower standards of perfection and therefore are a lot easier to please.

In the U.S. I'm a circus act, while in Mexico I am a superstar – Vive Mexico! The daily routine commences with almost a full house at each performance. We have the pleasure of performing with a full concert band of talented musicians. The musicians' union is very strong in Mexico, and they require a certain number of band members, plus strangely enough, two conductors. While one conductor leads the band the other one sits in back and harasses the playing musicians with little pranks – goosing them with a drum stick from behind as they play – another Mexican thing.

The Christmas season is in full swing in Mexico, and Eoin gives us a present of walking for the first time on Christmas day; from then on, there is no stopping him. The smog engulfing the city clears up enough for us to take Eoin for a walk around the city. We are pushing Eoin along in his carriage when some Mexican Indians – Mexicans with no Spanish blood who still speak Nahuatl, the language of the Aztecs – approach us and offer to buy Eoin. I ponder the offer and begin to haggle over the price when Camille storms over and puts an end to it. Of course, I'm just pulling her leg; but she doesn't think it's funny. During our walk, Mike the Dog decides to go off on his own, and we have to go looking for him again. Fortunately, neighborhood kids find him and bring him back to the circus.

Across the street from the arena is the German restaurant Fritz where we enjoy eating German-style food; but of course it still seems to have a Mexican taste to it. Mexican beef has a taste all of its own; it is so tough, the butchers in the meat markets pound the steaks with wooden hammers before they sell it to their customers. They say that a cow is what it eats, and so I wonder what a Mexican cow eats that makes it so tough. Aside from the food, all the walls of the restaurant are covered with artists who have performed across the street in the arena at one time or another. Shamelessly feigning celebrity status, I offer them my photo to put up on the wall with the rest, and they comply, but still insist that I pay the bill – *how rude!*

The last performance in the arena is a special night where all the performers return on stage to be serenaded by a mariachi band. The ladies in the show receive flowers and we all receive a standing ovation from the audience. It makes one feel good to be in show business as we all have our fifteen minutes of fame. Soon after, we are very busy packing up the show and preparing to leave for Puebla, a lovely Spanish colonial town east of Mexico City where the tented tour of the country begins. Not only do we look forward to performing under the big top, but to just getting out of the city to where we can breathe fresh air again.

The big top is large and has three rings, similar to the American-style circus, but with a few exceptions.

Inside the tent, a large trench is dug out of the ground close to the rings where the performance takes place. Inside the trench go the most expensive seats, close to the rings, but nevertheless in a hole in the ground. Another interesting observation I make is that there is no garbage pick up service for the circus. A huge pit is dug in the ground in the backyard of the circus for that purpose. During the engagement, one tosses all the garbage in the hole, which is then buried before the show leaves. During the entire engagement, there is a long rope tied to a stake with the other end dangling into the hole – so that any poor fellow who might have fallen in can extricate himself.

'Torpedo" the dwarf clown also digs fence posts around the backyard trailer area so that a fence can be erected to keep out hordes of curious town people. Lots of local kids hang around watching the spectacle of the raising of the big top, and many of them are put to work for free tickets to the show. Like with Duffy Circus, the show does not provide water so we have to send kids to beg water from the local inhabitants. Some of the more enterprising youngsters take to stealing water from one trailer and deliver it to another – *robbing Pedro to pay Paulo.* Of course the water is only used for washing while drinking water comes only from bottles. We have learned like every other visitor before, not to drink the water in Mexico. One unsettling observation I make – a herd of cute and cuddly burros being kept on the show, neither for performing nor for pets, but to be fed to the tigers. Unsavory as it might seem, a tiger has to eat what a tiger has to eat – even my nephew Mathew ate his pet lamb.

Local vendors surround the circus tent hawking everything from soup to nuts. One woman grills hotcakes, served with caramel sauce on top, which I sample every night after the show. Nights are beautiful in Puebla, and it's so refreshing to breathe in the clean, dry, desert air. After the last show of the day, we sit in our chairs by the trailer, sipping tequila and stare at a brilliant star-filled sky.

Eoin is now walking around and getting into everything. We have to maintain a constant watch on him to be sure he doesn't get into trouble. While performing, he is tended by other performers waiting outside the performers' entrance for their turn. For a toddler growing up in a circus, there is a potential for catastrophe. As careful as we are, Eoin still manages to get bitten by a horse.

Our social group is mostly among the American acts where Camille feels more comfortable speaking English, and finds it frustrating not to understand Spanish; but then she is not interested in learning the language anyway. Unlike myself, Camille suffers from culture shock while I enjoy mixing with the Germans and Mexicans alike so as to practice my language skills. Unfortunately, there are no French performers with us in Mexico.

The performances go on every day to large crowds until the last day of the engagement arrives and it is time to pack up and move once more to Guadalajara. Again as before, the tent is erected, holes dug in the ground, and we send little boys to fetch water. The circus lot, however, is on an empty lot in the middle of town where we again have to endure the din of city traffic. The engagement is not as pleasant as it was in Puebla, where outside of town, we could breathe the fresh air and watch an unblemished sky at night; but we make the best of it and, after a week, finish our contract with the show in Monterey. Naturally, during our sojourn in Mexico, we try to take in all of the tourist sights during our travel and off time. We visit churches, pyramids, museums and zoos and whatever else we think one-year-old Eoin would enjoy. He doesn't seem as enthusiastic as his parents, however, as we try to make our Mexican adventure a memorable one by storing up pleasant experiences – a movable feast to be enjoyed in reflection. A pleasant thought carried in the mind is as necessary for life as the water carried in the camel's hump

The Atayde Brothers ask us to stay on with the show for the season. However, we have already signed on for the Shine Circus tour of the U.S. and Canada, and besides, Camille has had enough of Mexico and yearns to return to civilization. After crossing the border in Texas, we stop at a restaurant and have a good old Texas-size grilled steak and water we can drink, but not before we are stopped by the border patrol who search our truck for illegal Mexicans – *how rude!*

Circo Atayde Hermonos (1971) "En la pista central! (In the center ring)

Chapter XI
Joys of the Road

The trip from Mexico to Oklahoma City is not noteworthy – just another long jump in the normal routine of the circus. Arriving at the fairgrounds, we meet an entirely different cast of characters with the Shrine Circus. Although complete strangers, we all share the same lifestyle of the circus performer, thus finding ourselves with another branch of our cultural family. Arriving on a new show is like coming home again – altogether different and, yet, the same old thing.

Our circus family father figure is Howard Suesz, a one time orchestra leader from Oklahoma who decided to have a tented circus called Hagen Brothers Circus. From there, he went to producing Shrine Circuses around the United States and Canada. Uncle Howard, as he is affectionately known, is one of many Circus producers who bids on contracts to produce a circus for the Shrine – a branch of the Masonic order that traditionally uses the circus for fund raising activities.[41] The Shrine Circus forms the back bone of the circus in America, and without them many a circus performers would be out of a job.

The Shrine Circus in Oklahoma City has a strange cast of characters. Performing in the center ring, set up on an ice arena, is an ice-skating act with Camille and I doing the juggling act in one side ring while Cùcciolo (midget acrobat), does his plate spinning act in the other. "Cooch" came to America with the Zoppe riding act after being traded for an elephant between John Ringling North and the Zoppe Italian Circus. Although small in stature, he had a big part in the movie *The Greatest Show on Earth*. He enjoys talking to Eoin who is almost his size, but is forever brushing off cigar ashes that he transfers to Eoin as he talks. Like all midget men in the circus, he likes to puff on a cigar.

Our ringmaster, Colonel Lucky, looks dapper in his red tails and top hat.

Back when I was doing club dates in Baltimore, I had worked with him when he was doing a whip-cracking act, dressed as a gaucho and speaking bad Spanish-inflected English. With his whip he would cut papers held from the mouth of his assistant/wife Joni. This was one of the last of the old-time vaudeville-type acts still being presented at the time on the club date circuit. Since then, Lucky has elevated himself from a dinosaur vaudeville act, into becoming a circus ringmaster/announcer with the Shine Circus, and even acquired the title of Colonel by joining the Kentucky Colonel Society. Ever the showman, Lucky stands out among the otherwise lackluster ringmasters in the industry.

Lucky and Cooch love to spring practical jokes on each other. We never know what is in their bag of tricks, as they both go to great lengths to pull a gag – just for a laugh. Colonel Lucky likes to arm himself with a blank pistol, just in case some of the animals revolt and attack someone in the audience.

The only attacking ever done, however, is by Kirby's chimps, which get loose occasionally, and have to be rounded up. Helping to round up loose chimps can be a dangerous thing to do – so I discover when I get my hand bitten for the trouble of trying to be helpful.

(One of the chimps can ride a bicycle. On one date, the circus sets up inside a football stadium with the chimps in the center ring and two dog acts in each end ring. While the chimp is riding around in the ring with the bicycle, one of the dogs walks over to investigate. Seeing the dog, the chimp rides over to investigate. The dog is spooked and runs away down the center of the stadium track with the bicycle riding chimp in hot pursuit. Now the center of attention, the dog and chimp race around the track. To the cheers of the audience, they make a full circle with the dog in the lead and the pursuing chimp close behind, before Mr. Kirby (from Scotland) calls back the cycling simian, and ends the race. The laughter and applause of the audience stops the show for a time.)

For those who want to be in show business and can afford the initial expense of a chimpanzee – go to a children's toy shop, purchase an assortment of toys (props), dress the chip up in children's clothes, teach him to play with the toys – pushing, a baby carriage or riding a tricycle, and *Voila!* a performing chimp act is born. Mr. Kirby's chimps, however, do more than the usual chimp tricks, but rather are sophisticated animals and talented performers – able to do some things that a human can't.

Dog acts, in contrast, are probably the least expensive act for a performer to put together. Except for the purebred varieties, most dogs can be acquired at minimal cost from any dog pound. Pound dogs are usually mutts that learn very well, are happy dogs and great performers. Many a showman who became too old for the physically demanding role of circus performer, continue their career in show business as a dog act because it's relatively easy and inexpensive to assemble, and always a winner with children.

Making one's living with animals can be precarious – not only do they require constant care, training and attention, but they can at times make the trainer look like a fool. A female in heat can cause cavorting canines to give any dog trainer a bad day.

Bandmaster Clem,[42] also a Kentucky Colonel and fine trumpet player, leads his wife Elizabeth on the organ, plus various drummers picked up in each town along the tour. On some of the outdoor circus dates, Clem doesn't bother unloading the organ from his camper, but rather parks the vehicle close by the circus rings. With the drummer sitting outside, Clem plays the show through his back door while pregnant wife Elizabeth plays the organ inside the camper. Colonel Lucky, Colonel Clem and Colonel Cooch form the Old Bastards Club, which is just an excuse to get together and drink – not that circus people need an excuse to drink; but it does put an air of respectability and sophistication to it. The act of raising a glass to ones lips is not just a way to pour liquid into the mouth, but rather a ceremony of significance, not to be to be trivialized – or so the Old Bastards believe.

Howard, the circus producer, owns three elephants and several tigers presented by Lou Regan who is always busy taking care of the animals and doesn't socialize too much with the rest of us. Lou once worked the elephants that appeared in many Tarzan movies made in Hollywood during the forties.

Being an elephant keeper is a full-time job. It may seem like the keeper owns elephants, but it is the other way around. The elephant owns the keeper whose job it is to feed and clean the animal and provide for its every need – like the worker ant whose only function in life is to feed and clean the queen ant.

There are lots of kids on the show and Eoin has lots of playmates. Like town kids, circus children tend to copy their parents' skills, and at an early age begin to learn to juggle and do handstands. Rather than the traditional children's game of cowboys and Indians, they like to play circus. Children who already are performing in their parents' acts are idolized by the other younger children who are not. Getting a child to practice an act is a lot easier than trying to get him to do his correspondence school (Calvert of Baltimore.) This is one problem that we don't yet have with Eoin until reaches school age.

Performing children delight in competing against other kids in the show – each one striving to outdo the other in an effort to gain more applause – something they learn from their parents who do the same thing while performing with their fellow adult performers in a display. One-upmanship is the name of the game.

During the opening "spec" (parade), circus moms put all the kids in costume and they get to ride on a float pulled by a lawn mower where they do get to perform for the first time by smiling and waving. This is not just to get the kids into the show, but so that the moms and dads know where the kids are. Finding a Shriner to babysit during this time is futile anyway, since they are all in the spec as well.

The Shriners, in their flowing robes, little red Turkish hats and other desert attire, love to strut their stuff in spec, more than the circus kids love riding on the floats. One of Eoin's playmates is Clara who has an older sister Rita who performs on the aerial web. They are children of the "Argentino" family (perch pole act). Dad, Luis, on the ground has a pole in a pouch around his waist then spins Mom, Tina, suspended by a neck swivel at the top of the pole. While playing the ice hockey arena in Niagara Falls, Ontario, Tina blacks out during the spin, and hangs limp by her neck from the pole. Everyone rushes out to rescue her, and she recovers to perform again in the evening show. Apparently her blackout is just a fluke – *nothing to worry about.*

After a tour of arenas in the U.S., the show enters Canada for a tour of Shrine dates, held in nothing but ice hockey arenas – a blessing for the circus. Since every tiny town in Canada has an ice hockey arena, there is always a town where the circus can be set up during the cold spring weather. While in Canada, Camille and I are introduced to the wonderful world of concessions when we are given the opportunity to sell balloons. Not having paid much attention to such things in our circus past, we are now delightfully enlightened by the revelation of the balloon demand potential in Canada. Strange, but true – if you put a toy or a balloon on a stick, it mandates a must-have spell, irresistible to children and parents alike. Suddenly, performing in front of an audience doesn't excite me as much as selling them something before and after the show. Soon, we find ourselves blowing up thousands of balloons in the ice hockey arenas trying to satisfy the lust of Canadians for air-filled rubber on a stick. Our fingers turn numb from twisting each balloon onto a stick as we engage in our labor of love. Amazingly, the money I make on concessions surpasses my salary for my act – *what a revelation!* Our business grows to the point of us hiring local kids to blow up balloons, and taking on a sales staff of two super salesmen – Bonny the Clown and Billy the Clown – nobody can sell balloons like a clown.

Bonny is an elderly lady with a dog act, doing the standard dog tricks. She and husband Phil from Mexico have been performing in the circus for many years, having done a perch pole act on the Ringling Circus. Later, while performing the perch act with the Hunt Brothers Circus, Phil on the bottom, holding the pole, steps into a hole – dropping Bonny to the ground, thereby crippling both her and the act. They continue in show business with the traditional panacea for a fallen performer, a dog act and/or clowning. Bonny is a grandmotherly type person who likes to tell it like it is and gives us an education in the dressing room: show business, child rearing on the road and life in general. Selling balloons is something that she does very well. Billy the clown is strictly an amateur who wants to be a clown, but doesn't know how to be funny. He does meet and greet during the come in, and plays ball tossing with the audience prior to the show; aside from that, selling balloons is his most important role.

The Rhodo troupe of acrobats working on the show came to America from Berlin soon after World War II. They are a large family – headed by two brothers, Hans and Bruno. Bruno had been a U Boat mariner, and survived the postwar years in Germany as a circus acrobat. Together with other family members, including Bruno's first and second wife, they not only perform in the ring but provide the backbone of the concession department: selling souvenirs and food. Remembering the hard times in Berlin after the war, they are hard working people, striving for a better life in America, and dreaming of opening a German restaurant[43] someday in Sarasota.

One unfortunate incident occurs to me in Sudbury, Ontario, when upon hearing Colonel Lucky announce my act, I run through the curtains to enter the arena, and smash my face into a pole hidden in the curtain – *sonamamitch!* Half dazed, I continue into the ring and begin performing on the wire.

Cooch, the light man, sees what I cannot – that I am bleeding profusely from the face, and does not turn on the lights to my ring. Cooch walks in to tell me of my predicament, and I leave the ring immediately with Camille following behind. Now realizing what had happened, I calmly walk out of the ring to a waiting ambulance, which takes me to the hospital where the doctor sews me back up. I am impressed with the Canadian health system. For a small fee, one buys National Insurance and the hospitals take care of everything without a hassle. My wound heals and I'm back in business again.

We arrive in Montreal in late spring when the snow has finally melted and the flowers are beginning to emerge. Mike the Dog gets loose again and does his regular disappearing act, alas picked up by the Royal Mounted Police who always get their dog. We are glad to have him back, but his wayward ways are starting to get on my nerves. Just as the weather is becoming enjoyable, it is time to leave the country, and begin a circus tour of open air arenas and baseball parks in the midwestern and western United States.

The weather is pleasant during spring, however we find ourselves playing Kansas, Nebraska and Colorado in July and August when the temperatures soar, and performing outdoors in the circus can be mighty uncomfortable; not only that, Eoin comes down with chickenpox – much to our chagrin. Eoin enjoys going around the show flashing the red spots all over his belly to any interested onlooker. While in Corpus Christi, Texas, Mike the Dog runs away for the last time. We spend all day looking everywhere for him but he is nowhere to be found. The poor dog must be confused by his constantly changing environment. Sadly, we abandon our search and continue down the road. I have mixed feelings – I miss the dog, but I'm glad he's gone.

The end of the season finds us in Salinas, Kansas, with only two dates remaining: Toronto, Ontario, and Columbus, Georgia – *Jesus Mary and Joseph!* We are not looking forward to driving to Toronto for a three day stand then all the way back to Columbus. The Shriners, however, have their circuses when it is best for them, but not necessarily good for the circus – so drive we must, and drive we do. After a grueling trip, we arrive in Toronto to discover that some of the acts never made it. Later they will claim that they broke down, but we think that they took a week off rather that endure the trip. Of course they forgo their salary, but some think the long drive just isn't worth it. Camille and Eoin and I do our duty and make the date – not only must the show go on, but balloons must be blown.

The show is a bit thin in Toronto, but we make the best of it, and nobody guesses that they are seeing half a circus – except the Grotto[44] who are not too happy about it. After arriving in Toronto, Cooch learns that his mother died in Sarasota, and so we all chip in to send him back home for the funeral while someone on the show drives his rig back to Columbus where he will rejoin the show. The show returns to the States and reassembles itself at the fairgrounds in Columbus, Georgia, the last date of the season.

From there, each of us shall go our separate ways until spring when we begin the Odyssey all over again. Three years and three circus seasons go by with the Shrine Circus tour pretty much the same every year. Like on any show, performers come and performers go.

Lou, the elephant trainer, is replaced by old friends, Rex and Eve and their two daughters whom I knew and worked with on the Clyde Beatty Circus. The Grimaldis,[45] Ken and Vesta, an antiquated, but still funny, musical comedy act from London are a welcome addition to the show. I haven't seen them since my college days in Boston while working club dates around town. In all these years, the act hasn't changed a bit since they played the Palladium in London during the Blitz (World War II).

Trapeze artist Jimmy Troy, who tries in vain to teach Camille to do a handstand, and his wife Cherie, who performs flawlessly on the Spanish web, leave the show for a permanent engagement at an indoor amusement park called Old Chicago.[46] In spite of the seasonal changes in show personnel, there are always kids on a circus and Eoin always has playmates.

During the off season, we resume our winter routine of collecting unemployment compensation from Florida, and working a few winter dates as they happen. We park the chicken coop in Mom and Dad's backyard and proceed to empty out the trailer from a season of shopping and collecting things for the day when we shall have a house of our own. With our lifestyle being what it is, it doesn't seem practical to own a house that one cannot live in – at least in the immediate future. Many performers lock up their houses while they are gone on tour, and spend the season worrying about what catastrophe is befalling their abode while they are away. That seems to me to be one headache that we can do without. Storing all our possessions in Mom and Dad's closets until we have a home of our own is convenient. We don't particularly like living with my parents, but there is no rent to pay, and I can help my parents maintain the house, which someday will belong to myself and little sister Sharon. It seems wise to look after our inheritance – and so I do. Camille tolerates the situation like the trooper she is, but I occasionally have to remind her of all the money we are saving and how soon we will be on the road again.

*

Orlando tourist attraction, Church Street Station, features the Rosy O'Grady pub, designed on the Victorian style of the early twentieth century – a polished wood interior, including a balcony with staircase, two bars, a bandstand, and saturated with old time atmosphere seen only in western movies. The attraction features a Dixieland band and unusual entertainment:

singers, dancers and an array of waiters, bartenders and busboys who all have some unusual skill to display – just the place for a juggler and unicycle rider during the circus off season. The club reminds me somewhat of the Gay Nineties in Minneapolis, but on a higher and classier scale. The band enters the bandstand in an unusual way by sliding down a fireman's pole from the break room above. Master of ceremonies, "Spats" Donavan, and "Red Hot Mama" Ruth Cruise, together with the band, put on a delightful, though antiquated, show. Mr. Snow the proprietor is looking for waiters with talent and that is where I come in.

A juggling waiter doesn't seem like a bad job, considering the tips involved – *I might be on to something here.* Hustling beer as a waiter is not really my cup of tea; however, I find it interesting that the drunken patrons are willing to give me a dollar to balance a newspaper on my nose – and so I do.

Unfortunately, that is the only lucrative part of the job. Mr. Snow pays less than the minimum salary and expects the waiters to make up the rest on tips. It sounds great, except that although I juggle clubs with the band, and deliver the beer on a unicycle, I am only rewarded with nickels and dimes – hardly a salary for a Las Vegas act like myself. For the show final, all the waiters grab a nations standard from different countries for the "waiving of the flag." Being the new kid on the block, I get to hold the American flag, and continue to stand waiving for another five minutes while Spats sings, "It's a Grand Old Flag." The other waiters put away what flag they were holding, and hit the crowd hustling drinks leaving me behind. By the time I'm finished waiving the flag, the drinks have been sold and the tips gotten, leaving me scrounging for a customer.

This is not a money-making situation, and if it weren't for the wonderful good time atmosphere and free beer for waiters, I think I would leave. The alternative at the moment, however, is to collect unemployment and mow the lawn in the backyard. My situation is about to improve, however, as Walt Disney World opens near Orlando and advertises for part-time Christmas parade personnel – whereby I say "good-by" to Rosie O'Grady and "hello" to Mickey Mouse.

The Magic Kingdom is organizing the Christmas parade and is looking for parade personnel and float drivers. After being interviewed by Dell, the parade producer, he offers me a job – driver of the Santa Claus float, which consists of an old Buick that has been covered over with a shell, upon which a sleigh is mounted, and decorated with fake snow and Christmas presents. Not only do I drive Santa, but I become Santa's helper, both during and after the parades. The jolly old fellow is portrayed by Eddie, an actor from Wales, in his early fifties who has come to Disney to portray Ben Franklin and to work in conjunction with the fife and drum corps in Liberty Square. He not only looks like Basel Rathbone of Sherlock Holmes fame, but he talks like him also. In keeping with the old British theatre tradition of keeping whiskey in the dressing trunk, Eddie continues that noble custom, but with a new twist.

In a little red pouch that Santa wears around his neck during the parades, he keeps miniature bottles of whiskey. As the parade lines up backstage, and we all wait patiently to go out onstage in Town Square, Eddie sits in his sleigh while I, the driver, sit unseen underneath in the pilot's seat. The floats are lined up for the Christmas parade each day, reminding me of B-17 bombers in England all lined up for take off for a raid over Germany. With cunning and dexterity, Eddie palms a miniature bottle into a handkerchief then feigns a sneeze, after which he brings the handkerchief up to his nose, takes a swig, then stealthily maneuvers the bottle back into the pouch with no one the wiser. I am aware of the situation since Eddie sends Santa's helper (myself) to the liquor store to buy his miniatures. During the parade, part of Santa's job is to "Ho! Ho! Ho!" on a microphone clipped onto his collar. Occasionally, Ed is too drunk to perform the jovial ejaculations properly so he hands me the microphone – as I drive, I'm doing the "Ho-Ho's" from below while he animates in synch above. Amazingly, no one ever catches on to the ruse, even though Eddie's inebriation is known, tolerated and even joked about. On one occasion while preparing for a parade, Eddie falls out of the sleigh, braking a rib, and has to be replaced for the day with a standby Santa. Thereafter, with his chest all strapped up and now wearing a required seat belt, he is able to make all the parades with, of course, the traditional painkiller in his pouch along with his ever-ready handkerchief. Although Eddie is the worst of the lot, other party animals abound in the Magic Kingdom – mostly members of the Fife and Drum corps, some Main Street musicians, and a few Disney character portrayers. Post-Christmas parade parties abound in a clandestine, unfinished room called "the den," located over Adventure Land, accessed by a trip over the rooftops of Frontier Land.

Stephanie (Snow White) is a pretty girl in her early twenties from Jacksonville who is having an affair with Main Street trumpet player Buzz who has a wife and kids at home. The wife occasionally comes to the Magic Kingdom, looking to confront the "other woman." Whenever she is sighted in the park, the alarm is passed to Stephanie who disappears through one of the many entrances, into the labyrinth of tunnels beneath the Magic Kingdom where the operational working areas are located. Although not exactly an alcoholic like Eddie, Stephanie has a bad habit of drinking gin and smoking marijuana.

Between parades I have nothing to do but explore the park and explore I do. The tunnel complex below the park contains numerous stairs leading to mysterious places where cast members can leave their working area, walk to wardrobe or the cafeteria or go home, without being seen by visitors in the park above. Like a little boy again in South Boston, I have an urge to know where each door is that leads into the tunnel and where it comes out. Not only that, but I need to swim in each swimming pool on the property and try the food in every restaurant. The two daily Christmas parades become routine except for the times when the Santa float is traveling so slow that the Buick engine loads up with carbon and quits – sometimes requiring a tow. Soon the New Year arrives, and the wonderful Disney Christmas parade comes to an end, and so does my float-driving job. It is now January 1974 and I have many things to do yet before we hit the road again in the spring.

Long after I'm gone, the den of iniquity is discovered by Disney management, and a notorious Disney house cleaning ensues. Eddie, Stephanie[47] and Buzz survive the purge and continue their entertainment roles, but not for long. Eddie goes from playing Santa Claus to portraying "The Old Prospector" – a gold mining character of the Old West who strolls round Fort Wilderness and interacts with the guests. The Old Prospector, however, appears to stagger rather than stroll, and while still in character, moseys into the Disney Village and bellys up to the bar for a swig of moonshine. Disney management is informed and gives the Old Prospector till sundown to get out of town. Eddie[48] is forced into retirement.

*

The Veterans Administration offers to pay my tuition for a flight instructor rating for which I enthusiastically sign up for at Herndon Airport in Orlando. Thereafter, I spend a lot of time and effort to become a flight instructor – my goal being like that of every pilot, to teach, therefore to fly for free. To become a flight instructor is a personal goal that must be fulfilled. However, on a practical note, there are more flight instructors than there are students, and an instructor without students must continuously hone his skill at his own expense while waiting for a student (paying customer) to come along. Although I attain the license, I find that there are no schools that need new instructors – as there isn't enough business to support the ones already employed. Having a flight instructor license, I discover, is like having a real estate license – everybody has one and nobody is making any money. Nevertheless, I continue to toy with the notion of someday having a career in aviation, until one day I get a call from a agent in Miami, who has a month engagement for me at a casino in Paramaribo, Surinam.

My thoughts suddenly turn away from aviation and towards a new adventure in the jungles of South America. Visions of Fred Astair and *Flying Down to Rio* fill my mind as I pack my wardrobe and props, and prepare for a new fantasy adventure. Unfortunately, the casino will only pay the airfare for myself and not my assistant, so Camille agrees to stay home while I brave a brand new world of tropical splendor and jungle paradise – *well, somebody has to do it!* Camille, like war brides before, will stay behind to maintain the home front while the Great Boston, world renown explorer, departs on another expedition to deepest, darkest Surinam, formally known as Dutch Guiana, sandwiched in between British and French Guiana – famous for the infamous prison, Devil's Island.

After kissing Camille and Eoin goodby, I drive my truck to Miami where I park it at the compound of friends Dave and Lois Hoover where they keep their lions and tigers. Dave, of course, carries on the fighting-style wild animal act that made Clyde Beatty famous. Lois drops me off at the airport, after which she drives my truck to her place, and I fly to Surinam on an island hopper that seems to stop at every island between Miami and Paramaribo. After each departure, the stewardesses proceed to feed everybody on the flight, and I manage to down a steak after each island visit. By the time we reach Paramaribo, I'm so stuffed that I never want to eat again – or so it seems at the moment. The airplane lands on nothing more than a strip cut into the jungle, and waiting for me is a car from the casino and a swarm of children who all want to carry my bags. The casino chauffeur meets me, shoos away the children, then proceeds to drive me into town on a dirt road.

Driving through the jungle is fascinating and beautiful, but I don't see any splendor. As we arrive in town, I notice that all the homes are built from wood, have quaint window shutters and are painted in bright colors. On the dirt streets of the town, I see hordes of black people riding bicycles or mopeds with a few cars and trucks, all traveling on the left side of the road like in Ireland. Along the sidewalks and back alleys, homeless dogs roam unmolested and ignored.

The country, being located near the equator, stagnates in perpetual humidity. On this part of the earth's surface, the air from the northern and southern hemispheres converge, and causes the air to rise, thus producing a condition of stagnant, super-humid air. Not a breath of wind blows, and the air feels so thick from humidity that one experiences a perpetual sweat, even when standing still – much like being incased inside a glass dome with no ventilation. There is neither air conditioning nor television, certainly not the paradise that I had envisioned during the flight. The locals seem to be well adapted to the tropical environment, but not I. Paramaribo, the capitol of Surinam, is quaint, but primitive, and can be walked from one end to the other in an hour. The jungle begins at the far side of the farmers market at the edge of town where mostly women come in their native costumes to trade and barter their wares. On the other end of town is the ocean with no beach; from there, the town begins with a large tree-lined park between two casinos. This is considered the upper-class area since there is an art museum there, and the residence of the Governor General (Viceroy) of Holland – the mother country.

The local residents, like in Mexico, close up the town in the middle of the day for a siesta, then reopen the shops again in the late afternoon. Most people speak English or the local language, which is a Talkee-Talkee-hodge-podge of Dutch and English with some African words from whatever dialect was spoken by Africans during the years of slavery. The population is a mixture of races from former Dutch colonies in Indonesia, and India, including descendants of former African slaves, some of whom escaped from slavery to live in the jungle in the old lifestyle that they knew in Africa – still residing there today.

South American Indians native to the area populate the interior of the country, still living in small thatched-roof villages as do their countrymen of African origin. There are very few white, Dutch-speaking residents of the country who work for the government in administering the country. Poor people live in a section of town that reeks of urine – not because they piss all over the place, but they can only afford the cheapest wood to build their homes, which happens to come from a tree they call pissy haut,[49] a carnivorous tree that emits a foul odor to attract and catch insects, which it devours. Although I find the smell revolting, the locals don't seem to mind living with it.

The casino where I am to perform reminds me of an old wooden hotel of Atlantic City vintage, once the top of the line during the age of Abe Lincoln, but now old and decrepit. Although ancient by American standards, it still maintains an ancient charm, reminiscent of a Hollywood rendition of gambling casinos in far-away, exotic places. The hotel/casino gives me free room and board plus a salary, so I plan to take the engagement in stride, and enjoy a new fantasy situation. Without my noble assistant, I'll have to draft a waiter to take her place; but being at the edge of the known civilized world, I don't think the audience will know that Camille isn't here. Other performers on the show come from strange far-away places, except for Carol, an American lounge singer from Dothan, Alabama, who unknown to me, happened to be on the same flight from Miami. The others entertainers include: a black couple from Jamaica who play piano and do a calypso-style song and dance routine, a one-armed artist from Belen, Brazil, who draws cartoons on a tripod as an act, and last of all a chorus of local children, dressed in their native dress who sing Surinam folk songs in Dutch. The show is backed by twenty black musicians, including four drummers playing different rhythm instruments, which suggest the sounds of the jungle.

The audience is a strange lot of characters: mostly men, people that one might expect to see in Calcutta, Istanbul, or Casablanca.

Smoke from cigars and cigarettes permeates the air, sending artistic streams of white, wispy contrails into the moisture laden air circulated by ceiling fans, which blend humid air and smoke into a great London fog with the density of Jell-O. They seem starved for entertainment and applaud enthusiastically after every trick. Other patrons gamble in the casino while the show is on or settle in at the lounge bar where several nice looking black girls guzzle drinks, listen to small talk from men, and provide special room service to those so inclined.

There isn't a lot to do in Paramaribo during the day, other than a couple of movie houses and the soccer game on Sunday, which the whole town attends, filling the stadium. Like crows filling the trees, those who fail to get in, sit and watch the game from the branches over looking the stadium. There is a more upscale casino/hotel in town – about the caliber of a Quality Eight Motel, with a swimming pool where I enjoy spending the day swimming, sipping rum and studying the Dutch language.

The people are friendly enough to the point of inviting me into their homes as they see me strolling around town. Naturally, I oblige just to satisfy my curiosity, and to sample the local cuisine. Just being an American and a performer at the casino makes me a celebrity of sorts, and I enjoy the attention and signing autographs; however, I am beginning to feel like I'm marooned on a jungle island and I count the days when I can return to civilization as I know it. We do one show a night and the days seem to drag on and on. Thoughts of escaping prisoners from Devil's Island not too far away drift into my mind as I await the day when my contract is up, and Carol from Dothan and I fly away to Miami. The place really is not all that bad, but not the tropical paradise that I had imagined; besides, there are things that I could be doing at home, and I miss my wife and son. My day of atonement arrives and I fly to Miami to be met by Lois, driving my yellow truck.

Chapter XII
More Joys of the Road

Camille and Eoin have been staying with Mom and Dad for several weeks since my departure to South America and nerves are wearing thin. Mom with her constant chitchat, and Dad, fighting the demons of depression from his irregular working lifestyle, continue to harass each other. Dad has been playing the hotels around Orlando for many years. The hotel industry, however, is a bumpy ride for musicians.

Whenever a hotel suffers a slowdown in business, the band is the first to get laid off – that's when Dad resorts to his cynical, grumpy-old-man mode, bemoaning the plight of the music industry and himself.

Yet, when he does return to work, he and the other musicians complain about working too hard, and not making enough money. Forgetting about when they were unemployed, the band schemes to work less, and demand more until they find themselves out on the street between gigs again. Mom, on the other hand, has found a new profession. She is now a care giver – tending the needs of a retired, elderly Colonel in Winter Park; thus the stability of the household is maintained now that Mom is again a career woman. Mom has found the perfect job, which entails talking to a captive audience – an old man, near death, who can't hide. The Colonel, however, is in such a state that he enjoys the constant sound of a voice.

Eoin is now three years old, and trooper that he is, eager to travel again – or as he puts it, "Let's go to the next town." Camille and I both are also eager to get on the road. Subsequently, our efforts turn to preparing for travel and a new adventure with a new show – The Royal Hanneford Circus – with whom we are to open the season at the field house on the campus of the University of Mississippi, "Ole Miss."

(The Hanneford Circus goes back to 1690, when Irishman Michael Hanneford toured the British Isles with Wombwell's Menagerie, the first show of its kind in that country. Succeeding generations carried on the circus tradition of showing under a tent and traveling the length and breadth of the British Isles with horse-drawn wagons. Then in 1916, John Ringling, of the Ringling Brothers Circus, invited the Hanneford family to perform in North America, and the family has been here ever since. Tommy, with German-born wife Stuppi, are the present owner and custodian of the Hanneford circus legend.)

Bandmaster Jimmy Ille, trumpet player non-pareil (without equal), is married to Tommy's sister Kay.[50] After Ringling bandmaster Merle Evans retired, Jimmy left his job at Circus-Circus in Las Vegas to conduct the Ringling band. During the Ringling winter dates in Florida, Jimmy would hire temporary and available musicians, including Chuck from Clyde Beatty Circus, to sit in and play the Florida engagements. Both bandmasters, having a reputation as drinkers, would have a contest between shows as to who could drink the most, and still function on the bandstand – Chuck's game being to get Jimmy to pass out so that he could save the day, and conduct the Ringling band himself. Jimmy endures nevertheless, and the show goes on with a disappointed Chuck who is resigned to always being a sideman, and never conductor of the Ringling band. Jimmy's tenure doesn't last long and he departs after being punched out by irritate general manager Tuffy, over Jimmy flirting with Tuffy's girlfriend Vicky.

Jimmy[51] tells me that he left the Ringling show because it was like being in the army, and he hated the Army. Tommy, of course, is the star of the show, as he mimics the "Riding Fool," an act made famous by his uncle, Poodles Hanneford. Struppi performs in the steel arena with her tigers as the "Queen of the Jungle Cats," while Tommy's mother, Katharine, still performing in her eighties, reigns supreme as "Queen of the Circus." Performing on the aerial web, and with Tommy's elephants, are Karin and husband Larry. Karin is from an Italian circus family that came to America many years ago to work on the Ringling show. Larry[52] had worked with me years ago at the Circus Hall of Fame when he was married to wire walker, Carmen.

Most Shrine circus producers advertise a three-ring circus, but the audience never sees performers in all three rings simultaneously. Tommy is the exception to this norm by having several three-ring displays in the show. Most of the performers are people that I know from having worked with on other shows. Coming together again is like a family reunion of sorts, many of whom we are glad to see again, and others less so. Rather than the succession of ice hockey arenas that we performed in while working for "Uncle"

Howard, Tommy books most of his shows in college gymnasiums. College campuses have more facilities and are generally more comfortable for both the circus and the audience.

Although we put on a terrific show, the jumps between dates, some being measured in days rather than hours, are back breakers. We spend more time in the truck going down the road than we do in buildings doing a show. In addition to that, our ever-growing collection of wardrobe, plus summer and winter clothing, is stuffed in every imaginable cubbyhole in the chicken coop, causing me to create empty space in the most imaginable places. On long jumps, Eoin sleeps in a bed made in an extension of the camper over the truck. A sliding glass window separates his entry into the extension from the cab, so every so often, Eoin will pop into the cab and ask, "Is this the next town?"

The show has an opening spec, with ponies pulling small floats designed after fairy tale characters. Eoin, dressed as a toy soldier, gets to ride a float along with the other kids on the show, all of whom are dressed in various Mother Goose costumes. He is in four-year-old heaven, especially after Struppi pays him in person, his salary of fifty cents a week. After a while, Eoin asks if he can have his own pony to ride in spec. When asked, "Where could we possibly keep a pony?" He responds innocently, "In the truck, of course." From then on we have a family joke that whenever we want to know where to store something, we exclaim that we can always put it in the truck with the pony. Eoin, who now sees the humor in it, likes to tease us by occasionally asking for the most outrageous things, which he intends to keep in the truck with the pony. He is well adapted to the road; but then he knows nothing else.

The show is booked at George Hammid's Steel Pier in Atlantic City, New Jersey, and I look forward to it with glee. The Steel Pier, once the Mecca of show business, is where everybody who was anybody once appeared and performed. The Pier, like the rest of Atlantic City, is now a shadow of its former self.

The glory years during the early nineteen hundreds when it was America's favorite summer vacation spot, are now faded and gone. The performance is set up at the far end of the pier where a grand stand is erected for an audience. Between the performing area and the grandstand is a gaping hole in the pier. This was once use during Olympic-style high-diving shows of former times.

The thought of performing on the same spot where Bandmaster John Philip Sousa gave his last concert is inspiring. We perform four times a day, along with the famous diving horse that follows the circus performance with a dive into a large tub of water. Mrs. Sonora Carver, the original diving lady, is with us every day, but now leaves the diving to her niece. She entertains us with stories of the good old days at the pier.

Adjacent to the horse tub are our dressing rooms, where within I notice a sign on the wall, warning performers to close their dressing room door during the horse dive. As the horse makes his dive each show, we soon learn to comply as a deluge of water splashes out of the tub, engulfing the dressing rooms. Even walking to the dressing rooms is an adventure of sorts as we have to navigate rickety old scaffolding and gang planks – protruding on the outside of buildings, and suspended over the ocean.

Between shows we enjoy the old-time entertainment of the boardwalk, offering traditional sideshows seen in carnivals and circuses of the past. Our most fun is eating fresh roasted peanuts while watching a Marx Brothers movie in a boardwalk theater across from the pier – something Mom told me that she had done when she was a young girl when she and her young sisters visited the Pier with Mimmay. I find it ironic that I am performing on the spot where my grandmother once enjoyed the music of John Phillip Sousa.

As the non-stop and never-ending circus season continues, we begin to notice that the days are getting shorter as fall approaches. The turning of the leaves and slight chill in the air reminds the circus folk that the season is winding down, and we can soon go home and rest. It is this time of year that we usually find ourselves in New Orleans for the Shrine Circus at a familiar building where I once took Olive to the Mardi Gras Ball. Although those day are long gone and almost forgotten, I still feel uneasy about whether Olive might show up at the circus and recognize me. Although not the only girl to have caught me with my pants down, I nevertheless feel nervous about a chance meeting; fortunately, she never shows up and I am relieved. Explaining a woman in one's former life to one's wife can be awkward – therefore, something to be avoided.

Camille and I have a quest: that is to eat in a different restaurant each time we visit the city, so that some day we can say that we ate in every restaurant in New Orleans – not exactly like the urge to climb Mount Everest because it is there – but an awe-inspiring goal and noble endeavor none the less. After adding another restaurant to our list of conquests, it is time to move on. The Hanneford Shrine circus tour soon comes to a close and it is time to jump over to other Shrine Circus dates for other circus producers in Texas, called in the industry as "The Texas Dates."

The Shrine Temples of Dallas, Ft. Worth, Austin, and Houston cooperate with each other by hiring one circus producer who assembles one show, which appears at each city in sequence. For a performer booked on the tour, it means a long tour of dates with a first class show of major proportions. The opening date is in Dallas at the State Fair Grounds where the giant statue of "Big Tex" stands at the main entrance waiting to greet us. It has been many years since I enjoyed playing a concert with the Naval Training Command Band here during the Texas State Fair. Now I'm back again, this time with my family of traveling troubadours where I am to perform in the center ring with the wire display.

Our second act (juggling and riding unicycles) has now expanded to include Eoin who rides on my shoulders for a finish trick. Children of performers are usually introduced to the audience at a young age in order to teach them the fine art of entertaining, also to get used to working in front of an audience, and to numerically enhance the act. Other performers like to tease acts with kids, about using their brats to get applause just to salvage an otherwise mundane act; but then we all do it, and of course the kids discover the joys of approval and applause for their efforts – as minimal as they may be. Playing circus by actually performing in one is a childhood treat, and Eoin takes to it like an elephant takes to water. With all the acts on the show who have children, Eoin has many playmates, and also competitors, since the kids love to try to outdo each other during a performance.

The performers' dressing room in the arena is a busy place, not only a place to get dressed for the show, but also a social club for the men and a gossiping klatch for the women – not that the men don't gossip too, and not that I know what goes on in the women's dressing room – never having dressed there before. Camille and I apply our former N.S.A. skills to gather intelligence around the show. When Eoin brings a circus chum in the trailer to play, we slyly interrogate the kid to find out what he knows from his parents. A dish of ice cream can extort a wealth of information. With the adults, two cans of beer will do the trick.

Another ploy we like to use is to state an already known fact then wait for the person to fill in the details. If they know something, they do, and if they don't, then they don't. Keeping one's ear to the circus grapevine and occasionally stirring the pot is the best entertainment on any show.

Of the many clowns that I know from previous circus encounters, with us on the Texas Dates are Gene Randow (tramp clown) and Ernie Burch "Blinko" (white face clown). The two buffoons together make a formidable comedy team in the ring, and backstage as well. In the men's dressing room, the two clowns proceed to pull their favorite backstage gag on unsuspecting performers – that of initiating a mock argument about nothing of consequence, drawing in others who are listening while they apply their makeup and change into their costumes. The two clowns then agitate and inflame the others in the room until an argument develops among the group. As the argument heats up, the two clowns feed the unwitting participants with retorts and contra opinions to stoke the fire of controversy. Soon a full-fledged war of words ensues as the dressing room is engulfed in turmoil. The two masters of mirth then do a quick disappearing act, leaving those in the dressing room to riot among themselves while the buffoons exit – laughing. Another clown coup is accomplished on the unwitting and naïve by two jovial jesters who have turned a tranquil backstage environment into a battleground of discontent. Stirring up a hornets' nest is what clowns like to do, and these two jovial jesters are good at it.

The show's producer, "Bad" Bob, not only directs the show, but controls the lights as well. From his vantage point at the lighting board, he signals a performer to hurry up by blinking the lights of that ring – something that performers find annoying. Bad Bob, however, doesn't mind annoying performers. The prop men who set up and work the show are performers who double in both capacities. Tipping the prop boys is a tradition in the circus, and if a performer doesn't give enough, soon Bad Bob is knocking on the trailer door demanding more – *how rude!* Although we all complain, we are all getting top dollar thanks to him, and he does book us an additional shopping mall date in between Shrine Circuses. Mall dates are fun since we can always see a movie and Camille loves to shop. Free performances at Shrine sponsored children's hospitals are expected during the engagement, and are given without reservation by the performers.

On the Texas Dates, we find ourselves with many old friends, and both old and new playmates for Eoin. Clara, Eoin's playmate from Uncle Howard's show, and older sister Rita are with us again, along with Mama Tina and Papa Louis of the Argentinos. Watching the kids grow up on the circus is an interesting phenomenon. Nothing seems to change until the kids and parents retire for the winter then reappear for a new circus season. Suddenly the kids have noticeably grown, and the parents are reminded that we too are growing older. Little Rita[53] is now changing into a woman and noticeably so. Performing in the circus is now becoming just a job, and we think about the things that ordinary townspeople think about as we walk into the ring with the spotlights shining and the band playing – just Mommy and Daddy going to work.

"What do you want for supper," says Camille smiling, as I mount the wire to begin my act. "Oh, I don't know," say I as she hands me my devil sticks and I begin to juggle. "Spaghetti sounds good," I say as I smile and bow to the audience. "We are low on propane gas," says she as she takes the sticks and hands me a saucer, which I then put on my foot and kick up to balance on my head. "Don't miss, we are running behind the other acts in the display. Hurry up!" says she as she hands me a cup to be kicked up and balanced on top of the saucer. "Better hurry or Bob will be blinking the lights," says she as I continue kicking up and balancing cups and saucers on my head. The tea pot lands on the stack of teacups and saucers, followed in the pot by a spoon and a lump of sugar. The audience applauds in approval as we finish the routine and bow with all the others in the display. As we exit the arena in the limelight, Camille repeats, "I'm tired of spaghetti – let's have something else."

"Fine!" say I as we prepare for the grand finale with the entire cast taking a bow. Thereafter, Mommy, Daddy and Eoin return to the Chicken Coop, home from work, another day in the lives of a circus family. Smoked chicken and ribs on the barbecue will be the entrée for the evening, followed by a shot of whiskey and a cigar, consumed to the sounds of elephants, lions, tigers and horses while Eoin plays circus with the kids – *life is good!*

The Dallas engagement is followed by Austin, Fort Worth, Houston and San Antonio, after which the whole show lays off for a week at the Kamp Ground of America in San Antonio, which offers special rates for elephants and bears. It is the end of October and Halloween. Eoin, along with all the other circus kids, dresses up and proceed to visit the trailer of everyone in the park – knocking on doors, asking for a treat.

Throughout the trailer park, a gaggle of geese follows the children as they make their rounds, gathering sweets from the campers. Later, they watch Halloween movies and cartoons, presented especially for the occasion, and shown on an outdoor screen. The air smells sweet, and while dozens of campfires glow, the sound of guitar music drifts through the air along with the occasional whiff of pipe smoke. The Halloween heavens are classic – a full clear full Texas moon on a black sky filled with glittering stars.

Another circus season has come and gone, and the gypsy lifestyle of constant travel now wanes. We prepare to disband soon as each of us goes our own way to our own destiny. Without realizing it, Eoin has seen more in four years than many people get to see in their lifetime. Eoin has known only the joy of the road, except for the short periods at home with Mom and Dad in Florida, and the short visits on the farm in eastern Ohio with Camille's Nona and Grandpa.

*

We are booked on the Puck Canadian Circus at the CNE in Toronto, sponsored by a Canadian cola company. Besides our acts, I am slated to portray Captain Cola, fighter of crime and thirst. Dressed in my hero attire, complete with mask and cape, I make my entrance like Tarzan of the Apes – swinging into the ring on a rope tied to a tree. The date is a fun job, and we enjoy working for Frazer and Little Mark (a dwarf). In order to promote the date, Frazer concocts a scheme to "audition" talented chickens to join the circus. He buys a flock of chickens and places an add in the newspaper announcing the pageant. Not expecting any candidates to show up, we are surprised when on the day of the fowl frolic, one girl shows up with a chicken that bathes herself. A large and enthusiastic crowd has gathered for the event and watch with amusement as each bird in turn is announced with fanfare, and brought out to strut their stuff.

The audience watches the farce pageant, amused and amazed as the contestants do nothing more than peck, scratch and cluck. Frazer keeps the gag running by reporting to the police the next day that performing chickens were kidnaped from the circus during the night. The press picks up on the story and the residents of Toronto are asked to search for the missing chicks. Frazer then hypes up the caper with a ransom note to the newspaper. The cluckers are eventually found, and gathered up by the police inside the police vehicle compound across the street where Frazer had tossed them the night before. The harried hens are returned to the circus where we all have a good laugh and a delicious barbecue.

*

Thanksgiving Day is coming up, but our off time at home will be short. California circus producer Patty has booked us on her circus traveling to the island of Jamaica. We are looking forward to the date, but there is much to prepare for. We fly out of Miami on a chartered jet with most of the cast on board. Animal people (chimps and elephants) will sail out of Tampa and arrive a day later. Aboard the flight is ringmaster Colonel Lucky from Uncle Howard's show, and an assortment of acrobats, jugglers and clowns – some people I know and some I don't. As we fly along to Jamaica, enjoying the camaraderie of the occasion, the flight becomes a real circus as we party on the way in our chartered jet. Patty has rented rooms for us in private homes in order to beat the much higher prices at the hotels.

Upon arrival, we are delivered to one of these homes where a black Jamaican landlady greets us. Arriving the next day, the ship with the animals and the circus big top and crew enters the harbor and is promptly unloaded and taken to the football grounds where the show is to be set up. Surrounding the big top is a ten-foot-high barbed wire fence, to keep out the gawkers. Each day, a bus makes its rounds picking up performers and delivering us to the lot where we play to full houses every day. At night the bus returns us to our house where reality rears its ugly head when Camille feels compelled to clean the house every day and shop for groceries at the market to prepare meals when we get home. Not only that, there is no hot water, but plenty of roaches. Although I find nothing wrong with the environment, our fantasy circus flight to Jamaica is blemished by the problems of everyday life. Camille is not pleased, and so we leave the house and settle into the high-priced Tororica Hotel, where we eat in the restaurant and sip rum by the swimming pool while a maid makes our beds – Camille is pleased.

Between our two acts, I take on an extra job of snow cone butcher (seat vender). The problem with snow cones is that over time the syrup poured over the ground-up ice oozes to the bottom of the cup, thus appearing to have none at all. I get nothing but complaints from my customers in the all-black audience who want more syrup on their snow cone. Not only that, but I have to suffer the indignity of them calling me "Boy." For some reason, audiences never catch on that the vendor whom they like to argue with is the same person in the ring that they cheer and applaud.

The show is successful, and a good time is had by all, but soon it is time for us to make the return flight to Miami. Assuming that nothing will go wrong, I make the mistake of sending my gear back on the boat with Monkey Joe who somehow makes room for it with his chimps. The boat arrives a week late, causing me a lot of anxiety since we have an engagement coming up soon. On the last day of my tight schedule, the boat finely arrives. We drive to Tampa, load up our rig and props, and drive to our next engagement, the Detroit Shrine Circus, where we arrive in the nick of time, just before the show at the fairgrounds is snowed in. Snow or not, the show must go on and it does.

*

Our New York Agent, Leo Grund, has us booked in Mexico City for a series of television spots during a four-week period. Upon arriving in Mexico City on a flight from Miami, José, who works for our local agent Raul, picks us up at the airport and take us to a hotel, which has been previously booked and awaiting our arrival. Our second trip to Mexico is more relaxed and comfortable since the country is now familiar to us, due to our last prolonged visit with the circus. Camille is still feeling a bit of culture shock, and of course, Eoin is always right at home wherever he is and taking in everything. My Spanish is now better than just being able to read the menu, and talk to a waiter; now I can engage in Spanish chitchat with just about anybody walking on the street. As I learned in Germany and France, speaking the language of the natives removes social barriers, and allows freedom of movement in a foreign environment.

If I show an interest in one's language, the people take an interest in me and go out of their way to be helpful. Furthermore, I find that a greeting or two in Chinese, in a Chinese restaurant in any country, will result in an extra egg roll – oh, the power of language!

After settling in at the hotel and enjoying a night out on the town, we arise the next morning to be met by José in the limo who proceeds to take us to the television studio for a rehearsal of the show Siempre En Domingo (always on Sunday.) We arrive at the studio, and witness an interesting phenomenon – many young people waiting at the studio entrance for celebrities to arrive so that they can take photographs and get an autograph. Sighting our limo approaching instills excitement in the crowd as if they are expecting a superstar. We emerge from the limo to the flash of cameras, and a group of young Mexicans begging for autographs – thinking that we must be celebrities, yet don't know who we are. Not wanting to spoil their illusion, we smile, wave, sign autographs and play the game. I am amazed at how a simple staged exit from a limo into a television studio can draw a crowd and provoke a public reaction. Even though we wonder how naïve people can be, we enjoy the attention never the less. After entering the building and checking in, we are assigned a dressing room – later, we rehearse with the band, and await the time for our performance.

While warming up backstage, along comes movie star Bob Cummings who thinks that I am someone that he once worked with in Las Vegas many years ago. Actually, the cup and saucer routine that I am practicing was copied from fellow performer and friend Dieter Tasso with whom Bob had worked with before. He apparently remembers the act, but not the person doing it. Not wanting to blow the gag, we engage in a long converalion with me pretending that I am Dieter, and Bob thinking that I am. Fortunately, I know Dieter[54] well enough to keep up the deception, which I find thoroughly amusing.

As the show unfolds, I notice that people in the audience are merely casual observers, eating their lunch, smoking, playing cards, knitting, writing letters and chatting among themselves. When a joke is told, the audience sits stone cold, while a laugh machine erupts with the required amount of levity. After a great trick, the applause machine takes over to sell the artistic endeavor. Even though I know that millions of Mexicans are watching, the detached audience sits there impassively, like a morbidly curious crowd, gathering around a car accident, staring at me as I perform in a room filled with empty people.

After our performance, the limo drives us back to the hotel where a surprise awaits. Agent Raul has found a cheaper hotel for us to stay at and we have to abruptly pack up and move to another part of town, and another hotel. Although we find this a bit awkward, we comply without complaining since Raul is paying the bill. After a few days, Raul calls again to ask us to move to yet another hotel that is even cheaper. During our stay in Mexico City where we perform on four consecutive Sundays, Raul has us hotel hopping every couple of days until finally Camille has had enough, and refuses to move again.

During our off time, we have more important things to do: visiting the German restaurant Fritz across the street from the Black Hole of Calcutta where I have the privilege of seeing my picture on the wall along with other artists who have performed at the Arena de Mexico. No one in the restaurant is impressed that my photo is on the wall, and again as before, I still have to pay the bill.

We walk around town and revisit the cathedrals, the museums and the zoo – all the sights which Eoin was too young to appreciate on our previous visit. On this occasion, nobody offers to buy Eoin from us. Now that he is five, perhaps he is too old – I guess we will just have to keep him. The television shows are a wrap. The limo picks us up at the hotel for the last time, and deposits us at the airport for a return flight to Miami.

We pick up our truck again at lion trainer Dave Hoover's compound

TERENCE O'BRIEN

where we always deposit our vehicle prior to a departure flight from Miami, and drive to Fort Lauderdale where a passenger ship awaits to take us and a group of other show people to an engagement at The Grand Bahamian Resort on the Bahaman Islands. The hotel gives us celebrity treatment by sending an ocean going yacht to pick up the whole show, transports us to the island and gives us a free room at that. The voyage takes a few hours, but the Gulf Stream in the Atlantic flow is calm and serene so no one becomes seasick. Actually, the only bad part of the engagement is that there is no fresh water on the island, necessitating tolerable, but not enjoyable, saltwater baths and showers. Eoin, of course, doesn't care whether a bath is salt water or fresh. He frolics in the swimming pool like an elephant in water. That night, we perform one show for a business convention and the next day sail back to the mainland where we pick up our truck and proceed to our winter home in Orlando with Mom and Dad. By this time, we have saved up enough money to put a down payment on a home of our own, and intend to scout various Florida locations for our future residence and dream home.

Chapter XIII
Mouse Adventures and Then Some

It has been an interesting and fun season and now with Christmas approaching I am looking forward to doing my annual Christmas job of driving Santa Claus in the Christmas parade at Walt Disney World.

However, my impending Disney experience takes on an unexpected and welcome new twist. Disney has revived the classic movie *Dumbo*, and in conjunction with that, a Dumbo's Circus unit will now occupy part of the Christmas parade in the Magic Kingdom with live circus acts performing on floats.

Rather than drive a float, I audition my act, and am hired along with Camille and Eoin to perform in the parade. A circus float, driven by batteries and operated by a hidden driver, is especially outfitted to accommodate my slack wire rig with me balancing on it, plus my lovely assistant, Camille. Other floats have other type performers on top: trapeze, performing seals, dogs, jugglers and acrobats. Eoin at 5 years old, the youngest performer in the parade, will ride around the float on his six foot high unicycle.

Many of the performers are old friends that we have trooped with on shows in the past. All this, plus the Disney characters from the cartoon make up the Dumbo section of the Disney Christmas parade of 1978, and what a parade it is. Unfortunately, being in the parade means that we can never get to see it, but to perform at Walt Disney World is the highlight of our show business career thus far. Those of us who are professional circus performers are privileged to park our house trailers on the property at the production center, behind the Pirates of the Caribbean attraction. Living in the Magic Kingdom is an interesting experience with something going on all the time. Eoin, of course, is in little boy Heaven, being the first person into the park in the morning and the last person out at night.

Because of a choir rehearsal with singer Perry Como, all the parade floats are removed from the shelter of the production center building where they are normally stored between parades. Left exposed to the elements, a thunderstorm descends upon us and drenches the parade floats just before the evening parade.

The time comes and we all proceed to man our floats – like pilots on an aircraft carrier manning their aircraft, ready to be launched on a mission. Neglecting to dry the top of my float, I mount the wire with wet and slippery wire slippers. I would prefer to balance on the wire with dry slippers, but it is too late.

As the parade moves out onto Town Square, the spotlights are on, the music is playing and thousands of people watching and taking photographs. For some unknown reason, the float ahead speeds up and puts some distance between us. At the same time, the float behind us has a problem and slows down so that as we round Town Square and turn on to Main Street, the float ahead has already reached the hub, and my float is all alone on Main Street with all eyes upon me. Now that I am caught up in the excitement of the spectacle, I sway sideways to and fro on the wire. Ordinarily this is not a problem with wet feet, since I have the wire locked in-between my toes. My float driver, knowing that we are lagging behind, rushes to catch up. Just as the float passes the Arribas Bros. Crystal Shop, the float hits the spot where the trolley tracks split from one to two tracks, and gives the float a sudden jolt just as I am at the top of my sideward swing. The wire is suddenly jerked from my foot, and I come crashing down, landing on my side on top of the iron braces of my rigging, breaking a rib in the process – *sonamamitch!*

The audience gasps as I lie there on the float with the wind knocked out of me. Not knowing what to do, nobody approaches the float. Camille, standing not far away, is taken by surprise and asks if I am alright. As I begin to catch my breath and rise from the floor, I feel a sharp pain in my ribs. Then in true show business tradition, I smile, wave to the audience and remount the wire to a burst of sympathy applause, enduring the pain of a cracked rib. The float driver underneath knows nothing of my predicament, and continues right along. Backstage, an ambulance is waiting for the parade to arrive, and takes me to the hospital where a lady doctor straps me up and sends me home.

For the rest of the engagement, I continue the routine as usual, wearing a special medical wrap around my rib cage, and trooper that I am, I never miss a parade. My noble gesture, however, goes unnoticed by Disney parade directors, and nobody ever asks me how I feel nor says, "Thanks for finishing the parade" – h*ow rude!*

Our parades become routine, and by this time Eoin has intimate knowledge of the Magic Kingdom – having spent all his time exploring all the secret exits and entrances to the tunnel, visited every attraction and ridden every ride. Having seen Eoin performing in the parade, Disney employees know who he is, and he is allowed to roam around, unchallenged. He even gets an employee discount on candy that he buys for himself in the shops. At five years old, Eoin is not only a performer in the circus, but a performer in Dumbo's Circus in the Magic Kingdom at Walt Disney World – a stark contrast to when I was five years old, living in South Boston, and roaming around the city in order to entertain myself. I feel enormous pride that I am able to give my son a wonderful childhood experience that I never had. Not knowing anything else, of course, Eoin thinks of it all as just another show in another town. Like all nice things, they soon come to an end, and it is time hitch up the chicken coop and go on down the road. Apparently they must like us, though, since we will be invited back again for the next two seasons.

The Calvert School in Baltimore sends us, along with the lessons for first grade, a manual for parents, describing how and what to teach. Camille and I take turns teaching the first grade, which we find enjoyable, but not Eoin. Like all show kids, he hates to do his Calvert school – requiring us to sometimes be forceful about it. For Eoin there is no escape and no excuses. Being the only one in the class, he cannot goof off without both his teachers (Mom and Dad) knowing about it. Furthermore, he is always the one called on to recite, answer, and respond – you name it, Eoin is the one. Poor boy, not only is he both the worst and the best in the class, he is the class. Besides the pure academics of reading, writing and arithmetic, there are the field trips to zoos, museums, battlefields, cemeteries, caves, ship museums, homes of famous people (dead and alive), theme parks, circuses and fairs all of which appear along the way during our circus odyssey around the country. He studies about Abraham Lincoln, and we take him to visit the log cabin where Abe was born, the house where he lived in Springfield, Illinois, Ford Theater where he was shot and the cemetery where he is buried. He learns about Mark Twain, so we visit his grave in Elmira, N.Y., his home in Hannibal, Missouri, Tom Sawyer's fence and Indian Joe's cave. He learns about the Revolutionary War, so we visit Bunker Hill, Concord Bridge, Paul Revere's house in Massachusetts and the battlefield in Yorktown, Virginia. We tour the homes and tombs of Hellen Keller, as well as that of Roosevelt, Truman, Eisenhower, MacArthur, the Rockefellers, the Vanderbilts, Buffalo Bill and Thomas Edison. Then of course, there is the Alamo, Niagara Falls, Times

Square, and four Bozo the Clown television appearances in Chicago with a side visit to the Chicago Zoo and the Industrial Museum.

The Smithsonian Institute in Washington hires us for an American Folk festival on two occasions where we perform as part of a salute to American vaudeville and the circus. During the weeks we are there, we spend our off time visiting all the exhibits there plus every other museum in town. In the Smithsonian cafeteria there is an exhibit of the old Nickelodeon cafeteria in New York where as a boy my father once took me to eat. I remember quite well putting a dime in the slot, opening up the door, and taking out a piece of pie. I explain it all to Eoin, but he is not impressed. We are hoping that Eoin is absorbing all of these experiences that most children never get. However, Eoin appears to be blasé about everything and does not display the same enthusiasm as his parents. I fail to realize that Eoin doesn't share his parents' passion for things of a historical and educational nature, but then neither did I at that age. By now, Eoin is riding a unicycle in the act and developing into a fine performer, standing head and shoulders over his dad – the head of his class.

*

We open the new season with the All-Star Circus, which plays mostly high school gymnasiums around the country, and is more of a vaudeville show than a circus; although we call ourselves the latter. The word circus sells more tickets than the word vaudeville apparently. In any case we have a band and a circus ring in front of a large curtain, and circus style acts including a baby elephant. As usual in the circus, we find ourselves working with people that we have worked with on other shows: from King Brothers Circus: Heins (leopard trainer and show manager) and his wife Patty (foot juggler); from the Hanniford Circus, Miss Ivy (trapeze), accompanied by her new husband (puma trainer); and from the Texas Shrine dates, Uncle Heavy with wife, Linda, and son, Grumpy (performing pigs), who all live together in a modified school bus. Linda says that the pigs are very clean, and hardly smell at all. Other performers new to us are Popcorn (clown) whose girlfriend/partner Randa presents a dog and chimp act, plus Mike who presents Baby Raja (elephant). What really sells the show, however, is the live band of young musicians who not only play the show, but are obliged to load, unload and set it up as well. The musicians sleep in a converted horse transporter with minimum comfort – thus another irritation and something to complain about. "I'm a musician, not a working man," is the usual lament of the band.

Being adventurous young men, however, they tolerate the physical discomforts and focus on the aesthetic joys of the road, as I once did in Ireland with Duffy Circus.

Show owner Jim and I have an agreement that I will have the concessions, for which I get a percentage of the take. Although it sounds good, it isn't. Since the show plays mostly high school gymnasiums, we never get more than a few hundred people attending a show, and from the gross, I have to pay two high school janitors twenty dollars apiece for the clean up after the show, plus ten for Patty to help us on the stand during intermission. Although I don't tell Camille, Jim also lets me take out twenty for her for assisting me (making popcorn and cotton candy). Camille loves to go shopping and spend money while I lean towards saving for a rainy day. If she knows she has it, she is sure to spend it – *maybe I'll mention it to her later*. Not tipping the janitors for clean up means no concessions allowed in the building, so I am forced to comply, which sometimes is not a money making proposition since my expenses are as much as I take in from the crowd. Always the optimist, I make up a lot of corn and floss in advance, hoping for a good house; but usually, I end up throwing away the unsold floss while keeping the unsold popcorn in plastic bags for the next engagement. The band, which has the unwelcome job of loading up the truck after the show, also causes me additional stress by inevitably leaving some of my concession stock behind in several towns. Being musicians and not "working men," their attention span on the loading job is short and their focus narrow. Not only that, but our wind jammers (circus musicians) consume more peanuts during load out than are sold to the audience during the show.

We have our hands full doing two acts, working concession, teaching school, shopping in town, doing laundry, sewing and cooking while doing one-night stands in school gyms with long jumps in between. Camille and I are totally consumed by our daily and nightly routine. The show not only must go on, but it goes on and on and on. There is something about the mystique of trouping that drives us to exhaustion, and we fail to realize the toll it is taking on our health and our lives – *Jesus, Mary and Joseph!*

In spite of the hardship, the joys of the road outweigh the minor grievances and we manage to put some money in the bank for our Florida dream home some day. One thing that makes us a close, happy family is the fact that we do everything together. We eat, sleep, play, work, travel, and do school all as a team.

The ultimate team players is the family who are all in this together – and so, survive and prosper. Our togetherness will soon increase, as Camille's nausea for coffee again announces that she is pregnant, and a new member of the troupe is on the way.

*

Meanwhile back in Orlando, Dad has been taking an interest in the circus from a musical point of view, ever since I had introduced him to Clyde Beatty bandmaster Chuck. Since then he has been playing Shrine Circus dates for Chuck around the country. With the demise of the big bands, Dad has been struggling to make a living in the Orlando area – playing weddings, and hotel cocktail and dining rooms. Now by being more versatile as a musician, he can continue working steady in another aspect of the business. Having mastered the piano and accordion, Dad is now a master of the organ used on all modern-day circuses. Dad also plays Shrine dates for Keith Killenger,[55] former Ringling bandmaster, succeeding Jimmy Ille who left the Ringling show because of heath reasons only to die conducting a Shrine Circus band during a performance. Dad was not there at the time.

*

While Dad is playing his circus dates, our show finds itself in the Boston area where we begin a scheduled lay off. Rather than spending the time in a state park, we decide to take a trip to Ireland. We contact old pal Walter who is teaching art history at Boston College, and now has five kids who speak English and German. Our master plan is to leave the chicken coop in Walter's backyard in Concord, and fly from Boston to Shannon Airport in Ireland where I intend to give Camille and Eoin a guided tour.

While maintaining his family responsibilities, Walter also has a school teacher girlfriend on the side, and takes me to her apartment to meet her. I feel uncomfortable visiting Walter's other woman, even though I find her pleasant and intelligent. I feel even more uncomfortable when back at Water's house, Regina casually asks me if I have met Walter's girlfriend, and what I think of her. Regina, with her doctorate in chemistry, now teaches school, and controls the purse strings knowing that Walter is on a tight leash, and is in no position to abandon her – an unusual lifestyle situation indeed. Each woman knows about the other and accepts the relationship without making a fuss. While seemingly unperturbed, she doesn't mind teasing Walter about his not-so-discreet liaisons with another schoolteacher. Walter can only smile and squirm as Regina turns up the heat, while I try to act nonchalant. Walter takes us to the airport to board a flight to Ireland and I breathe a sigh of relief to be away from the circus, Walter and the soap opera of life in America.

When I had lived in Ireland, I had always dreamed of returning someday and staying at the best hotels and living high off the hog. Upon arrival, I am surprised to find out that since I have been gone, the economy has undergone a drastic change, and the old prices that I had gotten used to are now history. Even the money has changed to the decimal system with an exchange rate unfavorable to the dollar.

Recalling my stay at a teach leabe agus bricfeasta[56] in Waterford for a half crown (the equivalent of sixty cents), I find that now, the contemporary price is forty dollars. Fancy hotels for us are now out of the question – *Jesus, Mary and Joseph!* Other changes are evident around the country: the horse-drawn vehicles are gone, along with people riding bicycles. The Theatre Royal in Dublin, the Savoy chain of theatres and the Metropole dance hall where I used to take Patricia dancing have all succumbed to the wrecking ball, including Nelson's pillar, which once stood proudly on O'Connell Street only to be blown up by the I.R.A. Like America before, television has come to Ireland, and changed the entertainment industry and the lives of those people making a living in it.

Jack Cruise continues to hang on in the business by putting on shows in the new Abby theatre, but to an ever-dwindling audience. Jack's usual theatrical abode, the Olympia Theatre on Dame Street, is so old that the ceiling came crashing in, forcing Jack to move. After repairs were made and the seats removed, the theatre became a rock and roll bar for the younger set with the audience standing where seats had once been before. Jack informs me that Patricia has moved to London to follow her dream and is singing at the London Palladium, the last of the theatre palaces still operating in the country. Camille, of course, is now foremost on my mind, especially now while touring Ireland while carrying a baby. Because of that, she declines to bend backwards to kiss the Blarney stone. Eoin does, however, and like myself, is bequeathed the gift of eloquence as expounded in Irish legend and lore. Furthermore, I show her and Eoin other significant places: where I lived, went to school, all my favorite pubs and restaurants, and where in each town Duffy circus erected their tent. Camille is underwhelmed, but tolerates my enthusiasm for reliving past experiences (fantasizing) – *by now she is used to it.*

While in Ireland, we are not able to find Duffy Circus; however, the Dublin Zoo, while not a tourist Mecca, is just fine for Eoin and for me too. We visit old friends from the Jack Cruise show, among whom is Pauline Forbes (former tap dancer), now a plump, middle-aged spinster who lives in a flat on Camden Street in Dublin with her mother and ten cats. Having tea with her and her mother in an apartment that reeks with cats is a stimulating experience. Although the apartment is neat and tidy, the feline stench is nauseating, and we can hardly wait to conclude our visit and return to the fresh air of Dublin town. The visit is very entertaining, however, since motor mouth Pauline likes to spread all the gossip in town, and I am an eager listener. We also pick up from her free theatre tickets to a historical drama in Gaelic, and Eoin gets a half crown as a gift – customary in Ireland for a visiting child.

Another character from another age is old friend Seán Mooney, a former well known theatre singer in Dublin, with whom I would drink every night after our Jack Cruise shows. Now, he lives alone, still a bachelor in his seventies in a flat with garbage piled up sky high in every corner. I don't know which is worse, an offence to the nose by an old spinster or an offence to the eye by an old bachelor. Nevertheless, we pick up more Dublin gossip, and drink lots of tea – Eoin gets another half crown. By accident we also run into Jimmy Mahoney, clown on Duffy Circus who had quit the show in mid-season after a dispute with the Duffys – still alive and well in Ireland – now planning to move to Australia to seek bigger and better things. We wish him well and continue along on our sightseeing tour.

Our stay, while satisfying, is too short, but then we have other commitments; and so, Camille, Eoin and I leave Dublin for Shannon Airport where we find ourselves standing in the airline check-in, right behind a Catholic priest. After standing together for a while, we make ourselves known and the good Father turns out to be none other than Father Sullivan, pastor of St. Augustan's church in South Boston, on his way home from a holiday. Like hearing my confession, he listens sympathetically to my tale of woe as a child at the hands of Sister Margaret whom he knows, after which, he replies, "She certainly must have done a good job, because you've grown up to become a fine lad."

*

Our tour with All-Star Circus has not yet resumed; however, we have picked up a short tour of ice hockey arena shows in French Canada from our agent Gaston in Montreal – something that I look forward to with pleasure since I will get to practice my French. The Quebec tour has a new cast of characters and new territory; otherwise, the circus routine remains the same as any other show, but with relatively small jumps between towns. As with other Canadian audiences, the circus going public remains enthusiastic and full houses greet us at every engagement. Performers on this show are more of the club date novelty act type, rather than death defying acts usually seen in a circus. Eoin mixes well with children on the show even though they speak French and he doesn't.

Children who speak different languages on a circus have a way of communicating with each other that can be puzzling to an adult who has to struggle with language barriers. Our tour of French Canada is short and sweet, without the hassle of personality clashes, competitive back stabbing, and everything that goes with the clashing of egos that occurs on shows where many people have to live close together for a long period of time. With that in mind, I look forward with apprehension, as we leave Quebec to rejoin the All- Star show somewhere in upstate New York.

*

The All-Star tour gets under way and the soap opera resumes. Randa, the dog act, splits with Popcorn the clown and teams up with elephant trainer Mike. A despondent Popcorn leaves the show and runs away to another circus. He is replaced by Coco Jr. the clown who arrives with his fiancée and Coco III, his son from a previous marriage. The happy clown couple gets married at a wedding chapel in New Jersey while dressed as clowns and standing on stilts, postponing the honeymoon until the close of the season. There is not a dry eye there, as the two clowns stand together twenty feet high and shifting back and forth to maintain balance and recite their solemn vows. (They divorce a few years later.) Uncle Heavy is not only overweight as his name implies, but also has a skin disease and suffers from stage fright, which causes Heavy to drink like he eats – heavily. Heins and wife Patty are having marital problems ever since Heins hired organist David – having fired trumpet player Bob after a spat about how to conduct the band. Organist David, who favors the alternate lifestyle, introduces Heins to new, erotic experiences. David not only knows how to manipulate the organ, but he knows all the gay bars and baths in the country, and takes Heins on personal guided tours. Heins' new hobby has wife Patty distraught. She leaves the show to return to Florida, and gets a divorce. Uncle Heavy dies in San Antonio – after which wife Linda moves in with Heins after Patty's departure. Patty hears about it and is furious at Linda. The sleeper truck, driven by trumpet player Big Gene, breaks down and needs to be towed. The tow truck, however, is too small for the weight of the sleeper and upon cruising downhill, the heavier truck pushes the lighter tow truck off the road and over a hill. Big Gene isn't a great driver, but then he is a musician not a working man. During a break, Big Gene has an amorous rendezvous with Patty in Florida, and is promptly fired by Heins when he returns to the show. Heins is furious at Patty for playing patty cake behind his back with a horn blower – even if they are divorced. Linda, finding herself in an awkward position between Heins and Dave, and not knowing which way to turn, takes stepson Grumpy and her pigs, and exits the scene later abandoning Grumpy to wallow alone with the pigs, as she runs off with a truck driver.

Somewhere during all these events, Camille leaves the show a few weeks before closing, and gives birth to our second son, Liam. Like Eoin before him at the tender age of one month, Liam, along with his mom, run away to join his dad and his big brother in the circus. The chicken coop now becomes a bit smaller as another passenger is added to the manifest.

The show is performing at the Canadian National Exhibition in Toronto, when upon calling home, Mom informs me that Dad has suffered a stroke while shaving to go to work with the orchestra at Mackinaw Island resort in upper Michigan where he has been employed for the summer. She is in Florida, I am in Toronto, sister Sharon is in Oregon, and Dad is in Michigan. None of us can do anything but hope that the boys in the band in Mackinaw will take care of the situation. The stroke is not fatal, and so his comrades in music put him on a plane for Orlando where Mom is waiting to test her care-giving skills. Dad survives the stroke, but never plays piano again. Unfortunately, he slumps into a state of despair; living out his final years bemoaning what might have been but never came to pass. Worst of all, he is forced to quit smoking and drinking – *Jesus Mary and Joseph.*

We now have our dream house in Kissimmee where we live during the winter off season – actually, the house is not finished yet, causing us to continue living in the trailer parked in our backyard.

Camille is not happy with the procrastination of our builder, and she lets me know it, but there is little I can do. In any case, our off time is short since we continue to work at Walt Disney World in the Christmas parades, and do the occasional Shrine Circus up north for various producers, called in the industry "winter dates." Resting at home is being unemployed while making money is traveling around the country – this is both our lifestyle and our dilemma. Not only do we work constantly, but also, during scheduled layoffs from the All-Star Circus, we have arranged to fill in empty dates by working concessions on the Ringling Circus.

We happen to be in the Washington area when the show closes for a few weeks. Coincidentally, the Ringling Circus is about to begin their Washington engagement. My childhood dream is being fulfilled. I'm about to work on the Greatest Show on Earth – well not exactly as I had envisioned; but selling cotton candy isn't all that bad – somebody has to do it. In any case, we will get free parking plus electricity and water for a week. Relaxing in a state park can be invigorating; but it isn't good for business. Duty to my family takes precedence over pleasure; and so, sell cotton candy I must.

We arrive at the Washington National Guard arena in the middle of the night, and creep quietly in the backyard where we park our trailer next to the performers' trailers, and plug in my cable to the shows electrical gypsy box. Our arrival is suddenly announced by blowing out all the lights on the Ringling show: too many trailers and not enough circuit breakers – the same problem on all traveling shows – *Jesus, Mary and Joseph!* Everyone is now coming out of their trailers to check their lights and asking, "Who are these people?" My face is red and I can only nod and mumble. We are not altogether strangers as our arrival on the show has been prearranged and many people on the show know us. Never the less, as new comers, we want to maintain a low profile and not rattle any nerves.

The next day, we check in with Memo with whom we had the pleasure of working in Mexico on the Atayde Circus when he was part of Bell family bareback riding act. In true circus tradition, after a few days on the show, everyone there knows everything about me. Although we are performers, we have to endure the indignity of being concessionaires, a lower class of people on the circus not exactly like the untouchable cast of India, but a more humble role in the hierarchy of the circus – slightly above a working man and just below a clown. Those on the show who know us are friendly while those who don't, ignore us – *how rude!* We are not there for the spotlight, but for the money, and so we go about our job of selling cotton candy in the seats at each performance. Our efforts pay off. Not only do we sell cotton candy inside the building during the show, but also balloons on the outside after the performance.

The balloon man is an our old friend Helmut from Germany with whom

I had worked club dates in the Washington area while in the Navy. At the time, Helmut did a comedy trampoline act with his wife and daughter. After the marriage of his daughter and the death of his wife, Helmut took to traveling with the circus as an independent balloon hawker, living in his car with his German shepherd dog, Lobo.

Apparently not a tough way to make a living, I soon discover that selling balloons outside after the show is nothing more than standing on the sidewalk, collecting money. Just like in Canada, the rubber goes like hot cakes and soon Eoin is pressed into service to cover an exit. He, too, at the tender age of six, discovers the excitement of exchanging a piece of rubber – no stick and not even blown up – for money. Our father/son balloon team soon becomes a game between us, as to who can rake in the most cash. Eoin now finds that he is making more money than his mom and dad pay him for riding a unicycle in the act. Now that he is aware of money, hopefully, he won't hit his dad up for a raise.

The general of the National Guard Armory likes to give the circus a hard time with his barrage of sanitation regulations. He doesn't allow trailers to discharge their gray water onto the grass – not the sewage from the toilet kept in a separate tank, but water from washing ones hands with soap – all the while tolerating enough tiger, elephant and horse piss to float a ship. We comply never the less, and discharge the water at night when nobody is looking.

Little Liam still doesn't know what to make of all of this.

He began watching his mom and dad and big brother perform in the Christmas parade at Walt Disney World. Not understanding what he was seeing, he began to cry as our parade float passed him and his sitter. As he got used to seeing us perform every day, he came to realize that a show is just something that happens every day, and although he doesn't know why, that is just the way things are. Now, every day on the Ringling Show, he sits under the watchful eye of a sitter, enjoying the circus as mom and dad roam through the seats selling floss. It must be such a strange world for a little boy, and yet it is the only world he knows.

*

With Washington and the Ringling Show behind us, we rejoin the All-Star "soap opera" Circus in Pennsylvania where a new cast of characters débuts and the plot thickens. Randa, with her chimp and dogs, departs the show along with Mike and Baby Raja, but not before the chimp bites Liam on the arm. Camille is angry and upset as the fire rescue team, who happen to be sponsoring the circus, take Liam to the hospital, after which he soon recovers. Everybody in the circus knows that chimps bite, not that they are ferocious, but that is their way of displaying displeasure – like mean little kids who want to get even – such as little Christian, son of Wanda Ward (trapeze artist) on Uncle Howard's Shrine Circus tour who would constantly bite playmate Eoin whenever they had a dispute.

Raul (from Mexico), his dogs and chimps, plus wife Tanya (hair hang) replace Randa. Stony (elephant) and keeper Mike (T) replaces Baby Raja and keeper Mike (R). Trombone player Lee replaces organist David, who is suffering from medical problems,[57] as bandmaster. Dusty the clown arrives, and so does "Magic Joe," Heins' long-time friend and crony along with his wife and son who come on with a reputation of conjuring up unrest and creating tension on shows. Last but not least, Bonny and Billy Earl (ventriloquist) joins us with his dumb cluck, Henrietta Chicken. The big, happy family convenes again and the show gets back on the road while Eoin and Liam have two new playmates, the children of Raul and Tanya, plus little Joe.

The season grinds on and nerves are on edge. It is only a matter of time until Joe's toilet on his trailer leaks. Not only does it leak, but also it smells to high heaven. No one wants to say anything so we all suffer in silence until I can't take any more and bring it to his attention. Joe immediately takes offence. In the meantime, Liam and his playmate little Joe begin to quarrel about childish things. The kids' quarrel intensifies until it spreads to the two mothers and they too become involved. Feathers are ruffled and sparks fly. The mothers go at it like chickens fighting in a pen: cackling, pecking and scratching – *Jesus, Mary and Joseph!* Joe volunteers to leave the show, but Heins negotiates a peace, and tranquility is restored for the time being.

Heins has become infatuated with a pirate-themed wire act, and for some time has been hinting that he would like to have him on the show. Our show is too small for two wire acts; not only that, but Magic Joe and his box jumper[58] wife are taking an unusual interest in my concession business. My senses tell me that something is amiss; but never mind, another break is coming up and I have other things to think about.

The O'Brien family performing at Walt Disney World (1978-1980)

Pal Walter with wife, Regina, and family (1975)

Chapter XIV
Helicopters and Soap Opera

Being a veteran and therefore entitled to V.A. sponsored education, I enroll in helicopter school at Charley Brown Airport in Atlanta. After depositing Camille, the boys and the chicken coop at her family's farm in Ohio, I make my way to the airport and settle into my helicopter training routine – sleeping at night in the truck parked behind the school while flying and attending class during the day.

My helicopter is called an Enstrom, built in Sweden and the instructor is a former medivac pilot, veteran of the Vietnam war. I have never been in a helicopter before, and only have two weeks to achieve a Commercial helicopter add-on to my already acquired ratings. We fly constantly, day and night, as I am determined to get my rating during the short time allotted – the shortest time being three weeks achieved by a former flight instructor at the school.

Coincidentally, the Shrine Circus is playing in Atlanta where I visit on occasion for a diversion, and to take a shower in the men's dressing room, which I am quite familiar with having played the date years before for Uncle Howard. Enjoying the camaraderie of old friends there, I sometimes park my truck there overnight, rather than behind the school at the airport. Strangely enough, I always seem to run into Blinko the Clown in the shower room – just as I did when we worked together on the Texas Shrine Circus dates. Coincidentally, he always appears in the hospital cafeteria across from the circus arena whenever I go to dinner. Circus people know, of course, that a hospital is the cheapest place in town to eat.

While visiting the show in Atlanta, circus fan Lucille, who has known me for years, sees me and I am invited to her home for dinner. Circus performers like nothing more than a free meal, and so I accept. She drives me to her home where I am greeted at the gate by her dog. "Don't worry, he doesn't bite," says she as I reach forward to pet the animal. The dog immediately lunges at my hand and chomps on my thumb. "Well, he never did that before," says an embarrassed Lucille. After an uncomfortable meal with my thumb throbbing, Lucille insists that she take me to a doctor for a shot. Not wanting to offend her, I comply. She later returns me to the arena where I wish I had stayed in the first place. I am reminded of a fan who invited trumpet player Ramon from the Clyde Beatty Circus to take a ride into town. During the trip, the car in which he was riding was involved in an accident, and Ramon returned to the lot in an ambulance and his neck in a collar brace – all for the want of free sustenance.

Back at the flying school, I continue to fly every day with a huge bandage around my thumb, which hurts as I mush on through the course until it is time to check out with an examiner. For some reason, the local examiner has a reputation of flunking the school's helicopter candidates on the pretext that the school teaches students to fly Enstroms, but not helicopters – something that I don't quite understand. The school chooses to play it safe with me and sends me to a friendlier examiner in South Carolina. My instructor and I have a long flight to go, and I am required to fly the bird for the entire journey. With my left hand on the collective, my thumb protruding and throbbing in pain, it seems as if I am holding the bird up in the air by my shear strength alone. As the flight ensues, it becomes apparent that we are lost, but not in any danger, we just don't know where we are. Without the proper instruments for navigation, we have to resort to circling water towers in several towns in order to read the name of the town and thus find it on a map. We arrive outside of some town in South Carolina, and I descend and land at a pre-determined cow pasture where the flight examiner is waiting to give me my check ride – *a walk in the park.*

As other students somehow arrive at the cow pasture to be checked out in the helicopter, I am driven to a local airport to be picked up by the school-owned airplane, and flown back to Atlanta with my license in my pocket and my thumb still throbbing in pain – but not so much as before. I manage to get my license in two weeks, thus breaking the school's record of three. *Give that man a cigar!*

Not being satisfied with that, and still having some government money to spend, we travel to Gettysburg, Pennsylvania, where I enroll in another helicopter course – this time learning the challenging external load capability of a Bell Helicopter. After mastering the Bell, now comes the expertise of picking up telephone poles and kegs of cement, flying around with them and then depositing them on a prescribed spot on the ground. After a week, I acquire the skill and the endorsement. Although proud of my achievement, I never fly a helicopter again and my licenses remain in my wallet to this day – something to sit on. Not only that, but trying to maintain my status in the Naval Reserve while constantly traveling has become a nightmare, and although I do the correspondence courses, I cannot attend the required drills and accumulate the required fifty points a year. Consequently, after being passed over twice for Lieutenant Commander, I receive my discharge papers – sorry, no cigar.

Eoin has never been to public school and now it is time to start Liam on the Calvert school. The thought of teaching two sons while driving down the road is disparaging. The earlier joys of the road are faded and our lifestyle now seems to be turning us into zombie-like creatures. The kids no longer like being cooped up all day in a truck driving down the road; but they accept it only because they don't know anything else nor have a choice. Eoin is an extrovert who loves the spotlight and the applause, while Liam, on the other hand, is shy, afraid of clowns, Santa Clause and the Easter Bunny. He will eventually overcome his fears someday, and perform in the family unicycle act, but that is yet to come. At the moment, he is only four years old.

*

The show plays the armory in Fall River and I brace myself for the onslaught of relatives. For some reason, my arrival in town with the circus creates a family reunion – like a wake or a wedding. Again they come in droves, and sit together like sardines in the chicken coop, glaring at each other with phony smiles while making small talk. Cousin Rickey, son of Mom's sister Anna, arrives with his fourth wife, and volunteers to help me with concessions. While selling popcorn during the come in, Rickey spots his father Ernie with Rickey's daughter Lisa from a previous marriage in hand, and ducks under the concession stand. Rickey later explains that father Ernie has split with Auntie Anna, and taken up residence with Rickey's third wife. Daughter Lisa thinks that Rickey is dead. Rickey further explains that dad Ernie is really Lisa's father not he – *Jesus, Mary and Joseph!* Rickey inserts himself with all the family visitors in the clown chicken coop, which now reaches critical mass, and the trailer automatically erupts, disgorging my dysfunctional family into the building to watch the show. The show goes on and a good time is had by all. All the while, cousin Rickey[59] watches the show from behind the concession stand hoping not to be seen by daughter Lisa who thinks he is dead. Camille and I are glad to have been there for a visit, and are just as glad to leave town, but not before we stop at our favorite all-night diner – The Night Owl – where we have our favorite hot cheese sandwich.

By now the country is in a recession: dates are getting fewer and fewer, the jumps are getting longer and longer (from New Orleans to Omaha for one show, then on to Georgia), the crowds are getting thinner and there are long lines waiting to fill up at gas stations – America has run out of gas.

We have now been on the All-Star Circus for six years and have a nice home in Kissimmee that we only live in a couple of months a year. It has become more and more difficult to close up the house and drive down the road. Each year, we feel as if things will get better, but they only get different.

Camille and I decide that we need a change of routine, and so book our next season with the T.N.T. Circus, a shopping mall show that stays at a mall for a whole week Camille's kind of show. I intend to inform Jim, who is expecting us again on the All-Star show for our seventh season, of our departure; however, due to mall booking problems with T.N.T., our new show delays its opening until late spring, leaving us with too much open time. We opt to open as usual with Jim and, when the time comes, change over to our new show. I am reluctant to tell Heins that I intend to open with the show and then quit in a few months, since he seems to be a bit unstable, and I'm afraid he might have Jim replace me right away, and send me down the road before I'm ready to leave to join T.N.T.

Since Dad had a stroke in Michigan, he is not the same man he use to be. He has lost his lust for life – bitter that he never made it big in music – and sits around all day waiting for the next stroke that will take him to the big band in the sky. One night, after watching an old Frank Sinatra movie on television, a story of a night club piano player who stays up all night drinking and playing music, Dad retires to bed, and during the night has another stroke. The timing couldn't be worse – Camille and I are preparing to open the season with Jim – *how can we leave home now?* We agree that Camille and Liam will stay home with Mom, while Dad is in the hospital. Eoin and I then drive to Georgia and open the show, which is basically the same as before, but now with a new dog act, Janos (Hungarian) replacing Raul who during the off season suffers an unfortunate accident.[60] Eoin substitutes for his mom as my assistant in the wire act, and does a real fine job; however, the unicycle act without Camille is like bourbon without ice. Nevertheless, we perform, and make it through the show to a round of applause – thanks to Eoin who always sells the act –

that's my boy. Magic Joe and his disappearing-reappearing wife avoid me as much as possible; but I catch him ogling my concession stand occasionally, and Heins continues to hint about his favorite wire act coming on the show. I sense a conspiracy afoot; however, I'm not concerned since I am just killing time until the T.N.T. circus opens in a few months' time, and I announce my departure from the show.

Eoin and I are only gone for a few weeks when the word comes that Dad has died. Heins tells me that I should go home, and take care of my family matters, and that Joe will take care of my concession stand while I'm gone. I want to tell Heins that I don't intend to come back; but I can't seem to get him away from his buddy Joe to talk in private – *well, no matter.* I'll call Jim when I get back make my apologies.

Little sister Sharon flies from Oregon to Orlando to help arrange for Dad's funeral. She plans a small service, and then will take the urn of ashes to Oregon where Uncle Bob has arranged for internment in the national cemetery in Portland. We all have mixed feelings about Dad. We are sad that he is gone – and yet, relieved. In the meantime, Jim calls to offer his condolences, and at the same time, beats me to the draw, and fires me before I can quit – *how rude!* Apparently learning of my intended departure, Heins plots with Jim to get rid of me, then give the concessions stand to crony, Joe. By this time, however, due to shrinking dates and small crowds, we are barely able to make a living, and are grateful to be departing for new horizons. However, the show still owes us back pay and travel expenses, which I will never see unless I get back to the show; and there is still a matter of dates to fill until our season with T.N.T. begins.

Fortune shines, as I am able to get some fill-in dates: a week at an American Culture Festival at the Smithsonian Institute in Washington and the television show, *CIRCUS*, in Toronto. Between now and then, I plan to drive to the All-Star show in Moultrie, Georgia, to pick up my money from Heins, then continue on to Atlanta, jump on the Ringling Show and do our regular fill-in concession job.

Unfortunately, in order to catch All-Star in time, we will have to miss Dad's funeral service. Be that as it may, supporting my family seems the right thing to do at the moment. Sharon carries on at home and so do we on the road. We stop at the Moultrie Civic Center and I knock on Heins's trailer door, and am surprised when Magic Joe opens the door and greets me in his shorts – Joe is now living with Heins in his trailer and is putting on his trousers to go to work. I feel awkward trying to talk to Heins with the illustrious illusionist loitering and listening so I just take my money and bid farewell to all my fellow performers, the boys in the band and the All-Star Circus from Hell[61]

We are still upset with the loss of my father, but being on the Ringling show and among friends has a soothing effect, which makes us feel secure – actually, being on the show is like being in an insane asylum, and we seem to fit right in. Again as before, we sell cotton candy in the seats for Memo for a few weeks until Ringling concession manager Bobby offers us our own floss stand. Working week stands, as we do with Ringling, is better than doing one-day stands with other shows. Rather than constantly driving to the next town we work all day cranking out cotton candy for the huge crowds that are attracted to the show. In order to handle such a large volume, I am forced to hire local kids to run through the audience selling floss for a fifteen percent commission. Since I am getting twenty-five percent while the show gets seventy-five percent, this only leaves me ten percent profit – except that which I sell myself at the stand. After realizing forty dollars a day for the both of us working all day, we begin to realize that this is not a high-profit-making endeavor. Adding to our stress, the town kids occasionally sell a board of floss, then rather than turn in the money and receive a new board, they deposit the board and their working shirt in the men's room, then scamper home – *the little rascals*. To prevent this from happening, we require that the kids put up collateral worth at least the value of a board, which keeps them from running away with the money. From time to time, however, they do manage to stick us with junk or stolen merchandise and run away with the money anyway – *the little bastards*. To add to my frustration, Bobby sticks me with Lesley who performs in the Black unicycle basketball act as the referee. Lesley enjoys playing cat and mouse games by sneaking uncounted floss on to his board when no one is looking, thereby selling them without turning in the money. We finally catch him and tighten up on our cotton candy security, but Bobby makes us keep him for unstated political reasons. We learn all the tricks and try to keep up with them, but we still are losing money. To add insult to injury, the show not only charges me rent for the concession stand, but holds back two percent till the end of the season in order to keep me from leaving the show; not only that, some buildings even charge rent for parking my trailer – *Jesus, Mary and Joseph!*

All is not gloom and doom, however, since I can make up the difference by working outside after the show for Helmut the balloon man, which carries us over the top. The boys, of course, have lots of playmates on the show that all have one thing in common other than the circus, they all hate doing their

Calvert correspondence school. They also like to watch cartoons on television. Liam likes cartoons so much that while we perform on the *Bozo* T.V. show in Chicago, Liam refuses to go into the studio to watch the telecast, preferring instead to remain in the trailer parked outside, watching his favorite 'toons and not even changing channels to watch Mom and Dad – *how rude!*

We are on the Ringling blue unit with German headliners Charley Bauman, tiger trainer, and Ursula Bochter, one of the few female,[62] wild animal trainers in the industry – and polar bears at that. Trying to keep up my languages wherever we go, I often engage them in German chitchat. Charley yells at me in German when I mistakenly park in his parking space. Coincidentally, Gunter Gabel Williams, animal trainer, yells at me in German whenever I park in his space on the Ringling Red unit.

Bobby has us busy, going from circus to circus and then to the Disney on Ice Show – also owned and operated by the Ringling organization. We change shows so much that we inevitably park in the wrong spot where ever we go. Elvin Bale[63] (trapeze act) arrives in one town to find a show-owned concession truck parked in his spot. After confronting the driver who refuses to move, he calmly returns to his coach, takes his pistol and shoots holes in all the tires of the offending vehicle, thereby getting himself fired by Mr. Feld (the big boss). Parking in the wrong spot on a large traveling show can cause a confrontation and angry words. While on the Clyde Beatty Circus, it even turned into a Cuban-Mexican war. One of the circus ten commandments is – "Thou shalt not park in another performer's spot." The Ringling Circus is a great show to watch; but working there can be exhausting and nerve wracking. We begin to feel the pressure of the everyday bedlam, the serving of large crowds of people, and the creeping paranoia from petty pilferage from our cotton candy stand. After a full day of listening to circus music and the constant din of hordes of people, falling into a deep sleep at night is no problem. We rejoice when the time comes for us to be on our way to other dates and less mental pressure. We leave the show in West Virginia and chart a course for Washington, D.C.

The Smithsonian Institute in Washington is our next adventure where we get to perform in a circus tent for the American culture festival where we get more respect as performers than we did as concessionaires on the Ringling show. At the Smithsonian, we are living national treasures – or so we like to believe. Camille and I always enjoy the Washington area, where we met and fell in love. The boys, on the other hand, are not keen on revisiting where we got married, and our favorite Chinese restaurant where we got engaged; however, being good boys that they are, they tolerate their parents' whimsical ways.

One adventure ends as another begins, as we face another long drive to Toronto to appear on the television show – *CIRCUS*. Toronto has always been one of our favorite cities, but the trip getting there is always a pain in the back (literally). Like the *Bozo* T.V. show in Chicago, the station allows us to park indefinitely on their property – saving us some inconvenience and expense. It is also a fun place to park since almost every act in the business comes there to park and appear on the show – similar to a funeral or wedding where you get to see everyone that you have ever known, friend and foe alike. The shows are taped in advance, and we will not see ourselves on Canadian television until we return to the country in a year's time.

Our next circus of destiny is in Rochester, Indiana, where we will join the T.N.T. Circus at the Rochester Mall. With plenty of time to make the date, we choose to drive home to Florida to check the house, have a short rest, then drive north to Indiana. In Georgia our perfect planning goes awry, however, when a bearing on the trailer burns out -*sonamamitch!* This is nothing new, since the other three bearings have already burned out at one time or another on the road – just more unwanted aggravation.

A Sunday breakdown on the road is the norm since no one works on that day who can help us. I pull off the road and stop, take off the offending wheel, then proceed slowly to a small town where I find a junkyard and an old gentleman who offers to replace the wheel. He can't get a new rim for the trailer until the next day, so with time running short, we opt to leave the trailer in his compound, drive to Orlando, then return in a few days to pick it up, and then continue on our way. We get to stay in our house (still not finished), but we have electricity for a week and relax before it is time to return to the front lines of life on the road. Leaving the house is always an emotional time. We would all like to stay home, but our public awaits – besides, we need the money.

Backtracking to Georgia, we pick up the chicken coop with its new wheel, then like the covered wagons of old traveling the Chisholm Trail, we drive to Rochester. All the way I am a nervous wreck, expecting a wheel to fall off any minute – stopping periodically to check the wheels and tires. Lady luck shines on us for no calamity befalls us during our pioneering trek westward to Rochester, Indiana. Finally during the night, we creep on to the Rochester Mall parking lot, and spotting a row of trailers parked along the side of the building, quietly move in behind them and retire for the night.

The show is operated by Kentucky Colonel Tegge, wife Louise who plays organ and son Timmy who plays drums and clowns. Show owner and ringmaster Colonel Tegge wears a mustache and goatee to reinforce the Kentucky Colonel image, and walks with a cane due to a childhood bout with polio. The show is rather small, with just a ring to perform in, a skirt surrounding the organ and drums, and a tiny dressing tent like that found on a beach, where we dress within. Our audience, the shopping public at the mall, must stand to watch one of the four performances given each day – there not being any seats. Other performers on the show include German jugglers Walter and Ingrid with whom I get to practice my German language skills. Walter had been on a German U-Boat during World War II and was confined in a prisoner of war camp in France. Unlike the German prisoners that I remember in South Boston who had had it relatively easy, Walter spins tales of hardship, famine and woe while under the custody of the French.

As small as the show is, it is well received by the shoppers and the malls go out of their way to make us feel right at home; so much so that Camille spends most of her time between shows shopping for things for our house in Florida. After a while, the poor chicken coop is crammed with items to be transported back to Florida. I do believe that Walter had more living space in his U-Boat than we have in the chicken coop – torpedoes and all.

Liam is now four years old and it is time for him to get a job. Camille makes a costume for him and his first assignment will be to walk around the ring during the opening spec – while smiling and waving to the crowd – the same job that Eoin started with at the Medina Shrine Circus in Chicago. Although Eoin took to his debut on the stage with a flare, Liam is terrified at the thought. It took him a while to get use to Timmy the clown, but now this is different – people will look at him and then what? We try our best to reassure him that nothing bad will happen. Ever-silent and brooding, he remains withdrawn – resigned to his fate. Doomsday approaches and it's show time.

Liam sits quiet and nervous, as all five of us (now going on six including Liam), pick up our flags and begin the grand entry of the circus: marching around the ring to the music of Timmy and mother Louise, while Colonel Tegge makes a pompous announcement as if addressing thousands of people. Camille has Liam by the hand for assurance as we parade around the ring.

While we all march in step, Liam mopes along beside his mom, his eyes to the ground trying to avoid eye contact with the audience, trying to grin, wave and walk all at the same time. Occasionally looking up, he sees friendly, smiling faces of families, with kids like himself enjoying the show. The ordeal is over for Liam as he leaves the ring then ducks into the dressing tent to change. He survives his first mission then withdraws to the chicken coop to watch cartoons. Suddenly he realizes that he is now a performer, and it wasn't all that bad after all, but that's today – what about tomorrow? Tomorrow comes and with it another four shows, and still the sky doesn't fall. After a while we notice that Liam and Eoin are the first ones dressed and ready for the show. Liam, the little trouper, suddenly likes the attention of the audience and the sound of applause just like his brother. We only wish that they would take to their Calvert School with the same enthusiasm.

One day, Timmy is late for the show and the band (Louise at the organ) will have to go on without the percussion section. Liam, having had a few drum lessons from Timmy, becomes the emergency stand-in drummer. Much to my surprise, Liam keeps the beat and catches all the tricks. Unknown to me, he has been taking his drumming seriously and learned to play the show. Being too short to reach the seat to sit down, Liam plays standing up with just his head protruding above the bass drum.

Half way through the show, Timmy arrives to take over, but not before the Colonel asks Liam to stand up and take a bow. "Oh, he is standing up," says the Colonel. The audience applauds and Liam, no longer suffering from stage fright, takes a bow – *That's my boy!* Next comes unicycle lessons and Liam is eager to learn – more so than his Calvert School lessons.

Our pleasant stay at shopping malls is marred by the fact that we have hundreds of miles to travel between them, and the price of gasoline is now over two dollars a gallon. From Chicago, we travel to Bemidji, Minnesota, then to Fort Worth, Texas, then back to Chicago, then Hagerstown, Maryland, then back to Chicago again – *Jesus, Mary and Joseph!* The problem with working strictly malls is that they want a circus when it is convenient for them, but not for the circus; but then, even the Shiners cause the circus the same inconvenience – making shows put on lots of miles at considerable expense, particularly hard now with the price of gas being what it is. We take advantage of the long driving periods to teach the kids to read since they have nothing else to do.

During our travels, we occasionally come across other circuses, and so while driving through Illinois, we happen upon Gerard Brothers Circus, owned by old friend Gerard Soules whom we worked with before on the Hannaford Circus, and also on the Disney on Ice show where he exhibited his beautiful dress-up dog act. Prior to that, Gerard had done a heel catch trapeze act, and a rather dangerous one at that where he hangs from the trapeze bar by his hands then flips up and catches the bar with the back of his heels.

During a performance on the Clyde Beatty Circus, prior to my being on the show, he comes close to falling, and decides to sell his act to Elvin Bale, preferring to perform closer to the ground with a slack wire act and, later, dogs. Along with Gerard is his alternative lifestyle companion Steve who suffers from a kidney aliment, and Billy McCabe (circus clown and cook). Billy has worked on many shows in the past including the pie car of The Freedom Train, which traveled around the country in the 1976 bicentennial celebration, displaying patriotic and historical documents. Billy became more known in the circus industry for his rib-sticking gravy – garnished on everything he cooked, rather than for his clowning. Although tasting well, it was more like a heart attack on a plate – typical circus cook house fare, rather than a nourishing meal. Some performers like to brag that some day they will own their own circus, and so Gerard does. It's not a smart move considering what the fickle finger of fate likes to do to circuses; but we all have our dreams, and so far the show is doing well.

A storm is brewing over the horizon and dark clouds loom over head, but Gerard and the boys make us feel at home and invite us to park overnight to socialize, after which we retire for the night with a steady rain coming down. For those of us in the circus who live in a trailer, the sound of rain on the roof is a pleasant soothing sound which lulls one to sleep, and makes one feel secure, knowing that all the townspeople have gone home, and there is no one outside standing in the rain ready to cause harm or mischief to the show – town hooligans don't stay out in the rain, getting wet.

After a pleasant visit, we wish them well and godspeed then depart the next morning.[64] We continue crisscrossing the country and find ourselves back in Maryland. In Hagerstown, the show parks behind a shoe store, which has just thrown away a bin load of shoes. According to the shop owner, they would display one shoe of a pair in a display window while keeping the mate in a box. Over the months, the sun faded the color of the displayed shoes, making them a mismatch with its twin, and therefore un-sellable. The shoe store owner dumps all the mismatched shoes in the dumpster behind the shop and next to our trailers, and invites us all to take what we want. Although we would never buy a pair of mismatched shoes, that doesn't mean that we wouldn't wear them if acquired for nothing. It only takes a bit of shoe polish to bring them back to looking spiffy again – that's just what we all do.

Halloween finds us at a big mall outside of Dallas where to spice up the show we all don spooky attire and present a Circus of Horror – to the delight of the audience. During our engagement there, we are visited by other performers, who park alongside of us and enjoy the ghoulish occasion – our favorite time of the year, since now the circus season is coming to a close and we all get to go home. Performers from other shows stop by to break their jump, socialize and enjoy free parking that the mall offers. Among them is Vicky Baker who performs an acrobatic act with her husband, themed as a ballerina and a toy soldier. They are working on a flying trapeze act, a dangerous undertaking, but circus people like to push the death-defying envelope to create more thrills and thus more marketability in the show business world.[65] Dallas is the last date of the T.N.T. circus, and so we each say adieu, wish each other luck, and depart on our separate ways. Another season lay to rest behind us with a short jump ahead and home to Florida and the new house.

The O'Brien family with Bozo and Cookie on WGN-TV, Chicago (1978)

Chapter XV
End of the Road

Uncle Donald, Dad's younger brother, had worked for many years as a guard for the First National Bank of Boston. Being divorced for many years with two adult children living in Boston, Donald dreams of retirement in Florida. After Dad's passing, Uncle Donald had remained in contact with Mom, and later they form a brand new relationship. He moves in with Mom. Mom always said that Uncle Donald wanted a mother rather than a wife; but he does the daily maintenance chores around the house – something Dad would never do. Mom always liked Uncle Donald, thinking of him as a younger version of Dad, which being brothers, he is. Although they never marry, they remain together for several years. All the while, Uncle Donald endures a barrage of Mom's constant chatter and criticism – something that Dad had gotten used to over the years. Dad had his own way of coping; but poor Uncle Donald has no escape – he doesn't drink[66] – *Jesus, Mary and Joseph!*

*

We are living in stressful times: the country is in a recession, unemployment is high, interest rates are high, the price of gasoline is high, and some shows are closing, never to reopen again. The money flows out as fast as it comes in as we struggle to make a living in show business – making only a small profit at the end of the season. If that were not enough, the Internal Revenue Service wants to audit my tax return.

We never pay taxes because we never make enough taxable income; but the computer doesn't understand, and sends me a nasty letter rejecting my deductions – *how rude!* Being audited by the I.R.S. is an interesting and frightening experience. I visit the local office and find that there are many other people waiting to explain their case; and so I pick a number then sit down and wait. I approach the girl at the counter and explain: the computer thinks that all the money that I made selling cotton candy on the Ringling show was profit, and that I had no expenses. I further explain to the lady about hiring kids needed to sell the candy, and paying them more than I got to keep for myself. She understands and is sympathetic; however, I continue to get nasty letters in the mail from the I.R.S. concerning the money that they say I owe them. My tax man in Sarasota files amended returns, but to no avail. I continue to state my case, but the I.R.S. computer has lost its mind and continues a vendetta against me by sending me threatening letters. Talking to the I.R.S. computer is like talking to my cat, and I'm freaking out. Eventually, the plug is pulled on the sinister computer, and rather than go to jail, I receive a refund – *Jesus Mary and Joseph!*

*

Spring arrives again and it's show time. We have a two-year contract with Tarzan, former lion trainer on the Mills Brothers Circus. He has recently bought a Shrine Circus company from Hubert Castle, former wirewalker and now former circus producer. Tarzan has a wonderful show, but a back breaking tour: Memphis, Tennessee, to El Paso, Texas, for two days, then to Minneapolis, Minnesota, then Missoula, Montana. Tarzan has so many dates that some of them overlap, causing a routing problem

Like many other Circus producers, he creates a second unit for what is called "pick-up" dates. All put together, however, it consists of only twenty weeks ending in June – not a full season. Even the twenty weeks turn out to be mostly half weeks, with half a week's pay. Circus producers shy against uttering the words "half week" while negotiating a contract, leading the weary performer to think in terms of a great season, rather than a mediocre one. Another irritating factor is that the show pays half in U. S. currency and half in Canadian – a Canadian dollar being worth only seventy-five cents.

The show opens in Spokane, Washington. According to the map, the northern route from Orlando to Spokane appears to be the shortest, but requires passing through mountains during early spring, which is not a good idea. Instead, we opt to travel the southern route direct to Los Angeles, then turn north to Seattle, then east to Spokane – quite a bit longer than the Lewis and Clark expedition of 1804. Undaunted by distance and fueled by adventure and new horizons, we hitch up the chicken coop to the yellow truck, hoist the main sail and cruise on a westerly course. We press on and on, day by day, stopping at night at a trailer park where we can rest up and swim in a pool.

Like Field Marshal Rommel's panzers (tanks) on their way to Al Alamein, we advance slowly, but surely, through the hot desert wind and over the baking cement highway. Not only are we all hot and tired, but I am growing tired of listening to Camille teach school and the kids bouncing around in the truck. Finally we descend though the mountains and cross the border into California where we rejoice at reaching the half way point of our odyssey, and celebrate by visiting Disneyland. Our ultimate destination is the circus in Spokane; however, we intend to break the jump with a visit with little sister Sharon and brother-in-law Cliff in McMinnville, Oregon. Sharon, a dance teacher and former nurse, has a lovely house with fruit trees, from which she makes jams and jellies. She also loves animals and keeps several dogs and cats.[67] Our family reunion is pleasant but brief since we still have a long way to go; however, we plan another reunion when we return to the area to play the Portland Shrine Circus.

We continue on our journey with another day's drive ahead of us, finally arriving at our opening of the season in Spokane. Arriving on the lot about the same time as us is the Fornasari family (musical clown act from Italy). As I greet Papa Fornsari, I notice that he has a new trailer and I express interest and curiosity. Papa informs me that the only reason he has a new trailer is because while passing through Atlanta, his other trailer was wrecked, and he was forced to buy a new one – *Santa Maria!*

Other old friends on the show are bandmaster Clem with organist wife Elizabeth, and son number two, Emil, who at the tender age of thirteen is playing drums on the show. Other son Greg[68] is conducting the band and playing drums on Tarzan's other unit. Elizabeth had been pregnant, carrying Emil during our time together on Uncle Howard's show, and now the kid is playing drums in the band on this show.

Suddenly, I am beginning to feel old. Other old acquaintances include André and wife René (wire walker and sword balancer) and Herbie Webber who walks across the wire with baskets on his feet and continues to repair his wire slippers – constantly sewing them up with new thread. Together we form the wire display, and a formidable one at that.

Managing the show is former flying trapeze act Reggie who once fell flat on his face during a performance, and has a flat face – making him look somewhat grotesque. Also on the bill is aerialist Mr. Sensation, the "Hedda

Hopper" of the circus industry. He not only is the queen of the air, but the guru of gossip who writes all he sees and hears for a circus trade magazine. Together with partner Bobby dressed like a genie just out of the bottle, they do a formidable aerial routine with an exotic, oriental flavor. Others on the show are those that I know by their reputation, but have never worked with them before.

The next day is show time; but I am not yet fully recovered from the long trip. Going a long time from the sitting position in a truck to standing upright requires some Bengay ointment. It's show time; the arena is filled with thousands of screaming kids; the band is playing; and the spotlights are on me as I mount the wire to give the performance that I have given a thousand times before. My brain must be asleep, because for a moment I have no idea where I am. I know that I can do the act in my sleep, but I never thought that I could sleep during my act. By the end of the week, I have recovered from my jet lag, but now it's time to load up the show, and travel to the next town – Missoula, Montana. Traveling east through the northwest during the early spring is a challenge of pioneering proportions.

We are driving towards Sioux Falls, South Dakota, during a spring blizzard – strong enough to stop a herd of buffalo. As I glance in my left rear window I see the chicken coop still attached, traveling sideways as if it were trying to pass the truck. I stare in disbelief, knowing the object in the mirror is closer than it appears. In such a situation one applies the trailer brakes in order to straighten out the rigs, rather than use the truck brakes, which would only aggravate the situation. Frightened by the experience, we pull off the road, and park for the night at a friendly filling station that lets us plug in our electric cord.

The blizzard covers the trailer in snow, but inside we are snug and warm. As I sip my bourbon and watch television, I'm having second thoughts about this show-must-go-on nonsense. Not only am I putting my family in jeopardy; but I am becoming a nervous wreck.

After digging out the trailer the next morning, we get underway again on the roads, which by this time have been cleared by the highway department, enough, so that we can get to the next town where we park at a snow-covered fairgrounds. Most of the show has already arrived and the kids on the show are already deeply engaged in making snowmen and having snowball fights. Before we even park the trailer, Eoin and Liam jump out the door of the truck, and begin to frolic in the snow with the other circus kids.

By now, my sideline balloon business has become full time. With the help of Eoin and Emile, we cover the doors of the buildings after the show, and as the public exits onto the street, we go into our rubber mode – selling balloon souvenirs to the happy circus goers for them to take home. The Shrines, however, do not approve of my balloon business outside on the sidewalk after the show since they feel that I am competing against them. My point of view is that after the circus patrons leave the building, the Shriners cannot get any more money from them, and I can – *so why not?* – nevertheless, they complain. Undeterred, we devise a clandestine hit and run balloon strike at each building where we suddenly appear on the streets from nowhere, sell all the balloons as soon as possible, then disappear before the "sons of the desert" spot us. If we should be observed and they complain, we have already taken in a hundred dollars – *so let them complain.* Playing hide and seek with the Shriners is like espionage – a game that we love to play.

The show plays in ice hockey arenas in northern Canada where only Indians and Eskimos live. Indians love the circus and love rubber balloons, especially if they are on a stick, but I don't understand why. I feel like an old-time fur trader taking advantage of the red man every time I take their money and give them a piece of rubber in return. In this part of North America the Indians speak their native language, and I enjoy eavesdropping on the conversations of the children. I wonder at the logic of playing towns like Moose jaw, Swift Current and Medicine Hat until we arrive and perform to a full house of enthusiastic people with lots of wampum. Driving to these places, however, is ridiculous – long drives over dirt roads with nothing but forest, mosquitoes and moose.

Flin Flon is so far up north (55° latitude) that everyone with a trailer leaves it parked at the fairgrounds in Brandon, and proceeds north in their trucks for the one day stand then return after the show to the comfort of our trailer, still parked unmolested at the fairgrounds, where we then collapse from fatigue. The boys, of course, take it all in; but the long trips in the truck are starting to get on our nerves.

The show returns to the States, touring around the Far West, finally closing at the Salt Palace in Salt Lake City. This is a big date with full houses where I give my best performance ever – it will also be my last. The show closes, we make our farewells, and everyone goes their different ways. It is early June and the season is already over. We have nothing booked until next year when we are scheduled to go out with Tarzan again. By now the joys of the road have been soured by seemingly endless driving; now suddenly, no work until next year. The boys have seen the country and then some; but they have never experienced a normal life of living in a town and going to school. Camille dreams of someday living in our home in Kissimmee – *so do I.* The thought of going though all this again next year is more than I can bear. We decide to run away from the circus and join a town.

We begin the long voyage home to Florida and stop to visit the Ringling show in Oklahoma City where we plan to park for a few days rest then move on. However, Bobby the concession manager needs someone to sell programs – and so I do. Camille is not pleased, particularly when they ask us to stay on the show after the Ringling engagement ends in Oklahoma City. Camille has had it with the joys of the road and is adamant about going home. I acquiesce, and so the yellow truck and the chicken coop make their way to Florida – our own hometown, another lifestyle and another adventure.

Our plans are to work at Walt Disney World where they were so nice to us in the past. With my experience in show business, and prior association with Disney in the Christmas parades, I plan to work in the entertainment department; and perhaps if I'm lucky, become a stage manager. We all have happy thoughts as we make our way south – surely nothing can go wrong – if I only knew – if I only knew – *Jesus, Mary and Joseph!*

Endnotes

[1] Opposite of escape

[2] Metropolitan Transit Authority

[3] **Geheim Staats Polizei** (Secret State Police)

[4] Derived from French: Ma Mére (my mother)

[5] Till next time.

[6] Years later, "sky master" Darryl tries to improve his death-defying sway-pole act by being transported to the top of the pole by helicopter rather than climbing up. One day the helicopter snags a pole cable, and the pole, the helicopter and Darryl come crashing down. Darryl survives, but never performs again.

[7] Years later, Queen Lee, who is a male prostitute on the side, is shot dead by one of his customers.

[8] Latin: Table

[9] **Schutz Staffel** (defense squadron)

[10] Close, but no cigar.

[11] **Volks Polizei** (People's Police)

[12] Close, but no cigar.

[13] Close, but no cigar.

[14] Pronounced "cove"

[15] Been there, done that.

[16] Greek: friendship

[17] Children's musical comedy – Theatre (U. K.) Theater (U. S.)

[18] Advertising slogan

[19] Gaelic: No girls here

[20] Very well, I shall marry you.

[21] French: Old Quarter

[22] Carnival organizations

[23] Military Transport Service

[24] After two divorces, Uncle Joe dies from a heart attack while playing a slot machine at a casino in Atlantic City. After divorcing Joe, Aunty Cookie remarries and is later widowed. Eventually, she smokes herself to death with cigarettes.

[25] Gaelic: Close, but no cigar

[26] Gaelic: Goodbye!

[27] Today, I am certified by the F.A.A. to teach the subject that I flunked.

[28] Extra money for extra work

[29] Weary Willy is the clown character created by Emmett Kelly.

[30] Bud dies at the age of eighty, and is buried in Tampa under a head stone that says, "J. FRED MUGGS, TOGETHER IN LIFE, TOGETHER IN DEATH." In addition to Bud, Roy and Jerry are also listed on the stone, awaiting their time. The chimp will be buried with them.

[31] Jutta marries Ned Toth, nephew of Frank McCloskey while Bridget marries Assistant Manager Johnny Pugh, who one day becomes sole owner of the Clyde Beatty – Cole Bros. Circus.

[32] For many years thereafter, former concession people I happen to meet still call me "Mike." – *I'm not Mike – it's the dog – the dog!* We continue to refer to Mike the Dog to distinguish him from Mike the Clown and Little Mike.

[33] Prodding stick with a hook on the end

[34] Circus argot for toilet. Mike empties the septic tank of the public toilet – hence the name.

[35] Circus slang for riot.

[36] Carmen and Larry have a young daughter, Lisa. Larry, however, has a roving eye. Carmen divorces him then remarries Hunkey, a bear trainer who turns out to be a child abuser, and is eventually shot dead by step-daughter Lisa, who then has to do some time in the slammer.

[37] Toby is booked on a circus in Hawaii. While awaiting a flight at the Los Angeles Airport, he is injured by a terrorist explosion from a bomb placed in a locker.

[38] Rudy will one day drink himself to death.

[39] Big George and Big Bob Raborn, his assistant, continually argue as to who is Big Top Boss. The matter is settled while erecting the Big Top, when the pole being erected by the elephant touches an electric power line above, and Big Bob and the elephant are electrocuted.

[40] Atayde Brothers Circus

[41] Although implying that money raised by the sale of tickets to the circus goes to children's hospitals, an investigative reporter of the *Orlando* (Fla.) *Sentinel* later reveals that money raised for the circus supports only the Shrine Temples.

[42] Clem played in the Marine Corps band in the Pacific Theater during World War II, serving also as a litter bearer – what military musicians did during combat operations.

[43] One day, the Rhodos realize their dream. They buy the old wrestling arena in Sarasota, and turn it into The Old Heidelberg Castle, which enjoys initial success, but has no parking space for cars. To solve that problem, they buy adjacent land at an exorbitant price, which gives them ample parking space, but high monthly payments. Struggling to make ends meet, Hans neglects to pay his taxes, and goes to jail for tax evasion. Bruno dies, then the restaurant goes bankrupt and succumbs to the wrecking ball.

[44] Another branch of Masonry that sponsors the circus

[45] Ken and Vesta are tragically killed in a road accident in Orlando, Florida. Their performing dog "Twinkle Toes" survives.

[46] During a performance at Old Chicago – an indoor themed shopping and amusement complex – Jimmy falls from the trapeze to his death.

[47] Stephanie doesn't report to work for a few days, and is found dead from an overdose in her bed at home in Windermere. Buzz now despondent, abandons his family and runs off to Las Vegas.

[48] Eddie Hugh drinks himself to death and is buried in Orlando. Revelations from wife Evy reveal a perfect heart but a destroyed liver – a classic case of alcoholism by a classic actor and a classic guy.

[49] In talkie-talkie, pissy haut means piss bark.

[50] Later, Kay develops cancer from an abscessed tooth and dies. Daughter Nellie, by a previous husband, is adopted and raised in the circus by Tommy.

[51] Jimmy played trumpet in the army, and landed in Normandy with the Allied invasion of France. Years later, I see Jimmy, now a street musician, playing trumpet for hand outs in Jackson Square in New Orleans.

[52] Later, Larry dies of Lou Gehrig's disease, and Karin remarries a Danish

watershow diver who is later killed in a road accident. Karin remarries again to find herself swimming in a tank with sharks in a carnival attraction. The marriage to the shark man is of short duration. She then goes to Germany to present elephants with a German Circus.

[53] Later, while performing at a shopping mall in St. Paul, Minnesota, for Bad Bob, seventeen-year-old Rita falls to her death.

[54] While working club dates in Minnesota during my college years, I worked with Dieter's wife, Connie Armstrong (trapeze), and her parents, who did a knock about comedy act. After marring Dieter, Connie tragically breaks her neck and dies in a car wreck, while traveling to do a show.

[55] Wife Kathy keeps his ashes in an urn bearing his hat and bow tie, which she casually displays to visitors at their home on Casey Key, Florida.

[56] Gailic: Bed and breakfast guest house

[57] Years later, I meet David on another circus where he confides to me that he is dying of aids; then shortly thereafter, he does.

[58] Show business argot: magician's assistant

[59] Cousin Rickey eventually dies from dirty needles while taking drugs.

[60] Raul takes his truck in for a welding job under the vehicle. Somehow, a spark ignites the gas in the tank, and there is an explosion, consuming the vehicle and everything in it, including the animals.

[61] Heins goes to Las Vegas with trombone player Lee and Dusty the clown where they have a falling out as to who will sleep with the clown. Heins abruptly leaves the show, and now completely out of the closet, goes to work as a bouncer at a gay bar in "Faghdad by the Sea" (Sarasota.) The show goes broke and folds. Jim divorces, remarries, divorces again and dies of natural causes. Patty remarries to Chris (trumpet player in the band) and opens a trailer repair shop in Deland. Partners Dusty and Lee move on to other circuses.

[62] Eloise Berchtold is another well-known female trainer of lions and

elephants with whom we work at the Illinois State Fair. Later at a Shrine Circus in Canada, her elephant kills her during a performance.

[63] While being shot out of a cannon on a British circus in Hong Kong, Elvin misses the net, breaks his back and is confined to a wheel chair thereafter.

[64] The circus flops; Billy dies of aids; and Steve dies of kidney failure. Gerard goes to Las Vegas with his dog act, and later teams up with another partner who murders Gerard and then goes to jail.

[65] Later during practice on their new act, Vicky takes a bad fall, lands in the net on her neck and becomes a paraplegic. Her husband remains by her side as they retire from the business.

[66] Later, Mom talks Uncle Donald out the door, never to return. He dies in a retirement home in Ft. Lauderdale.

[67] Later, Sharon puts the cat in the garage while she goes downtown. She also puts an electric heater in with the cat to keep it warm. The cat tips over the heater; the garage catches fire; and her house burns down – *Jesus, Mary and Joseph!*

[68] Later, son Greg goes to China with a show and, without telling his family, marries a Chinese girl and stays there.